SECRET BILLIONAIRE

THE CAROLINA SERIES BOOK TWO

JILL DOWNEY

Secret Billionaire

The Carolina Series
Book 2

by
Jill Downey

Cover Design Copyright © 2020 Maria @ Steamy Designs
Editor April Bennett @theeditingsoprano.com

DEDICATION

Becoming an aunt has been one of my
biggest blessings in life!

This is for Grace and Finn... love you both so much!

BOOKS BY JILL DOWNEY

Books by Jill Downey

The Heartland Series:

More Than A Boss

More Than A Memory

More Than A Fling

The Carolina Series:

Seduced by a Billionaire

Secret Billionaire

Playboy Billionaire

A Billionaire's Christmas

The Triple C Series:

Cowboy Magic

Cowboy Surprise

Cowboy Heat

Cowboy Confidential

1

Faye served a round of beers to the table of guys still lingering. The place had cleared out. They and the solo patron at the bar, were the only customers left. She set the six beers in front of them and had turned to leave when one of them called her back.

"It's our boss's birthday." The guy nodded his head toward the man Faye had been drooling over the entire night. "Since Jesse here, can't seem to take his eyes off of you, how about you make his day and give him your phone number?"

Faye grinned at the gray-haired man who'd thrown his friend under the bus.

Hands on her hips she said, "You behave yourself, ya hear. I don't give my number out...even if it's an extra hot birthday boy."

They all guffawed with laughter, then the teasing began in earnest.

"Hear that Jesse? Extra hot!"

"You might actually have a shot," another one chimed in.

"His name's Jesse Carlisle, and I'm Stan, his fore-man." He tipped his beer bottle at her.

Faye curtsied playfully and then stuck out her hand towards the embarrassed hunk. "Pleased to make your acquaintance. Happy Birthday. I hate to be the bearer of bad news guys, but this is last call," she said, as she laid their bill on the table.

Jesse tipped back his chair and looked up at her through ridiculously long lashes and smiled. "Don't listen to these guys. They're full of hot air."

"What business are y'all in?"

Stan answered for them. "Construction. We build houses."

"Maybe I should take that back then and give Jesse my number after all. I've been dumped. I had a construction company all lined up, and they just up and quit on me."

The five men all looked curiously at Jesse waiting for his response.

He shrugged and said, "That's brutal. This is the busiest time of year for construction. You're going to have a tough time finding someone else."

Faye was not the least bit surprised that he didn't step in and offer to help. She knew the timing was horrible.

"Don't I know it."

The building, once a favorite dive bar for the locals, had been closed and neglected for years. She renamed it The Pelican and had big dreams to bring it back to life with live music, open mic nights, great tasting bar food. Since the kitchen required a major overhaul, her customers would have to be content with peanuts, potato chips and jerky for now. There was still a ton of work to be done and she was trying to be patient. It was hard to not feel overwhelmed.

"My dream is to restore the outdoor seating area. I had hoped to have that done in time for tourist season this year." She sighed, "Oh well. It didn't stop you boys from coming in tonight."

Jesse's forehead furrowed as he listened to Faye. "I can give you a couple of numbers of some workers I know, but I can't promise anything," he said.

She put a hand to her heart. "You'd do that for me?" She laid on the southern charm.

"I'll drop off a few cards this week."

"That would be great. Can I use you as a reference?"

His amber brown eye's crinkled when he smiled at her. "Of course."

Stan looked out at the pier and said, "It's a shame to waste that outdoor space. You've got the perfect location."

The deck was adjacent to a marina, and when the renovation was completed, customers would be able to drive their boats up, secure their vessels and come through her own private entrance. However, before that could happen, the covered deck needed repaired, possibly replaced, then stained and sealed. Right now, it was a lawsuit waiting to happen.

They were interrupted by the guy at the bar who yelled, "Can a guy get a fucking beer around here?"

Faye reluctantly returned to the bar to serve him.

"Last call," she said to him, her voice clipped.

He glared at Faye, waving his hand dismissively. "Yeah yeah, I heard ya."

She rolled her eyes and pulled a fresh frosty mug from the cooler and filled it from the tap. "Here ya go. Are you ready to cash out now?"

"I'll wait til I'm done."

"Suit yourself."

She glanced over at the table and caught Jesse staring at her. Her cheeks grew warm. He was gorgeous but even more than that, he seemed like a sweetheart. Hopefully, she'd be here when he dropped off those business cards. The guys all reached into their pockets as they divvied up the bar tab. Leaving a pile of cash on the table, they stood up to leave.

Jesse stopped at the bar to say goodbye. "I didn't catch your name."

Her pulse raced. "Faye LeBlanc."

"Nice to meet you Faye."

"Yeah, you guys were fun. Happy Birthday."

"Thanks to you it was." His eye's lazily ran over her face, briefly settling on her lips, before he turned to follow his friends out the door.

Faye blew out a long breath as she finished wiping down the bar. She turned off the music and the pleasant sounds of the whirling ceiling fans, and the clinking of the pull chain were like a lullaby. The backdrop of water lapping at the deck only added to her sleepiness. She rubbed her eyes and yawned. She'd been up since seven that morning. There hadn't been that many customers today, but the last three months of renovating a dilapidated building and opening for business were catching up with her.

She couldn't wait to crawl between her cotton sheets. All she could think about was her soft pillow and cozy bed. The only thing standing between her and sleep was the last holdout, the guy on the bar stool. He was still in no hurry to leave despite the fact that she'd announced last call, turned up the lights and turned off the music. Since he was impervious to her hints, she was going to have to use the direct approach to get him to leave.

Smiling, Faye shrugged apologetically and said, "I'm fixin' to close. I'm going to have to take your beer if you don't down it now."

His bushy salt and pepper eyebrows looked like two fat caterpillars as they drew together in a scowl. "Is that so? I paid for my beer and I ain't leavin' 'til I finish it."

Her irritation intensified her southern Carolina drawl, "I'm not trying to be rude or anything, but when I announced last call, you had plenty of time to finish a mug of beer."

He glared at her. "I reckon you think you're gonna be the one to haul my ass out of here?"

She put her hands on her slim hips and tilted her head, "I reckon so."

His cheeks, already ruddy, flushed even more. About to argue the point further, he abruptly threw back his head and drained the glass. Banging the mug down onto the bar top, he stood up and sauntered to the front door. As he grabbed the door handle, he snarled, "Oh, I forgot something." He pulled a few coins out of his pocket and tossed them at Faye. They clattered noisily to the floor at her feet.

"Snake in the grass!" Faye muttered to the empty room as the door slammed shut behind him. Her hands trembled as she locked up. *What a jerk!* She rubbed her temples, feeling a headache coming on. She grabbed an ice-cold bottle of Heineken from the cooler and sat on a bar stool, taking a long pull of the full-bodied beer. The combination of icy cold and strong bitter taste of the import hit the spot. As she relaxed the tension faded along with her headache. *Stress.* As she looked around, she tried to be happy that the interior at least, reflected her artistic flair with jazzy colors, whimsical marine animals and nautical décor. Her pure grit and elbow grease had paid off.

Faye finished her beer and tossed the bottle into the recycle can. She closed out the cash register and finished cleaning the bar glasses. Grabbing her back-pack from under the counter, she turned out the lights and locked the door behind her. Her feet ached from standing all day in flip flops, but she only had to walk a couple of blocks to get home.

She stepped out and took a deep breath, the smell of the briny ocean air at once calming and exhilarating. A chill went down her spine when she saw the silhou-ette of a man leaning against a truck. As her eyes adjusted, she realized it was the same man she'd booted out earlier. She could see the glow of a cigarette as he took one last drag and ground it out under his boot heel. He took several threatening steps toward her and she backed away, hands suddenly clammy with sweat.

Before he reached her, a low sexy voice coming from the direction of the pier said, "Is there a problem Faye?"

Voice quivering, Faye said, "I'm not really sure."

The man behind the voice stepped out and stood under a light. She was grateful to see that it was Jesse Carlisle. His leisurely approach couldn't disguise his protective bearing, almost panther-like, as he sized up the threat.

"You got a reason to be hanging around here after hours?"

"Same as you I reckon."

"No, I don't reckon. I suggest you get in your truck and head on down the road if you know what's good for you."

The man puffed out his chest and sneered, "Why don't ya mind yer own business pretty boy."

Faye was relieved that the threatening stranger was no match physically for "pretty boy", who happened to be built like a quarterback. Jesse had broad shoulders, bulging biceps, thighs that filled out his faded blue jeans to perfection. The other guy, although burly, had a beer belly and sticks for legs. Besides that, he looked like he hadn't seen the inside of a gym for a decade plus. She'd place her bet on the hottie.

He must have done his own assessment and had come to the same conclusion, because he held up both hands and said, "Hey now, there's no need for you to get your hackles up, I was just gonna offer this pretty little lady an apology. I think I mighta outworn my welcome earlier."

By this time, Jesse was standing slightly in front of

her, using his body as a shield. He was so close she could smell him, an intoxicatingly masculine earthy scent of cedar mixed with soap. Her fear had dissipated somewhat, and now she was aware of her pulse racing for a completely different reason.

He crossed his arms and said, "You go right ahead and apologize then."

"Um, miss, I don't know yer name...well I'm sorry I was a little short with ya earlier. I didn't mean no harm."

She glared, "You mean when you threw the money at me?"

He squirmed shifting from one foot to another as he glanced at her bodyguard and said, "I was teasin ya. I'm sorry if ya took it wrong." He reached into his pocket again and pulled out a couple of bills thrusting them toward her.

Her hands balled into fists. "I appreciate the gesture, but no thanks."

"Come on, take it."

"I think we both heard the lady say no. Why don't you get in your truck and leave or else I'm going to have no choice but to knock you to the middle of next week."

He kept both hands up as he backed away, "I'm leaving. No need to pitch a hissy fit." Turning to Faye he said, "No hard feelins?"

Faye's lips tightened as she fought the fear that had her gut tied in a knot. "No hard feelings. Drive safely."

Tipping his red ball cap, he hopped into his truck and drove away.

Faye slumped the minute he pulled out of the parking lot. The adrenaline rush from fear followed by her physical response to Jesse, left as suddenly as it had come.

Seeing Faye sway, he put his arm around her waist and said, "Hey are you okay? He's gone now."

"I'm feeling a little dizzy is all." She clung to him for support.

"Where's your car?"

"I walked. I only live a couple blocks from here."

"I'll take you home. You should never be out alone and walking this late at night, I don't care how close by you live," he said irritably. "I know you just met me, but would you at least let me take you home? If not, is there someone you could call to pick you up? I'll wait with you until they get here. A boyfriend maybe?"

Her eyes glistened with tears and her hands shook uncontrollably. "No boyfriend, and I wouldn't want to wake my roommate up. I would love a ride home. That was so scary. I don't know what would have happened if you hadn't shown up...thank you so much." Teeth chattering, she held out her trembling hands. "Look at me, I'm shaking like a leaf."

His large hands swallowed up her delicate fingers, the warmth of his touch both reassuring and jolting at the same time. Her body seemed to respond of its own accord.

"I'm right over here," he said. She felt his hand curve into the small of her back as he led her over to a motorcycle. "I almost want to lecture you about accepting my ride, and about being too damn trusting."

Handing her his helmet, Faye pulled it on and fastened the chin strap. "No need for the lecture. I trust my instincts. I'm seldom wrong about people."

Grinning he said, "Somehow as a defense strategy, 'trusting your instincts' doesn't reassure me much."

He threw his leg over the bike then she hitched up her skirt and crawled on behind him. Her nose crinkled and she said, "Where do you want me to hold on?"

He glanced back and gave her a devastating smile, "Best if you wrap your arms around me and hold on real tight."

Her breath quickened as his warm gaze captured hers. "Um...okay." She reached around him and encircled his waist, her hands flattened against his hard-toned belly. She could feel his body heat as her breasts pressed against his back. His scent made her want to bury her nose into his shirt. With her legs snug against him, she could feel his muscles rippling with every movement. She was shocked at how much she craved the warmth and reassurance of touch.

He fired up the bike. "Where to?"

She pointed. "That way."

"Hang on tight. Left it is."

She didn't know what was going on. Her whole body tingled, and she was overly aware of his body heating her skin where they touched. She had never had such a strong visceral reaction to a man before. She felt excited and alive, her fear forgotten for the moment, replaced with a fluttery sexual tension in her belly. "Turn right at that stop sign, then I'm the third townhouse on the right."

He pulled next to the curb and shut off the motor. "Nice digs you got."

"I'm crashing with my best friend right now. All my

money is tied up in the bar. You can't beat the view that's for sure."

"Look at those stars," he said, before getting off his bike and giving her a hand. She removed the helmet and handed it back to Jesse. The ocean breeze stirred tendrils of her hair that had escaped its clasp.

Looking up she said, "It's beautiful, isn't it? It always makes me feel so small...in a good way."

He looked down at her, his expression suddenly serious, "You're beautiful."

Her breath caught as their gazes locked.

"I meant what I said back there, about not walking home alone this late at night."

"Believe me, I heard you. That was frightening. From here on out, I'll take my bicycle."

The air was thick with awareness. The ride over had tousled his coppery brown hair and she wondered how it would feel to rake her fingers through it. Could he really see everything she was thinking and feeling or was it her imagination working overtime? Talk about feeling stripped bare. Geesh.

Suddenly self-conscious, she broke eye contact. Her emotions pinged all over the place...from fear to desire and back again...yet she felt drawn in by this man, somehow safe, cared for... and above all, she felt like a woman. The chemistry between them was insane. He got back on his bike.

"Um...well...I don't know what to say or how to thank you. I've never been rescued before."

His eyes flickered with some emotion, then he put on his helmet and started up his motorcycle. "I'm glad to have met you Faye LeBlanc. I'll be your protector anytime."

"I owe you a beer or two on the house. You'd better take me up on it or I'll never forgive you."

Eyes glittering, he said, "I'll be there to redeem them, make no mistake about that. I'll drop those cards off tomorrow."

She felt her belly flip flop. "Good night then."

He reached his hand toward her face, then pulled it back. "Good night Faye."

She hugged herself as she watched him drive away.

~

*D*amn *but that girl is fine!* He circled back around to make sure he saw lights come on inside. She woke every latent alpha male instinct he had. She was slim and willowy, *delicate*. He was surprised by how attracted he was to her because generally, he went for the voluptuous curvy type... Maybe he'd finally learned his lesson on that score.

The dark smudges under her eyes only made them stand out more. *Her eyes!* Almost the color of a cornflower. The most vivid blue he'd ever seen. His jaw clenched remembering them wide with fear, which had made him want to pick her up and carry her off to his lair.

He was glad he'd listened to his gut feeling about the guy at the bar. It had paid off...big time. He'd decided to make sure she made it safely to her car. Except she didn't have a car. *What the hell had she been thinking walking home alone at one o'clock in the morning?*

It had surprised him how badly he had wanted to beat the shit out of that asshole. He'd noticed the guy ogling her all night. Not that he was innocent on that score. He'd been aware of her the entire evening. How she'd moved, gracefully...like a dancer, her smile, her laugh.

She could have stepped right off the cover of a magazine. She'd had on some gauzy skirt with a side slit that went all the way up her long sexy thigh. Her spaghetti strap top had plunged daringly low in the front and left her midriff bare. The outline of her nipples pressing against the fabric had made him hard.

The short ride to her place wasn't nearly long enough. His body had practically hummed with pent up energy. Feeling her breasts press into his back and her warm hands on his belly had stoked a fire in his groin. He wanted more.

He could still feel the heat from where her slim arms had wrapped around his torso. Almost like he was branded. Next question, how to get this woman to agree to go out with him. His mind flashed to an image of her tangled blond hair fanned out across his pillow, her plump lips wet juicy and willing.

Unfortunately, time was a limited commodity. Both his crews were working full throttle and he had several jobs he had to put bids on in the morning...which, glancing at his watch, was only a few hours away. Tired but revved up, he'd be lucky to get in a couple of hours sleep before his alarm went off at six am.

She needed some security lights. It was way too dark in that parking lot. But *that* fell under the category of none of his business. He hoped that tonight would be a wakeup call. Maybe when tourist season was in full swing it'd be safe with all the people mingling about, but now it was deserted this time of night.

Fuck me! He had enough to worry about... how was it that in the length of one evening she managed to burrow under his skin. He couldn't stop thinking about how vulnerable she was working at that bar by herself. Even as he told himself that it wasn't his responsibility, a flash of her big blue eyes, wide with fear made it impossible for him to listen. He shook his head, she had cast some kind of spell over him and dammit, he wasn't sorry. Suddenly he related to how Tarzan must have felt. He knew he'd have to revisit that safety conversation with her when he cashed in on his free beer.

2

*A*fter a crazy morning, Jesse finally found the time to check in on Faye. The door was open, so he let himself into the bar. He could hear loud banging coming from the back room and found her in the kitchen on hands and knees hammering a nail into a wooden shelf.

Leaning his head inside the door he said, "Knock knock."

Her hair was pulled up into a ponytail and she had a bandana headband tied at the nape of her neck. She wore a white tank top under faded bib overalls. And all he could think about was taking them off. His mind went straight back to the feel of her breasts pressed against him.

Startled, she bumped her head when she heard him. At the sight of him her whole face lit up. She sat back on her heels and grinned, then held up the hammer like a trophy. Her cheek was streaked with dirt.

Eye's sparkling, she greeted him. "Jesse! You're here."

His pulse quickened at her warm welcome. "Yes. Checking in to see how you're doing...um...you know after last night." He didn't know why he was suddenly tongue tied.

"I'm okay. Everything seems better when the sun is shining."

"You've got that right. What are you working on?"

"I'm finishing off this shelf I made, then at least I can cross one thing off my endless list."

His eyebrows rose, "You built that yourself?"

Standing up gracefully in one smooth motion, she set the hammer on the shelf, then wiped her palms against her pant legs. "Yessir, all by my lonesome."

"I'm impressed," he smiled at her, utterly enchanted.

"What brings you here in the middle of the day? Are you ready for a cold one?"

"If you can take a break, I wouldn't turn it down."

She undid her ponytail then shook out her hair. As she brushed past him, the air practically crackled between them. The top of her head came just about to his chin, which put her about five-eight if he had to guess. Her arms looked like pencils to him, all feminine, skin silky smooth and soft...made him want to find out just *how* soft. He caught a faint scent of flowers, fresh and clean, delicious.

"What's your poison?" she asked.

"How about a Heineken?"

"My personal fave. I think I'll join you. Let's go out and sit on my rickety deck. I have a couple of lawn chairs we can sit on."

"Sold."

Spying the chairs leaning against the wall, he set his beer on a plank and fetched them. Opening her chair first, he swept his hand inviting her to sit. He followed suit. He leaned his head back and guzzled half the bottle in one swig.

"Thirsty much?" she drawled.

He wiped his forearm across his mouth, then grinned. "I'm a guy, what can I say?"

"Yes, you are definitely a guy." Her eyes flickered as they lingered on his lips. He felt his dick respond.

"How long have you had the bar?" he asked.

"Coming up on three months. Open for a couple of weeks."

"Quite the undertaking. This place has been abandoned for years."

"Yep. A smarter person would have demolished it and started over, but I'm just a tad bit sentimental. I decided on the preservation route. I'm questioning my sanity at this point."

"I think it's admirable that you want to preserve a part of our southern heritage. This place is as old as dirt. I'm all about history and the vibe of a place. If these walls could talk—you know what I mean?"

She smiled at him, revealing dimples, as her eyes lit from within. He swallowed hard. "So, what happened with the contractor?"

A fine line appeared between her brows, "I have no idea. He came, gave me an estimate, told me when he could start, then he never showed. After I left a half dozen messages, he called back and said he was tied up in another project and couldn't get to mine. Basically, I'm screwed. I can't find anybody. I'm doing what I can do by myself and practicing patience." She laughed and said, "YouTube has been a gift from the Almighty! I have dreams for this place." She took a sip of beer gazing out over the water.

"This location is prime. I think you made a wise investment."

She gripped the bottle tightly, "Thank you for saying that. You're the only one. Most people think I'm nuts. I guess time will tell."

"You've gotta start with a dream."

She turned her gaze back to him and searched his eyes as if looking for something. She must have found it because that warm smile lit up her face again, wreaking havoc with his pulse.

She sighed leaning back into her chair, "I was born a dreamer. That's the easy part for me."

Jesse took a long look around, the rotted deck planks, the dilapidated railings, the roof that's shelf life had expired twenty years ago...the sagging overhang, and God only knew what else was hidden from view. He gritted his teeth trying not to jump in and offer to help. He had stacks of work upon work that he wasn't caught up with in his own company. He had no business offering his services...and yet...

"I can help," slipped out before he could stop himself. *You dumb ass! How the hell are you going to help!*

Her eyes widened as her mouth opened in surprise. "You can? Really? Aren't you swamped?"

"I can make it work. I'll have to make a few arrangements, but yes, I'll help."

Shrieking, she jumped out of her chair and leaned down to give him a big hug. "Bless your little heart! I'll pay you anything. I will give you free beers for the rest of your life. I will name my firstborn after you."

Jesse laughed, a warm feeling spreading throughout his body. "After I take care of a couple of things, we'll have a business meeting to hash out the details of what you're hoping to get done this season. Then I'll give you an estimate. How's that sound?"

She clapped her hands together then twirled around in a circle. "Are you kidding me? It's like a miracle. And I'm going to owe a beer to that piece of work from last night."

"I should be able to stop in here first of next week." He didn't know who was doing the talking, because it couldn't be the business owner, Jesse Carlisle; *he* knew that he couldn't bite off one more thing. But dammit, it was worth every little bit of inconvenience he was about to experience, to see her face light up like that. What was it about this woman that made him go all knight-in-shining-armor? He'd never hear the end of it from his crew.

"Should we shake on it?" she asked.

He held out his hand and she slipped her palm into his. She gave him a lopsided grin. "You probably just saved me from financial ruin. Thank you, Jesse."

He winked at her and said, "My pleasure." *You dumb ass, you've really fucked up royally this time. Too late now, not a whole hell of a lot you can do about it.* But truth be told, he didn't want to take it back. His body hummed with excitement. He felt invigorated and realized it'd been too damn long since he'd felt this alive. He'd make this work and the bonus? He'd be able to personally make sure she was safe.

"I'd best be getting back to work. I've got to tie up a few loose ends before I can start here."

Faye clapped her hands together again and let out a squeal, almost a squeak, which made his heart skip a beat. *Adorable.* Dammit, keeping his hands to himself was going to be a challenge. She lit some kind of fire inside of him. She must have seen it on his face because suddenly she became still. Their eyes locked and the only thing that felt real was the electrified air between them. She blinked and the moment was gone.

Clearing her throat, she said, "I'll wait to hear from you. I'm here every day from about eight in the morning until closing time. I'm not open for business until four during the off season. Gives me time to work on things."

"Good to know. I'll see you around."

She beamed at him. "I'm so excited I could burst! You're making my dreams come true Jesse Carlisle."

He had a spring in his step that wasn't there a day before and he found himself whistling as he climbed onto his motorcycle.

3

------

*F*aye stood on her tiptoes at the very top rung of the ladder and stretched as far as she could to reach the ceiling tile that needed replaced. She bit her lip in concentration knowing she was in a precarious position, her balance hovering on the edge. *Someone has to do it.* For the first time it struck her how much she really was on her own. Which is how she wanted it. *Right?* Today was a typical Monday...everything that could go wrong so far had done so.

It had started when she'd parked her bicycle by the back door. Someone had decided to spray paint profanities and graffiti all over the exterior wall. Hard to not take it personally. Then her beer distributor had made the delivery but had shorted her order...she wouldn't make it through the week even if business was slow. At least they had promised to return the following day. From there she'd discovered that her freezer had conked out. A setback, but at least it hadn't been stocked with food yet. Adding insult to injury, she'd hammered her thumb when she was nailing down a loose floorboard. It still throbbed.

"Hey sis, you're going to break your neck!"

She turned and saw her brother Griffin standing in the doorway.

"Griffin!" Quickly climbing down the ladder, she ran over to give him a hug.

"How's it going?"

She rolled her eyes, "It's a disaster really. And I don't want to hear any I told you so's or so help me I'll hammer your toes."

Griffin grinned, then he noticed how tired his sister looked. "You look like shit sis."

"Turns out owning a bar is more than just pouring drinks and making conversation—who'd have known?"

"Me, for one, and all your friends, oh and who can forget dear old Dad, and brother Kyle for starters..."

Laughing she held up her hand. "Stop! Message received. I'm just venting anyway. I'm actually enjoying it. Call me crazy."

"That among many other things."

Looking him up and down she said, "By your country club golf attire, I take it you didn't come here to help out."

He smirked, "Hardly. I just came to check on you."

"You have to swear to keep things between us! No reports to big brother and especially not to Daddy! Do you hear me?"

"Yes, sis I hear you. My lips are sealed." He pantomimed locking his lips and throwing away the key.

"Be serious! You have to promise."

"Yes, I promise. Listen sis, hear me out, what I lack in mechanical skill I make up for in my hefty bank account. I'd like to donate to the cause."

Faye straightened and put her hands on her hips challengingly, "I told you I'm not accepting any family money. I'm doing this all on my own...of course I'm not forgetting my trust fund was the seed money to begin with."

His lips twisted, "Yes if you don't remember that little gem, Daddy will be sure to remind you."

"So far he's staying completely out of it."

"Only because his primary residence is now in Palm Springs."

"I don't know Griff; I think he's mellowing in his old age."

"I'll concede he's better than he used to be...not by much though," Griffin said.

They both turned when the front entrance door opened and there he was. *Jesse.* Faye's face heated and her whole body tingled. She pressed a hand to her throat as he stood there flashing that killer smile... gleaming white teeth...*he should have to wear a warning sign.*

His eyes narrowed speculatively when he saw Griffin standing next to her.

"Hi Jess, come on in," Faye called out. "This is..." she cleared her throat, "A friend of mine, Griffin Jones." She gave her brother a warning look catching his attention before he could say otherwise. He recovered quickly, hiding his surprise and held out his hand. Jesse grasped it firmly and the two men sized each other up.

"Hey Jess, what's up?" Griffin said.

Jesse nodded his head toward Faye, "Here for a consultation with Faye."

Griffin raised his eyebrows, "A consult huh? What about?"

Discreetly kicking him with her toe she said, "Griffin was just leaving. I'll walk him out and be right back." She grabbed Griffin's arm and tugged him out the front door.

The minute the door closed behind them, she glared at him and hissed, "What was that about? It's none of your business what we're about to discuss."

He grinned and winked, "Your cheeks are all red. Where did this dude come from?"

"I repeat, none of your business. I've got to get back in there. Remember, you're *not* my brother! You're an old friend. That goes for *anytime* you're in the bar. And my last name is LeBlanc *not* Bennett, Got it?"

"Why the deception?"

She gave an exasperated sigh, "A multitude of reasons. It's not *really* deception, after all it *is* mom's maiden name. Besides I told you, I don't want anyone to know I'm associated with the Bennetts and I don't want my crazy ex to be able to find me. But mostly, I want to be judged by my own merit and not as a spoiled little rich girl. I want to be liked for who I am not for what I can buy. Besides it's different for a guy, rich and powerful is a bonus. For women, it either intimidates the good ones or attracts the one's that just want to use you. Men like to be the one with the power."

He grinned rakishly, "Is that so? I've never quite looked at it that way. I've got my own version of that...

do they like me for my dazzling looks and charming personality or do they just want me because I'm rich?"

"As if you care. You'll use whatever it takes to get the girl. You flaunt it!"

He held his chest like he'd been wounded, "Ouch! That hurts."

She bit back a laugh, "You're a little too big for your britches little brother. One of these days you're going to fall hard, and we'll see how cocky you are then."

He winked at Faye. "Doubtful... but what's wrong with a little confidence anyway?"

"Confidence is fine. It's the arrogance that's so obnoxious. But I love you despite that."

A flicker of hurt crossed over his face but was quickly veiled as his lips curved up in his familiar cocky grin, "Of course you do. What's not to love?"

"Just remember what I told you!" Faye reminded him.

"I'll remember. Back to you, it's eventually going to come out you know. You can't hide who you are forever. Fuck 'em. Who cares what people think anyway?"

Jaw set, she folded her arms across her chest, "Me."

"Okay but don't say I didn't warn you. Lies have a way of coming back and biting you in the ass. The secret billionaire, ha, that's a good one!"

She rolled her eyes, "Now *why* would I expect anyone in my family to understand. Thanks for your support Griffin!"

His eyes still twinkled as he tried to school his face to look serious. "I'll take it to my grave, no bullshit."

"You'd better. I'm going in for my meeting. See you later."

"Later, Ms. LeBlanc" He shook his head chuckling as he got into his Porsche convertible and drove away.

*J*esse's eyes glittered, "So how good a friend is he? The other night you said you didn't have a boyfriend," he said, the minute Faye returned.

"And I don't. He's a childhood friend." Faye mumbled, avoiding eye contact. She could feel her cheeks heat up from the lie, and quickly changed the subject. "Let's take a tour of the place and I'll share my vision...then we can go from there."

Not to be brushed aside so easily, he continued, "You sure that's all he is?"

Faye looked up into his eyes. "He's just a friend. More like a brother."

"He looks like a movie star. Kinda hard to believe you wouldn't have an interest."

"Trust me on that, I've known him my whole life. It's nothing like that. Strictly platonic."

"If you say so."

"I do."

"I guess I'll have to take your word on that. Show me what ya got."

"Let's start outside with the deck and pier," she said, leading the way.

He squinted in the sun, appraising the space and the potential. "It's as bad as I remembered it. I suggest a complete tear down. All the planks will have to be replaced as well as the railings. A lot of the boards are rotted."

"I figured. I'd love to have a mini-bar outside for overflow, would that be reasonable?"

"I've got a few ideas. I'll draw them up for you tonight. Today I'll get some measurements so I can give you a price point. Sound good to you?"

"Yes." Faye spun around her arms wide. "I want to have lots of palms and potted plants and colorful flowers and twinkle lights hanging from the ceiling and arbor," she ticked off her list excitedly.

"Arbor? What arbor?"

"The one you're going to build for me," she said, smiling, using every ounce of charm she possessed.

When he smiled back, his eyes were molten pools of brown with golden amber flecks that practically burned a hole straight through her. When he stared at her mouth, her belly felt like she was on the downhill side of a roller coaster. Unconsciously, she touched her lips with her fingertips.

His eyes flickered then he looked away. Pulling the tape measure off his belt he squatted down. He used the pencil that'd been tucked behind his ear to jot down figures on a notepad.

"You want to hold this end for me?" he asked.

"Sure." She grabbed a hold of the blade he held out.

His white teeth clamped around the pencil as he backed his way to the other end of the deck. Faye practically salivated watching him, his movements agile and sure. The sun glinted off the natural highlights in his hair, his skin already bronzed by the sun. Her gaze wandered over his muscular physique, not an ounce of fat on him. She was daydreaming about whether he normally worked with or without a shirt when he cleared his throat, startling her out of her reverie.

"You can let go of your end now. I got it."

Her face heated with embarrassment, "Oh sorry, I was thinking about how great this is going to be when its finished." *This lying was getting to be a little too easy.*

He winked playfully, "Sure you were."

She opened her mouth to protest when she was side-tracked by a loud boat cruising up to the dock. She glanced over her shoulder and caught the man on board the craft staring at her. He wore a bandana over his bald head and the white muscle shirt displayed arms that were covered in tattoos. His skin was weather-beaten from a lifetime of too much wind and sun.

"Can I help you? Faye asked.

"This your place?"

"Yes."

"You haven't been open too long have ya?" He said, more of a statement than a question.

"Nope, several weeks."

"Do ya mind if I dock here for a couple of hours? I've been using this dock since this place was abandoned. I'm kind of sorry someone bought it. It's been mighty convenient."

"I guess it wouldn't hurt this one time."

His lips twisted, "That's generous of ya," he said.

His smile didn't reach his eyes. In fact, his eyes were dead, she couldn't see any light in them. A chill went down her spine. Like she'd told Jesse the other night, she was rarely wrong about people.

Jesse had been quiet up until that point, but he

stepped in now, "Yeah as a matter of fact, *very* generous. You docking here for a reason?"

"I've got to get some supplies. You got a problem with that?"

"Nope, just asking. Wouldn't want to see my friend here taken advantage of."

"I'll be an hour, tops. After today I'll make other arrangements."

"Good idea," Jesse said.

Faye looked at Jesse from the corner of her eye and she could tell that he'd had the same visceral reaction to the stranger that she'd had. She could see how tightly coiled his muscles were...ready to pounce if need be. She touched his arm and he immediately softened. Looking down at her, their eyes locked and his flickered with some emotion she couldn't name. He watched the man hitch his boat and jump onto the dock, then walk across her deck to the pier that ran the length of the marina. He disappeared from sight.

"All of a sudden I feel like I'm a creep magnet. What's going on?" Faye laughed nervously.

"People get set in their ways and think they have a right to anything they want. The concept of private property must have gone right over his head. Once I build the new deck, we'll be able to gate that entrance off so nobody can trespass when you're not open."

"That would be awesome."

"I don't want to sound sexist or anything like that, but I don't like the thought of you being here alone all the time."

She slipped her arm through his and said, "Well, I declare. Aren't you just the sweetest southern gentleman, Jesse Carlisle? That's why it's good you're going to be here to protect me. Let's have ourselves a beer."

The corners of his eyes crinkled as he smiled, and she could feel him relax under her hand. Frankly, she was relieved he'd been here when that guy showed up. She didn't want people to know that she was here alone as much as she actually was. With Jesse starting on construction, she wouldn't have to worry about that for now. Then when tourist season started, she'd have to hire help. Her isolation would be minimal. She was glad of that.

4

"What do you mean I'm in charge?" Stan's mouth hung open in disbelief.

"Listen Stan, you don't really need me, you know what you're doing. I'll let the guys know that you're the one in charge of this project. They all respect you," Jesse said.

"You're the brains of the outfit. I'm just the brawn," Stan replied.

"Yeah right. You're an engineer without the degree. You've got this bro. I've taken this other job on and it's kind of an emergency."

Stans eyes narrowed, "What job?"

"You remember Faye the owner of that new bar we were at last week? She really needs my help. She's desperate. I couldn't turn her down."

"Wouldn't happen to have anything to do with how attractive she is now, would it?"

Jesse grinned sheepishly, "It doesn't hurt."

"It's not like you to put pleasure before business. You know how far behind we are."

"Honestly, I don't know what I was thinking. I was telling myself to keep my big mouth shut the whole time, and then my lips started moving and what came out was 'I'll help'. Damnedest thing."

Stan smirked, "Yeah I know what was doing the talkin' and it wasn't the brain in your head."

"I'll owe ya big time. I'll still be available day and night if you have something come up. I'll check in...I won't completely abandon you guys."

"You know you're gonna catch hell from the guys. They're going to have a field day with this one."

Jesse shrugged. "I'm already prepared for that."

"Well it's your company. I'm just the foreman. You do what ya think's best. At least it's the guys' favorite new hangout so we'll get to watch over your shoulder after quittin' time," he grinned wickedly.

"Lucky me. I may have to pull one of the guys here and there for some of the work. Most of it I think I can handle by myself, but there are a few things that are a two-man job."

"Like I said, you're the boss and you sign the paychecks."

"I just don't want to put the rest of you in a bind. We'll figure it out."

Stan's eye's twinkled as he responded, "No worries here. We do all the work anyway. You just micro-manage us. And I'm happy for ya. You've been crying in your beer for too long. Take it from me, find yourself a good woman and settle down. Don't let Kelsey manipulate you. She had her chance and fucked up.

It's time to move on. You still get to have a life, too. How long's it been since you and Kelsey split anyway, a year?"

"About that, but who's counting?"

He clapped Jesse on the back and said, "Time to put the past behind you and have a little fun. You deserve it. You work way too hard my friend."

"This is still going to be work. It's just better scenery than working with the likes of you guys. Plus, she really needs the help. She'd probably have to shut down before she even got started if I hadn't jumped in. She said as much. She said I'm saving her from financial ruin."

"Ha! Nothing gets the loins more fired up than a damsel in distress."

"Yeah, well there's a lot of work to be done."

Stan guffawed, "We'll see how much work ya get done with that beautiful blonde as your backdrop."

Jesses forehead furrowed, "Not much choice, the place is falling down. Listen, thanks man. I appreciate your understanding."

Stan squeezed his friend's shoulder, "No problem boss. I'm happy to help ya out. You'd give any of us the shirt off your back and then some. You already have. Don't worry about a thing."

Jesse smiled from ear to ear, "I'll finish up the last bit of work at the Blakes', then I'll be free to get started on Faye's place."

Stan grinned, "Nothing wrong with doing the right thing, buddy. She looks like a good strong wind would blow her away."

"I thought the same thing. I must admit, I do feel

manly around her," Jesse joked, flexing his biceps and sticking out his chest, cracking them both up.

"We've got your back. I'm happy to see that spark in your eyes again."

He grinned. "What spark? There's that overactive imagination of yours again," Jesse said. "Let's get going. I want to fill in the rest of the crew. It will be a bit of a juggling act for you because you'll be handling both crews, but the condo complex is underway and going smoothly... should be fine."

"I know where to find ya."

Jesse held his hand to his forehead in a mock salute, "Thanks Stan."

5

Faye shivered despite the fact that she was layered and bundled up in a bulky sweater against the chilly air. She gazed out over the balcony at the night sky, the sound of the ocean waves soothing her frayed nerves. She sighed then took another sip of wine.

Maddy frowned. "I'm worried about you."

"Me? Why's that?"

"I think you're setting yourself up for a fall. You should come clean with Jesse about your real identity. Especially if you like him."

She shrugged, "How can I? It's too late for that now. Besides it shouldn't matter. I'm just me. My family background doesn't define me."

"But how do you think he's going to feel when he finds out? And he *will* find out eventually."

Her chin jutted out stubbornly, "By the time he does, I'm hoping he'll know me for who I am, not for being a Bennett. It's really nobody's business anyway. I've hired him to do a job. If I want to keep my personal business to myself it's my prerogative."

"He's a guy. Don't you think he might feel a bit foolish when he finds out that you're worth billions? I'm sure he thinks he's helping out some down-on-her-luck girl who made a bad investment."

"And he is! Besides that, my daddy's worth billions, not me."

"Really Faye? You're lying to yourself. You can live in that fantasy bubble all you want but when Daddy and Mommy go, you'll be a billionaire."

"Hopefully that's a long way off. Now quit your worrying about me. I know what I'm doing."

"If you say so. Problem is you've got all of us lying as well. Someone is bound to slip up. I'm afraid it's going to be me. I'm a lousy liar...just so you know."

She glared playfully at her bestie, "It'd better not be you."

"I'll do my best but no promises. Now when do I get to meet this gorgeous hunk that's got you all aflutter?"

"Stop in anytime."

"I'll do that." Maddy's eyes narrowed, "I haven't seen you this sparkly for a long time. I think you might be finally moving on from your past."

"Let me put it to you this way, I'm glad I left Julian on the other side of the planet. I have to admit, the other night freaked me out. When I saw that shadowy figure in the parking lot, my first thought was that it was him."

"I'm sure. Understandable after what he put you through."

"I feel bad for him but his obsession with getting me back was crazy."

"You have to try and let go of all that. He's in New Zealand, you're here. It's okay to trust that you're safe again."

"Maybe... the other night set me back. I had thought I was moving past it all, but I had a nightmare last night. I haven't had one of those for months. The fear was right there in a snap."

"You'll settle back down. I'm glad Jesse is around. That makes me feel a whole lot better."

"Me too."

"How are you feeling about the bar?" Maddy asked.

Faye toyed with a lock of hair, "I'm hopeful again now that I have a contractor on board. He's a real hard worker and seems to know what he's doing."

Maddy laughed, "Thank God! You didn't really have a whole lot of options. Beggars can't be choosers."

"I lucked out."

"Are you happy here? Back in the States I mean. I'm so happy that you're back that I forget about your feelings."

"Yes, I'm glad to be home."

"Do you miss New Zealand?"

"Sometimes, but I'm glad to be back close to family and old friends. I missed it here. I hate the way I left there. ...it ended on such a bad note...but at least Julian's out of my life for good. I'm not sure I'll ever go back there."

"Wasn't Fiji your favorite place in the world anyway? Who needs New Zealand?"

"Second to New Zealand. Didn't you read my

blogs?" she said, laughing as she stood and stretched her arms over her head.

"Every last one of them...Faye LeBlanc. For five years I lived vicariously through you. How pathetic was that?"

Dimpling, Faye said, "That's what friends are for. Seriously Mads, you are my grounding force in life."

"Gee, why am I not thrilled with that role?"

Faye swatted at her friend's arm, "I don't know what I'd do without you. You keep me sane. Between my crazy family and my crazy ex-boyfriend, you should feel like you're the lucky one."

"You make a good point."

"I'm going to hit the sack. I'm almost afraid to...I don't want another night of bad dreams... *but* I have to try, I've got a ton to do tomorrow," Faye said, she covered her mouth as she yawned loudly.

"You can always sleep with your light on... Speaking of work, I wish you'd take a car instead of walking. After what happened in your parking lot, I'd hoped you'd be extra careful."

"Don't worry on my account. I've been biking instead of walking *and* I'm carrying pepper spray."

Maddy rolled her eyes, "Well that's sure to keep you safe. But it's better than nothing."

Faye wiggled her fingers at her friend, "Night. Try to stop in tomorrow."

"I'll try. I'm going to sit out here and finish my wine." She tipped her glass toward Faye. "Here's to pleasant dreams and no nightmares."

6

Faye could hardly believe that it had been two weeks since Jesse had started working for her. They'd discovered that they worked remarkably well together. In no time at all they'd fallen into a comfortable rhythm albeit with an intensely sexual overlay.

"Faye!"

She walked outside onto the deck for the third time in the last hour, hands on her hips, trying hard not to smile, "Can I help you?"

"Could you *please* turn on some country tunes? This pop music is driving me bat shit crazy! You're killing me."

"Anyone in particular you'd like me to stream, your highness?"

Positioned on his hands and knees, and no shirt, he looked up at her grinning, and her breath hitched at the sight of him. "Brett Young station."

Her eyebrows rose, "Anything else?"

"Some water when you get the time. And I might need your help in a few minutes. I need to do some more measurements and figure out exactly where you'd like to see this bar and arbor placed."

"Let me take care of the music first, then I'll grab some water for you."

He winked. A sure sign he knew he was being a diva. "Thanks, darlin'."

"Anything to keep the help happy."

He chuckled. "When I agreed to help you out, I had pictured you on your hands and knees, by my side, handing me nails... I'm lonely out here all by myself."

She rolled her eyes, "And they say women are high maintenance."

"Your point?"

"I'm not inside twiddling my thumbs you know," she teased.

"You sure about that?"

Her eyes narrowed and she was about to let him have it when she saw the gleam in his eyes. She didn't go for the bait this time. Shaking her head, she went back inside to do his bidding. After changing the music, she reached into the cooler and grabbed an ice-cold bottle of water, hesitated, then pulled another one out for herself.

When she returned, Faye found him sitting on the deck floor, legs extended, leaning back on his elbows. His muscular pecs and six pack abs were on full seductive display. Same pencil tucked behind one ear. Her earlier curiosity about shirt or no shirt was answered.

His torso was a golden-tanned washboard...matching the parts she'd already admired.

She swallowed hard then leaned down to pass him the water. After plopping beside him, she crossed her legs and took a long swig. She looked out across the water. "Heaven on earth isn't it?"

His gazed followed hers and he nodded, "Pretty much."

Faye was quiet, taking in the moment. The sun shone, and the temperature had climbed into the low seventies. The briny sea air and squawking of the shore birds were hypnotic. The slight breeze stirred her hair, tickling her cheek. She brushed it back. Brett Young crooned in the background about mercy and a broken heart.

"This must be why there is such a thing as island time," Faye said.

"Yep."

She heated as he turned his attention back to her. His eyes burned a trail across her skin. She met his gaze —*big mistake*. His eyes smoldered with desire. Her belly flip-flopped and she suddenly became aware of a warmth between her thighs.

"Faye," he said gruffly.

She pulled her knees up and wrapped her arms around them before burying her face. He reached out and traced his fingers across her bare arm, sending jolts of electricity through her entire body. Lifting her head, she whispered, "Jess, I don't think this is a good idea."

"Why not?"

"Because technically, I'm your boss...and I don't

want to lead you on. I'm not entirely healed from the last breakup."

"How's that?" he asked gently.

"Bad ending to my last love story."

"Do any of them ever end well?"

"This one was particularly ugly."

"My last wasn't any picnic either, trust me on that." He took a long pull from his water bottle, suddenly pensive. Faye studied his sculpted jawline, which looked as if he'd missed his morning shave. She liked the light sexy stubble. She already regretted opening her big mouth. She could kick herself for bringing up the ex. He was her past. This bar was her new life.

She reached out and touched his arm, "Hey, you got all quiet. I'm sorry that I brought up the past. I really like you Jesse, I do. I won't deny that there's wild chemistry between us. I'm just not sure the timing is right."

"Because you're my boss and all." His eye's glittered. "I promise that I won't accuse you of harassment."

She pushed him against his chest, "Well aren't you just funny as all get out? You know what I mean...why complicate things? We're doing just fine as we are. I think we make a great team."

"I agree, but things are already complicated. I'll have to call you out if you say otherwise. I want you and I think you feel the same."

"That may all be true... but I still don't think it's a good idea."

"Again, why not? We're both adults. I'm not wrong that this attraction goes both ways, you just admitted it."

She smiled, "No, you're not wrong."

"Is there someone else in the picture?"

"No," she answered softly.

He sat up and leaned in close, kissing her cheek. "I promise to take it slow but I'm going to warn you, I don't give up easily." He brushed a lock of hair behind her ear then trailed his fingers across her cheek. Their gazes locked, only a few inches between them. His breath against her face smelled clean and slightly minty. She couldn't help it...without conscious thought she pressed her lips softly against his.

He drew in a sharp breath, then whispered, "Faye." He ran the pad of his thumb over her bottom lip, staring intently into her eyes.

Blushing she said, "I'm sorry, I'm giving mixed messages."

"I like this message much better."

From a distance they heard someone yell, "Get a room."

Faye started giggling. "Do you think they're talking to us?"

He jumped up easily and grinning held out his hand, "I'd bet on it. As much as I'd like to take his advice, I'd better get back to work. This deck isn't going to build itself."

He helped her up and rather than release her, he pulled her against his chest. She slipped her arms around his neck. She could never grow tired of looking at him. His eyes were warm pools of liquid gold, like whiskey, and the streaked highlights in his hair matched as if they'd been brush stroked by an artist.

His soft curls lifted in the breeze, he flashed that sexy smile and she knew she was a goner.

*J*esse met Faye's eyes and was utterly enchanted. *Damn it!* She had cast a spell for sure. Her bedroom eyes were almost his undoing, bright blue fringed with those long dark lashes, looking up at him like he was an ice cream cone she wanted to lick. His throat tightened.

"I could get lost in your eyes," he murmured. He was an inch away from picking her up and carrying her inside to finish what *she'd* started. Lush moist lips tempted him to dip back down for another taste.

He had to... just one. Leaning down he brushed his lips against hers. *So soft.* He smiled at her sharp intake of breath. As he rubbed his hands up and down her bare arms, her warm soft skin made him want to kiss every inch of her. She parted her lips and her tongue darted out, brushing against his mouth. *So sweet.* He drew it in, sucking gently. She kissed him back.

His hands drifted down from her waist and he held her tight against his hardness. Her fingers scorched the skin of his chest. He reluctantly ended the kiss. Resting his forehead against hers, he caught his breath before burying his nose in her hair. Her floral scent almost drove him over the edge.

She stepped away and he shoved his hands in his pockets to keep himself from pulling her back into his arms.

She avoided meeting his eyes. "We should get back on course. Now, where were we? Didn't you mention something about needing my help with measurements?" she asked, still slightly breathless.

He gave her a lopsided grin and played along, "Why yes, Ms. LeBlanc that's exactly what I said." He reached out and brushed her hair back. "Let's go inside first and I'll show you a couple of drawings I came up with and see if it's what you had in mind for the arbor. First thing in the morning, I'm going to get to that barricade and block off the entry from the dock. I should have done that right away. Some of my tools were messed with during the night. We don't need anyone else trespassing around the construction site."

"I'll buy a couple of signs from the hardware store to keep people out." Faye added. She turned and led the way inside.

"Good idea," he said. Jesse enjoyed the view as he followed Faye inside. Reaching behind the bar he pulled out his backpack and withdrew a cardboard roll containing his drawings. Spreading them out onto the counter, they bent over them together. He was aware of her bare arm brushing against his and had to force himself to concentrate. He pointed out where he thought the mini-bar should go.

Tilting her head, her brows furrowed, "Wait is this toward the back end? I pictured it toward the front."

His strong tanned fingers traced the drawing. "Yes. See, here is the exit onto the patio, and here is where I think the bar should go."

"I guess I can visualize that. I trust your judgement."

He casually draped his arm across her shoulders, "It's going to look great when I'm finished with it."

"I have no doubt."

"That's good then. When we're done with this place it will be the *only* place to go for a good time."

Faye grinned, her eyes sparkling with excitement. "That's what I'm talking about."

7

*C*ould it really be Friday already? Impossible...
and yet it was. She was thrilled with the
progress they'd made on the outdoor area. She
honestly felt more alive than she had for a long time.
When she pedaled into the parking lot, Jesse's motorcycle was already there. She felt guilty that she'd over-
slept and was an hour later than she'd intended to be.

She secured her bike to the rack by the back
entrance. Seeing that damn graffiti made her spitting
mad every time she had to look at her ruined wall.
Damn delinquents. That was at the top of her list of
things to accomplish as soon as possible. She'd put it
off for too long. At least it was in the back, hidden from
the public's view.

Of course, her schedule would depend on what
Jesse had in mind for her today. Regardless, she was
going to re-paint the damn thing this weekend if it was
the last thing she ever did.

Slinging her backpack over one shoulder and juggling the carryout coffees and cinnamon rolls from her basket, she stepped inside. It felt deserted and she called out, "Jesse?"

No answer. She set her pack and goodies on the bar. Everything was opened up and the ocean breeze had chased away any residual staleness lingering in the air. It was still chilly, but it was sunny and supposed to reach the upper seventies. *Perfect!*

"Jesse?"

"Out here," he called.

She still couldn't see him, but she grabbed the coffees and stepped outside, following his voice.

He was hidden from view, crouched down in a pit between the large stilts below the deck. Half of the planks had been removed and the deck level was at about shoulder height.

"You've got to see this, it's the darndest thing," he said, ducking back down.

"Good morning to you too," she said,

He glanced up at her and grinned sheepishly. "Sorry, I'm just trying to figure something out here." He hopped up beside her and accepted the cup of joe she held out.

"Cream and sugar, right?" she asked.

He winked, "You really get me." He took a sip, eyes sparkling as he peered at her over the rim of his cup.

"What's got you puzzled?"

"Give me your coffee," he said, placing it on the deck next to his own. He jumped back into the pit and turned for her. She sat on the edge and he splayed his hands around her waist, lifting her down next to him like she was as light as a feather. He didn't release her right away. Pulling her against him, he tipped her chin.

"I've missed you...and you're late." He planted a kiss on the tip of her dainty nose. She fit perfectly against him. She resisted the urge to snuggle into the warmth of his body.

"I'm sorry, but did I miss something? When did you become the boss?"

He grinned and released her, squatting down next to a large wooden crate. There was stamped lettering which read 'Mexican Stone Craft'. "I found this after pulling up some loosened deck boards."

"What's inside?"

He lifted the lid which he'd earlier pried open with a crowbar. Faye leaned closer, peering into the crate.

Her eyes widened, "It's a statue."

"Yeah and what's it doing here?"

"Who knows. I wonder how long it's been sitting down here?"

"Could have been here for weeks or years. Anybody's guess."

Her forehead furrowed, "It almost looks like somebody built a little room down here. That's so weird."

"There's more. This whole ten by ten space was enclosed and protected from any rising water levels."

"Why would someone go to that amount of trouble?" She said.

He squatted down and picked up a newspaper from a pile on the floor and read, "*World series goes to Cincinnati Reds.* This is from 1975. And look at this box of cheap trinkets. It's like something you'd see at a street market."

She put her hand on his back, peering over his shoulder. "Strange. And all those canned goods. Think I could serve them at the bar?"

"Ha! This is an old building. Think about the prohibition days. Smuggling, rum runners, they'd need a place to stash their booze."

"It could even have been a supply storage area. Depression-era hoarding," she said.

"Could be. I think we should use this statue in the bar somewhere. It's cool, looks vintage," Jesse said. "You're artistic. You could paint it to match the rest of your wild color scheme."

"That's a great idea. I just don't see having the time to take that on with everything else. I'll call Amy, an artist friend of mine, and see if she'll paint it for me." She frowned, "If it's an antique I wouldn't want to ruin it though."

"I don't think it's worth much, looks like an ordinary old clay figurine of some Mayan God. Next problem, how to lift the damn thing out of here. I'm going to have to round up another guy to help me. It must weigh over a hundred pounds."

"This is so exciting...and mysterious. Makes me want to go on a fact-finding mission about the history of this place. Too bad I don't have the time."

"That could be a future project, maybe in five years or so," he said, chuckling.

Faye reached in and ran her hands over the decorative statue. A sudden chill ran down her spine and she shivered.

"You cold? Here, take my jacket. I've worked up a sweat, I don't need it anymore."

He held it for her while she slipped her arms into the sleeves. She leaned her head back looking over her shoulder at him, "Thank you."

"Anytime. By the way, thanks for the coffee."

"I've got cinnamon rolls inside."

"Sold!" He jumped back out of the hole and gave her a hand up. Grabbing their coffees, he beat her inside to the pastries.

He was already sitting at the bar ready to take his first bite by the time she sat down. "Hungry?" she asked.

"Always. I've got to keep up my strength."

"For sure, because as you know, I've got a mile-long honey-do list for you. I still can't believe I was lucky enough to snag you."

His gorgeous caramel eyes crinkled as he bit into the pastry. "Maybe you should wait until the works done before you get all excited."

"I still can't believe you found the time to work me in. Every other place was booked up for the next year. I promise to promote you like crazy after you're done here."

He choked on his roll and grabbed the coffee to wash it down. He looked at her from the corner of his eye. "Good thing you came along to rescue me then isn't it?"

"Don't be modest! You're the one who rescued *me!* I'm just glad to be able to help you out as well as benefit myself. Winning!" He put his hands behind his head, triceps flexed and defined, and looked at her. He opened his mouth to say something, but she interrupted him, "I am so curious about that statue! Who do you think put it there?"

"I have no clue."

"It brings out my inner detective."

"Well Nancy Drew, we've got bigger fish to fry. I'll see if I can round up someone to help me get it out of there sometime today."

"Do you have someone that can help?" she asked.

He glanced down as if considering her question then said, "I'm sure I can round someone up."

"That's good then. My bro...friend Griffin might be able to help but he's not much into manual labor. He'd rather get his workouts in the gym or by playing hard."

"No offense, but he did look a little highfalutin. Don't worry, I'll figure it out. What's on your docket this morning?" he asked.

"If you don't need my help right now, I thought I'd go into town and buy some paint for the back wall that got defaced."

Standing he said, "I won't be needing you this morning...not for labor anyway."

She bit her lip as their eye's met... the intensity of his gaze took her breath away. He reached out and brushed a crumb from her chin then leaned down and kissed her cheek. She felt his warm breath against her face, his lips a soft caress. She could smell hints of aftershave cologne...spicy. An ache she couldn't define settled in her chest. Her whole body tingled with longing and she wanted more. Her lips parted and taking it as an invitation, he covered her mouth with his own.

"We shouldn't," she whispered against his lips.

"We should."

She was still perched on the stool as he tilted her back in his arms. He moved to the hollow of her throat, and then licked and kissed his way around to her neck and shoulder. She gasped with pleasure and buried her fingers in his hair. As he was tugging her tee-shirt up, the front door jingled. Jesse groaned, then straightened and reluctantly pivoted to put his body between her and the door.

Glancing back and seeing Faye's dazed expression, he took over, "Can I help you?"

A young man who looked to be about eighteen, give or take, stood in the doorway. "Yeah. I'm looking for the owner."

Faye tugged at her shirt then stood. "Hi. That's me. Faye LeBlanc."

"LeBlanc?" he said, as his brows snapped together.

Smiling she walked toward him and held out her hand, "Yes, I just bought the bar a few months ago."

After releasing her hand, he looped his thumbs in his front pockets. "I'm looking for work. Are you hiring?" There was something about him...Faye couldn't put her finger on it.

He was a gorgeous young man. His arms were heavily inked, with tribal tattoos disappearing under the sleeves of his tee-shirt. And, despite the fact that *he* was the one asking *her* for a job, he came off as if he'd be doing her the favor, almost challenging her as he boldly met her eyes. Despite his cocky attitude Faye was intrigued.

"Not until business picks up. In another few weeks I'll be needing some extra hands. What did you have in mind?"

"I'll do anything. You won't find anyone as good as me. I'll bus tables, wash dishes, take out the trash, clean, whatever you need."

"Have you ever worked in a bar or restaurant before?" she asked, her voice gentle.

His eyes narrowed. "No, actually this would be my first job. But that shouldn't concern you, I'm smart and I learn fast."

Faye said, "If you want to jot down your name and number, maybe we can talk in a couple of weeks. How's that sound."

He lifted his shoulder in a half shrug, "Whatever. Is this a nice way of blowing me off?"

Jesse had already walked over to the bar and grabbed a notepad and pen. Handing it to the kid, he watched over his shoulder as he jotted down the information. Despite the kid's outward bravado his hand shook slightly as he wrote.

"Tyler huh?"

"Yeah."

"You have references?" Jesse asked.

His eye's flashed, "Sure. I can get those for you."

"You can bring all that with you when we sit down and have a real interview," Faye said.

"Thanks Ms. B-LeBlanc."

Smiling she said, "Call me Faye. It's casual around here."

He lowered his head and nodded, "Most folks call me Ty."

"Okay Ty it is. Thanks for stopping by, and no I'm not blowing you off. You'll get an interview."

For the first time since he'd arrived the corners of

his mouth turned up. "You won't regret it, ma'am...I mean Faye." She held out her hand and he shook it.

"What's your tat say?" he asked.

Faye showed him the inside of her forearm. Ty cocked his head and read the delicately scribed words out loud, "*Don't dream your life, Live your dream.* Sick."

She pulled her tee shirt collar aside to reveal a second elegantly scripted cursive tattoo. It sat right under her collar bone. "This one's my favorite, *Sometimes when you fall you fly*...my daily reminder."

"True-dat."

"See you in a couple of weeks Ty. I'll be giving you a call."

He jammed his hands in his front pockets again and left without another word.

"Awkward," Jesse said.

"He was darling! Just nervous. Poor kid. His first job search," Faye said.

"Seemed like a tool," Jesse argued.

"He's young. Aren't most young guys full of themselves? And don't you go judging a book by its cover. His bravado is covering up his insecurities."

Jesse's eyebrows rose, "And you got all that from a five-minute conversation?"

"Yes, I told you I've got a sixth sense about people."

"If it were me, I'd be crossing him off the list of potential employees."

"There was something about him... I can't really put my finger on it, but I'd like to give him a chance. I have a feeling he hasn't had too many of those."

Jesse's eyes were pools of warmth, "That's one of the many things I like about you. Not only do you have looks and brains, but you're also kind." He stared at her lips, "He's probably okay. His timing was a little off, but I won't hold that against him."

Faye felt her cheeks grow warm and her pulse raced, "Well I'd best get going or this day will be shot."

"Yeah, you best," he said in a low sexy voice.

"I won't be gone long."

"I'll be here."

8

*J*esse made a call to enlist the help of Joe, one of his younger and stronger men on the crew. He explained his predicament and Joe agreed to help. "Hey, could you do me a favor and not mention how busy we are?"

Joe couldn't hide his curiosity. "Why not?"

"Long story. Somehow, she's under the impression that the reason I have so much time on my hands to help her is because I'm a down-on-his-luck contractor. I haven't had time to correct her assumption."

"That's a good one. Your secret is safe with me bro."

"It's no secret, it's a misunderstanding. I'm not sure how it even happened. Nothing I ever said to give her that idea."

He chuckled, then said, "The longer it goes on the harder it is to fix. But hey, it shouldn't matter anyway. It will just be a bonus when she finds out what a catch you really are."

"I just want her to hear it from me."

"I understand. Women are from a different planet. Ya never know what's going to set them off."

"That's what I'm afraid of."

"Island's small, I wouldn't wait too long."

"I won't, I just won't have time to talk before you get here to help with this statue."

"I'll be there in about an hour."

"Thanks, see you then."

He scratched his head as he surveyed the amount of work in front of him. This secret compartment was an interesting distraction, but he had a shit-ton of work to do. He picked up his crowbar and began pulling up more decking.

~

Faye loaded her supplies into the basket attached to the handlebars of her bicycle. Her two gallons of paint were stowed in the plastic milk crate attached at the back. She had one more stop before heading back to her bar. The bank. She hated to do it, but she was going to have to dip into her trust fund again. It couldn't be helped.

She had wanted to pay Jesse a percentage up front, but he'd insisted that he could wait until the job was complete. He probably didn't make a whole lot as a contractor. She was shocked at how low his estimate had been. He seemed to be charging her next to nothing. She was going to make him accept a deposit; after all, she was the boss.

She was also going to tell him that he should raise his rates. Hell, she'd be paying her bar help more than he was charging her, and they mostly relied on tips. But what did she know? It was his business not hers. She'd give him a bonus when the work was done.

She entered the small hometown bank, and the manager came out of her office to personally greet Faye.

"Hello Faye! How's the bar coming along?"

"That's what I'm coming to talk to you about. I need to transfer a chunk of change from my trust account into my checking."

"No problem. I'll handle it personally. Come on back to my office." Turning, she motioned Faye to follow her. "Now how much are you thinking?"

Faye chewed on her lip. "I was thinking around ten thousand dollars. That should cover it for now. I've hired a local contractor and I thought I should advance him a little, to at least cover materials."

"You're lucky you found someone. Everyone is booked out for months. The building and remodeling business is booming. Who'd you hire?"

"Jesse Carlisle."

Her eyebrows rose, "*The* Jesse Carlisle? How'd you manage that at the last minute? He owns one the most sought-after construction companies in the area. In fact, he's usually booked out a year ahead."

Faye's eyes went wide. "He *is*?"

She responded as she continued to enter the information into her computer. "Yes, Carlisle Premier Construction. He's built many of those expensive condo and townhouse subdivisions in the bay area. Not to mention those million-dollar homes on the north end. Local small-town boy makes good. He went away to school then his dad, Big Hank, had a heart attack, so he quit school and came back to run the family's' construction business. Took it from a small remodeling enterprise to the successful business that it is now."

She managed to squeak out, "Million-dollar homes? Are you sure we're talking about the same guy?"

"I only know of one Jesse Carlisle on the island."

Faye was stunned, realizing her mouth had been hanging open, she pressed her lips together. As the shock wore off, she became increasingly angry. He'd deliberately misled her. Her anger obscured her judgement, making her forget her own deception. He'd presented it as if he'd only have to move a couple things around to accommodate her, when in fact he owned one of the largest construction companies around. *How gullible am I?*

~

The stereo was blaring country tunes as Joe and Jesse lifted the heavy figurine onto the deck above them. Voice strained, Joe said, "Damn dude, you weren't kidding about this being heavy!" Sweat dripped off his brow. After hoisting it out they climbed up onto the deck.

"It's cool though, don't you think?" Jesse said.

"Yeah and kind of creepy." Joe's eyes narrowed as he studied the statue. "The guy looks pretty pissed off to me. Maybe he'll ward off all the asshole customers for your girlfriend."

"Don't get ahead of yourself. Who said anything about girlfriend? Right now, she's a customer."

"Yeah right. That's why you're already trying to manage her moods."

Jesse laughed at that. "You've got a point. That does seem like a boyfriend kind of move."

They were both startled when a male voice interrupted them. "That's a pretty ugly looking statue." The stranger lit up a cigarette as he looked around appraisingly. Standing below them on the pier, he blew out a stream of smoke and asked, "Is Faye around?"

"Nope, she's out running errands," Jesse said. "Can I give her a message?"

Rather than answering Jesse's question, he asked, "Who are you, the boyfriend?"

Jesse's hackles stood up, suddenly on the alert. "Do you have a message for her or not?"

"Just tell her an old friend stopped by. I'll try and catch her later." He flicked his cigarette into the water and left.

Jesse and Joe exchanged a glance and Joe shrugged. "That was weird."

"Never a dull moment."

~

*N*either heard Faye return until she was standing in front of them, hands on her hips and sparks flying from her eyes.

In her deepest southern drawl, she said, "Why if it isn't Jesse Carlisle of *Carlisle Premier Construction!*"

Jesse and Joe exchanged a look then Jess said, "Faye, do remember Joe?"

She glared, "One of your crew?"

He looked heavenward, "Yeah."

Joe smiled awkwardly at Faye. "I was here for the birthday celebration a few weeks ago. Great place. You're going to kill it. This location is everything."

She glared at Jesse before turning to him, "Thanks."

Joe tugged at his shirt collar, "Jesse, where do you want this monstrosity to go?"

"Yes *boss,* where do you want Joe to put the damn thing?" Faye said through gritted teeth.

"Faye, I can explain..." his voice trailed off as she turned on her heel and stomped off.

"Let's just load it in my truck for now. You can meet me at the shop later to help me unload 'the damn thing.' Faye's friend is going to paint it to match the rest of her bar decor."

"I don't envy you one bit dude. She's madder than a wet hen. Makes me glad I'm single."

Jesse raked his fingers through his hair and expelled a long breath, "Looks like I'm going to remain single. Let's move this bad boy."

After they'd wrestled it to the truck bed, Joe yelled goodbye to Faye from the front entrance, "Nice meeting ya, Faye."

"Thanks Joe," she yelled back, not bothering to come out.

He rolled his eyes, "Good luck man. Call me when

you're ready to unload. If you need anything else, you know where to find me."

Jesse looked over his shoulder and gave a lopsided grin. "I may be back on-site sooner than I thought after this."

Joe shook his head and practically sprinted to his truck.

9

Faye was putting her hair up into a ponytail when Jesse walked into the kitchen. "Faye..." She glared up at him. "Hear me out."

"What's to hear out. You must think I'm a real ditz!"

"No, I don't think that. But I honestly don't know where you came up with the idea that I was under-employed."

Crossing her arms, she arched her brows and said, "Oh really?"

"Really. Can you tell me when I ever said that?"

"I feel so stupid right now. I'm thinking that I'm helping you out and it turns out you're rescuing *me*." She stomped her foot, "I don't *want* to be rescued! I want to make it on my own merit."

He tilted his head. "I'm confused, what's the difference between you hiring me or that other construction company that bailed on you?"

"They didn't misrepresent themselves."

"Neither did I. If I did, tell me how. What did I say?"

"How about today...earlier, when I was blathering on about giving you good recommendations? You must have been laughing so hard inside." Tears shimmered in her eyes.

"Look I tried to correct you, but you interrupted me. Then the moment was gone."

"I'm humiliated, embarrassed...I don't need your charity."

A tear escaped and ran down her cheek. Jesse felt like he'd been punched in the gut. He had to fight not to pull her into his arms. His voice soft and low, he said, "Faye, I'm sorry. I don't know what else to tell you. I never intended to mislead you. You made the assumptions about me. I could be mad at you for thinking I was some dumb worthless schmuck."

She impatiently brushed away her tears. "I don't even know who you are. Why didn't you tell me you built all those developments?"

"Because it never came up. You didn't exactly ask for my resume. Besides, I still think of myself as a small family business."

She glared at him, "Why did you even agree to lower yourself to work on a dive bar?"

"I'm not going to answer that and bury myself further."

"Why? Is the truth that hard for you?"

"I wasn't born yesterday. If I tell you why it will only piss you off more."

"Was it because you felt sorry for me?"

"Partly," seeing her stiffen he said, "Now hear me out. Yes, I felt bad for you. But it wasn't pity. It was a macho guy thing as much as anything. There may have been some ego involved... I'll admit, I'm a sucker for a beautiful woman in distress. You're trying to get something going here. You were desperate and I wanted to help. End of story."

"I assumed that since you could rearrange things so easily that you weren't very busy, and you certainly didn't say anything to make me think differently."

"Let me get this straight. Now I'm responsible for your assumptions? I can *maybe* see where you came up with that idea, but it was never my intention to mislead you. I have a feeling this isn't really about me anyway. You don't have anything to prove to me."

Her eyes narrowed, "Meaning?"

"Meaning that you've mentioned that your family doesn't approve, and that you don't have any support or help."

She raised her chin, "That falls under the category of none of your business. And I still find it very odd that you never mentioned you owned a big construction company."

"I was sitting in your bar with five guys that told you I was their boss. As I recall, initially I didn't volunteer for the job. I was going to give you references."

Her mouth opened in surprise, then Jesse could see the lightbulb go off. "Oh um...that's true. You didn't."

"Did I really act like I was trying to hide something?"

Her shoulders sagged, "I guess not. I'm sorry." She buried her face in her hands, "Can we please just forget this whole thing? Can you forgive me for jumping to conclusions?"

"Nothing to forgive. I'm sorry too. I should have pushed it earlier when I realized your mistake...and I didn't."

She peered up at him, "Jesse, can I ask you something?"

"Shoot."

"Do you think I'm crazy to try to make a go of this place?"

He put his knuckles under her chin and tilted her head up, "You want to know what I think? I think you've got gumption. And you know what else I think? You could have yourself a little gold mine here."

She gave him a watery smile, "Thank you for saying that. I'm a bit overwhelmed at the moment and I hate feeling so dependent on someone else."

"No more or no less than anyone who needs a contractor. You're already open and selling alcohol. The rest is just the icing on the cake."

Still glassy eyed, when she smiled at him it was like the sun peeking through the clouds after a hard rain. "I'm really grateful you agreed to take me on, Jesse of Carlisle Premiere Construction."

"I'm really glad too, Faye LeBlanc. Truce?"

She nodded her head yes, "Truce." She looked away, biting her lip, then said, "Now where do you suppose we should put our statue when he returns from his makeover?"

"He'll have to be prominently displayed, front and center. He's quite impressive."

Faye looked up at Jesse through her lashes. "Jess, I hope I didn't embarrass you in front of your friend."

"Nope. I'm sure my whole crew will have the blow by blow account, but I can handle them."

Faye grinned, then impulsively stood on her tiptoes and kissed his cheek.

"What was that for?"

"Because you're a sweetheart."

He gave her a salacious grin as his eyes scorched her body from head to toe.

"My future just got a little brighter," he said.

"Don't press your luck."

Chuckling he left her alone in the kitchen, her beautiful face tugging at his heart.

10

Faye had just regaled Maddy with the latest turn of events surrounding Jesse Carlisle, which had Maddy shaking her head in disbelief. "Can you explain to me how you could have been so upset with Jesse when you've been lying to him about your entire life? Isn't that the pot calling the kettle black?"

Faye sighed heavily. "I know, I saw red and it clouded my thinking...I was so embarrassed... in my own defense, I didn't stay upset for very long."

Arms folded across her chest, Maddy said, "I'm not trying to be overbearing here, but you'd better fess up to him, and soon, or you're going to blow it!"

"Blow what?" Faye said, feigning innocence.

"Yeah right. As if you don't know what I'm talking about. Hot guy, major chemistry, I've haven't seen you this alive since you moved back."

Hugging herself she said, "He is pretty wonderful."

"Well then…"

Fidgeting nervously, she said, "I just can't. It'll change everything…and what am I supposed to do? Just blurt out 'Oh by the way Jesse, I forgot to mention, I'm an heiress to billions'?"

"Yes. I get that some guys couldn't handle it, but if he's that guy, he's not the one for you anyway. In my opinion it's not that big a deal. The bigger deal is your coverup."

"I just feel like it's nobody's business anyway. I do feel bad that I lied about my real name, but why would I go around and talk about my family's riches? Who does that?"

"Whatever. You're going to do whatever you want anyway, why should I waste my breath?"

"I'm sorry Maddy. I know you mean well, but it'll be fine. You'll see." Faye reached out and squeezed her friend's arm.

"I hope so. I don't want to see you get hurt again."

"I know."

"I don't see the difference between what you were so angry about with him and this. If I were him, I'd want to know the truth. I hope you know what you're doing."

"Not really. Basically, I'm winging it, but hopefully he'll understand. We need a little more time getting to know each other without money entering into the picture. You know that money pushes buttons, the way people think and feel about it is complicated. It's one of the biggest issues in most marriages and divorces…I want him to get to know me, being just me, Faye

LeBlanc. I kind of like it. I wish it could stay this way forever."

"When you put it that way, I guess I kind of get your point. So when do I get to meet this guy?"

"Since it's your day off tomorrow, why don't you come into the bar? I can't have my bestie left out."

"If you're sure you trust me not to mess up. I'll pick up barbecue for all of us from Smokies and we can hang out."

"Perfect!"

"What time?"

"Make it noon. I'm nervous for you to meet him."

Maddy grinned. "I'm nervous because I'm afraid I'm going to blow your cover."

"Just remember, it's all really early, who knows what's going to happen. We have a strong attraction for sure, but it could fizzle out."

Maddy smirked, "Keep telling yourself that."

"Just don't make a big deal out of it."

"Course not. I'm heading to bed. I'll see you at noon tomorrow. Keep it down in the morning because I'm sleeping in."

"Lucky you. See ya and don't say anything to embarrass me!"

Maddy's eyes gleamed, "Would I do something like that?"

"Yes! Go to bed."

Laughing, Maddy rose and headed to bed.

After pulling on a thick sweater, Faye poured herself a glass of wine and slid open the French doors, stepping onto the balcony. It was chilly but the sky was crystal clear, and the stars were fully on display. She could see the distant lights of the marina and sighed with contentment. Sipping her wine, she relaxed and let herself decompress.

Things were going smoothly at the bar, and she was relieved that she and Jesse worked so well together. They both did their own thing then came together when it was required. They were attempting to keep things on a

somewhat professional standing. Kind of sort of. That was the hard part. They were playful and flirty, but the heat level was at fiery hot, and if they gave in to it, they'd be all over each other and the bar would never get done.

Since tomorrow was Saturday they would quit early. She had advertised karaoke and thought that might bring in more customers. She wanted to have a little break before her bar shift started.

Her musings were interrupted by a movement along the shoreline. She could make out the silhouette of a man standing there. It almost seemed like he was staring her way. She shivered but not from the cold. Spooked, she grabbed her drink and went inside. Peering out from behind the safety of her locked door, she watched as the man stood with his back to the sea, facing her condo. She inched away from the door and moved to the kitchen window so she could observe without feeling exposed.

She could see the glow from a cigarette as he held it to his lips for a drag. He stayed for about five more minutes then walked away, heading in the direction of the marina. Her heart was racing, and a stern admonishment to herself about her overactive imagination did little to dispel her unease. That was just plain creepy. Faye don't even go there! This is your PTSD from your last relationship. You are safe!

Rinsing out her empty wine glass, she headed for bed, even though she was convinced that sleep at this point was merely a fantasy. She was pleasantly surprised to find her eyelids drooping after reading only one chapter of her book. She turned out the light and fell into a deep troubled sleep. Dark shadowy figures lurking in corners, sinister statues coming alive, coins being tossed in her face, and graffiti covering every inch of her bar inside and out, had her tossing and turning all night. When her alarm went off, she could hardly drag herself out of bed. It was going to be a very long day.

11

Faye threw on an old pair of cut-off jean shorts and a faded CSU tee shirt that she didn't mind getting paint on. She was determined to get that damn wall done today. Her pulse fluttered when she pedaled into the lot and saw Jesse's motorcycle already parked there. He had beat her again. Today was his day to pick up the coffee and as promised it was waiting for her on the bar counter, along with a cream cheese croissant, her favorite.

"Good morning beautiful," Jesse said cheerfully.

"Is it?" she joked.

"Yes. Any day I get to spend with you is a good one."

"I was out like a light the minute my head hit the pillow, but I still feel like I didn't sleep a wink"

Jesse studied her face, a line appearing between his brows. "You do look tired. Something troubling you?"

"My imagination. There was someone on the beach last night and I could have sworn they were looking right at me standing on my balcony. In the light of day, I realize it was probably just someone out for an evening stroll."

His eyebrows drew together, "You sure about that?"

"Pretty sure. It was dark and they could have been looking anywhere. I just got shook."

"And maybe it's the Neanderthal in me, but I want you to be extra cautious. Look, I'm not trying to increase your anxiety but as a woman, you have to stay alert. Your bar got vandalized with graffiti, you've had a run in with a patron... when in doubt trust your gut."

"You're freaking me out a little."

"Don't mean to do that, but I care a lot about you, and I need you to be safe. Don't be paranoid, just pay attention." His eyes narrowed, "That reminds me, some guy stopped in looking for you the other day, when Joe and I were moving the statue. Wouldn't give a name just said he was an old friend."

Faye's brows drew together. "What did he look like?"

"Tall, dark hair, dressed like a hipster." Jesse grinned, lifting one shoulder.

"Great, you could be describing my ex." Worry clouded her features.

"Hey, it's gonna be okay." He held out his arms. "Come here." She stepped inside his embrace and buried her nose into his chest, breathing in his maleness. It comforted her. He was solid and strong. She relaxed.

Her voice muffled against his shirt she said, "I feel safe with you...sheltered."

"Your ex live around here?"

"No, he's in New Zealand. At least that's where I left him."

"Pretty safe bet that it wasn't him then." He leaned back and tipped her chin up, studying her face.

"Why don't you take the day off? You have to work late tonight, and I don't really need you for anything that I can think of."

"No, I'm okay. It's better if I stay busy." She yawned and stretched her arms overhead. "Nothing a good cup of coffee won't fix. I'm going to paint over that graffiti today. That shouldn't be too hard."

"I can do that for you."

"No! You have enough to do. That is something I actually *can* do."

Jesse flashed his irresistible grin, "I'd rather have you around anyway. I was trying to be unselfish."

"I like being with you too." Her cheeks felt warm as she looked up at him, "Really that's at the top of my list of favorite places to be."

Jesse took a step back and theatrically put his hand to his chest, "Be still my beating heart."

Faye giggled. "You're so cheesy. Oh, I almost forgot to tell you, my best friend Maddy is coming by with lunch at noon. She's super excited to finally meet you."

His eye's sparkled with curiosity. "And just what have you told her about me?"

"Nothing much, just about how average you are, you know mousy hair, faded eyes, boring, unattractive..."

His eyes gleamed, "Is that so?" Before she could move quick enough, he picked her up and threw her over his shoulder, carrying her outside to the edge of the deck and dangling her over the water.

Giggling hysterically, she cried out "Put me down!"

"I don't think so. Now you were saying?"

Sprawled upside-down butt in the air, she was completely at his mercy. "I take it back. Your hair is a glorious crown!"

He tickled her, "And?"

"Smokin' hot bod! Eye's the color of the finest whiskey...*put me down!*" she begged, gasping for breath from laughing so hard. He answered by flipping her off his shoulder and into his arms, now cradling her against his chest. His eyes burned with desire as he gazed into hers. He dipped his head down and kissed her softly. Her breath hitched.

"Go on..." he said against her lips. He sat down, holding her on his lap. She could feel his hardness pressing against her bottom.

Faye, breathless and aroused, had never felt so feminine or sexy. In Jesse's arms there was only them. She cupped her hands behind his head and returned his kiss. He wasted no time and plunged his tongue inside. She opened her mouth wider, enticing his thrusting tongue to explore further. His hands sought her soft skin and slipped underneath her shirt. His palm brushed across her flat belly, exploring her torso until he reached her breast, rolling his thumb across the silk clad nipple. She gasped with pleasure, so aroused she thought she might come right then.

Breathless he called her name softly, "Faye, you're perfection," then continued his exquisite torture.

Her whole body trembled with want. His ragged

breath matched her own, and when she looked into his eyes, they were heavy lidded, pupils dilated.

"You're all I can think about," Jesse said, his voice low and rough.

Forgetting where they were, as he lifted her tee-shirt, she pulled his head down to her breast, while slipping her other hand under his shirt. Her desire surged as her fingertips touched the softness of his skin covering strong solid back muscles... *here...real...now.* She needed this...to be grounded in the present, not consumed by fear. He pulled her bra aside drawing her nipple into his warm mouth. He latched on and suckled greedily. She arched, raking her hands down his back, calling out his name.

"Jesse, please!" He groaned then lifted his head, and tugged her shirt down, eyes flickering with regret.

"Faye, not here, not now. When I make love to you for the first time, I want it to be special."

She covered her face with her hands. "I'm sorry. I got carried away."

He pulled her hands away and stared intently into her glazed eyes. "I hope so. I want you to get carried away. Never apologize for that. But Faye, if you don't get off my lap very soon, I may need a change of clothing, which I don't happen to have with me."

She scrambled to her feet. Not meeting his eyes, she said, "I'm going to go paint."

"I'll go jump into the cold ocean." Not getting the smiling response he wanted, he stood up and put his hands on her shoulders. Face still warm with embarrassment, she stiffened but let him pull her into his arms. He sniffed and nuzzled her hair then nibbled on her ear until she squirmed and giggled.

"That tickles."

"Since the bar's closed on Monday, what do you say we go on a date. We'll spend the whole day together playing... followed by dinner at my place, maybe just pizza delivered, but what do you say?"

She gazed into his warm eyes and said the only thing she could possibly say, "I'd love that."

"Good, it's a date." He kissed the tip of her nose and she went to mix up paint.

Jesse watched as Faye headed to the back room and raked his shaky hands through his hair. He blew out a deep breath. *Damn*, that had to be one of the hardest things he'd ever done.

She was like a unicorn. Magical, irresistible, exquisite. He was all messed up. When he'd told her that she was perfection, he'd meant it. Her body had responded to his slightest touch, like the finest tuned instrument.

12

Faye had just poured her paint into the tray when Jesse stepped outside to tell her he was heading over to the hardware store to pick up something he'd forgotten.

His mouth tightened when he looked at the ruined wall, "I'd like to get my hands on whoever did this."

"You and me both!" Faye said. "Every time I look at this wall, I'm boiling mad all over again!"

"Listen, I'll be right back."

"Take your time, I'm not going anywhere."

"I locked the front door so nobody can walk right in."

"Thanks, see ya when you get back."

"Be good." He brushed her cheek before turning and sprinting to his truck.

Faye sighed. Why did he have to be so damn perfect? How was she supposed to resist temptation when he had such dreamy eyes and lush lips? She dipped her roller in the pan and soaked up some paint before covering over the profanities. As she applied the first coat, she couldn't help but roll her eyes. *Someone was a genuine poet.* No imagination what-so-ever.

Suddenly her roller stopped, and a chill went down her spine. There in the center of all the swear words was a red heart with J Loves F smack in the middle. She had to put the roller back in the pan because her hand was shaking so badly. *Girl get a grip! You're starting to get paranoid. It could be anyone.*

Faye sat down hard on the stoop. Closing her eyes, she took a few deep slow breaths to calm her nerves. Shaking it off, she knew it had to be a coincidence. Those initials could be anyone's. Hell, for that matter they were Jesses initials as well and she knew he hadn't done it. That thought calmed her down instantly. Between the lack of sleep and the long hours she'd been working it was no wonder her mind was playing tricks on her.

She stood back up and quickly swiped her roller over the offending heart and chose not to grant it any significance. Determined to bury her fear, she said out loud, "There, all gone!"

～

*F*aye was just finishing the second coat of paint when Maddy arrived with lunch. She poked her head outside. "Chow time."

"I'm coming," Faye said. "Jesse's on the back deck." Stepping down off the ladder she set her brush aside and put a lid on the paint can, then followed Maddy inside. Her stomach growled in protest. The croissant she'd eaten that morning was long since digested.

"Let's eat outside," Maddy suggested.

Drying her hands off on a bar towel, Faye said, "I'll grab us some bottled water, unless you'd rather have something else?"

"No, water's fine," Maddy replied.

As they stepped outside, Maddy looked over at Faye wide-eyed and mouthed the words, '*Oh my God!*'

Faye grinned from ear to ear. "Jesse, Maddy's here with our lunch."

He looked up at them, then stood. A six-foot-plus, shirtless, muscle-bulging, sweaty, sex bomb of perfection.

Maddy's mouth hung open until she caught herself. Faye made the introductions. "Jesse this is my bestie from high school *and* my roommate, Maddy."

Jesse held out his hand, his expression warm and welcoming, "My pleasure to finally meet you. I'm hoping you can help shed some light on this enigmatic beauty beside me... as only a bestie can do."

Maddy cleared her throat and tittered nervously, pushing her glasses further up on her nose, "Um well as they say...what happens in Vegas stays in Vegas."

Really? Faye rolled her eyes at her friend. *She's going to blow it. She looks guilty.*

Faye clapped her hands over-enthusiastically, cheeks flushed she said, "Let's see what you've got... I'm starving."

Jesses scratched his head, puzzled by the sudden awkwardness. "You girls must have some wild stories, is all I can say."

They both laughed a bit too hard at his comment and he intercepted Faye shooting daggers at her friend.

They sat on the ground in a circle as Maddy pulled out the barbecue sandwiches. "I've got slaw and baked beans and extra barbecue sauce if you want to add any."

"Did you remember my pickles?" Faye asked.

"Y'all think I'm stupid or something? I wasn't about to listen to you pitchin' a hissy fit through the entire lunch." She took out the foil containing the pickles and tossed them to Faye.

Faye smiled as she ripped open the foil and grabbed one, hungrily biting into the crunchy dill snack. Her lips puckered, "Tangy, just the way I like them."

Jesse was busy slapping more barbecue onto his sandwich and then piling slaw on top of that. Faye loved watching his hands. She always judged a guy's hands... she knew it was weird... but his definitely passed her test. They were tan, strong, and very masculine. His nails were trimmed short, well-kept but not fussy. She knew how they felt against her skin and blushed just thinking about it. Jesse took that particular moment to look at her and she felt her cheeks grow hot.

His eyes flashed as they raked across her face. Her skin felt seared everywhere his gaze touched. When he had settled on her lips her breath hitched and she quickly busied herself with her sandwich.

Maddy cleared her throat and said, "So Jesse, I hope you know you're my hero for rescuing my friend here."

He winked and said, "Could be she's the one doing

the rescuing." Taking another big bite, he wiped his forearm across his chin, swiping off some sauce.

"Do you have a clone?" Maddy asked. They all laughed, breaking any residual tension that had been in the air. "But really, you're doing a great job here. I can't believe how much you've gotten done in just a few weeks... and all by yourself."

"Hey, I've got a great side kick here," he said, nodding his head toward Faye. "What do you do for a living?" Jesse asked her.

"I'm an accountant. Boring to most folks, but I love crunchin' numbers."

"She's being modest. She's more than just an accountant. Her office is one of the most successful local businesses around. She has five accountants that work for her and she has some of the biggest companies accounts around here."

Maddy blushed at the compliment, "Quit blowing my horn. I'm just a numbers nerd that was lucky enough to stumble on my niche."

"That's great. There aren't enough women-owned businesses. I'm always happy to hear about them."

"I repeat, do ya have a clone?" Maddy said.

Faye beamed. This was turning out better than she could have hoped for. After the initial discomfort, they settled into an easy flow of conversation. Maddy brought up Faye's travel blog and got her to open up about some of her adventures.

"Hm. A writer, a world traveler...even more intriguing. There are many layers to the beautiful Faye LeBlanc," Jesse said.

Maddy started gathering up their trash and said, "She's layered all right. Real thick if you get my drift?"

Jesse's mouth twitched as he jumped up and grabbed the trash from Maddy. "Here let me take that. Thanks for picking up our lunch. How much do I owe you?"

"No way! Don't even go there. It was my idea. You can buy next time."

"Deal."

"I'll let you guys get back to work. It was great meeting you Jesse. Take care of my friend here. She's special."

"You've got nothing to worry about from this end."

"Thanks Mad." The girls hugged and then she left.

"That went well."

"I like your friend."

"I'm glad. Now I'll go clean up my mess. I'm done with the painting. It only took two coats."

"Good, I could use another hand when you get a chance."

"Sure thing."

She pivoted to go, but he grabbed her arm stopping her, "Faye, is there something you're not telling me?"

She looked down, not meeting his eyes. 'What do you mean? What makes you say that?"

"Just a hunch. Never mind. Just get your butt back out here. I'm missing you."

Her eyes clouded for a second as she battled with herself, then the moment passed and she said nothing, because he'd already picked up his drill and walked away.

13

That evening, Jesse's jaw dropped when he and a few of his crew walked into the Pelican. The place was packed and noisy. His first clue was the full parking lot...but wow. Almost at full capacity. She needed that outdoor space yesterday. If this didn't motivate him to get it done, nothing would. The karaoke hadn't started up yet, but the DJ had his sound system streaming at ear-splitting decibels with people trying to shout over the din. Typical Saturday night bar life.

He scanned the room until his eyes homed in on Faye. She was behind the bar filling up a frosty mug of draft beer, with another dozen thirsty drinkers waiting in line for their refill. She tucked behind her ear a lock of hair that had escaped her high ponytail.

He stood inside the door unable to look away, as if in a trance. She moved with grace and efficiency, working fast but not rushing. She laughed at something one of the guys said to her as she passed him his cocktail. He suddenly snapped out of his study and turned to Stan and said, "Hey I'm going to jump behind the bar and help out. Get in line. I doubt there will be table service tonight, I'm afraid."

When he stepped beside Faye she startled until she saw it was him, then her whole face lit up. Full-blown dazzling white smile, dimples and all. He could see the relief dance across her face.

"Hey! What are you doing here?" she said, trying to talk over the racket.

He shrugged, "Came to see the prettiest girl on the island."

"Boy am I ever glad to see you!"

"Mutual. Want me to just dive in?"

"Yes!"

Just then they were interrupted, "Is this your honeymoon or a bar? Can I get a refill?"

Her eyes twinkled at him before she turned to take the order. She looked good enough to eat. She had on some long slinky maxi skirt with a side slit that sat low on her slim hips and hugged her like a second skin. Her sleeveless top was cropped right above her navel, exposing her flat belly and a sexy navel piercing. She wore what he thought looked like Jesus sandals, since they crisscrossed and wrapped partway up her slim shapely calves. A ton of bangles mixed with beaded bracelets jingled as she worked.

He faced the crowd and jumped right in taking orders. Most people were drinking beer, but he did have to mix a couple of fancy drinks. His old college days of bartending were coming in handy.

Between the two of them they caught up quickly, and by the time the DJ had set up for karaoke, they were in good shape. She jerked her thumb toward the door and yelled, "I'm going to give Ty a call and see if he's ready to start tonight."

"Good thinking. I'll watch the bar while you make the call." He shouted back.

"Thanks, I'll go outside so I can hear. I'll be right back." As she slipped behind him, he slung an arm around her and gave her a quick squeeze. His hand touched the bare skin of her waist and he went rock hard. Her lips parted slightly as their eyes met and he could see hunger there that matched his own. *That's good then.*

~

"Ty, it's Faye LeBlanc. How would you feel about starting tonight? We can work out the details later. I'm slammed."

"Sure! I can be there in twenty."

"Great. I really appreciate it. Wear your running shoes." She hung up, relieved that he could make it on such short notice. This was a big dose of what it was going to take, and she realized she was woefully unprepared. She needed to start interviewing next week for a part-time bartender and server. She already had the busser. Tyler would get added bonus points for his readiness to help out last minute.

Thank God Jesse had shown up when he did. Her body quivered when she thought about his burning eyes trailing across her body. As thrilled as she was with the crowded bar, she couldn't wait to be alone with Jess on their date Monday.

Her belly did a flip flop as she opened the door and saw him behind the bar, all smiles, biceps bulging as he shook the cocktail mixer. She didn't even mind that the woman waiting on her fancy drink was practically drooling. Who could blame her? *Sorry chick, Tonight, he's all mine.*

"Hey Ty, could you empty the trash cans into the dumpster around back? They're almost overflowing."

"Sure."

"Just through the kitchen and out the back door. Thanks," Faye said.

She watched as Ty wheeled the trash receptacle from behind the bar. He had bad-boy written all over him...literally and figuratively. Brooding, with dark, almost-black hair spiked up and wild looking. Vivid blue eyes with ridiculously long lashes. Tats out the wazoo. Would have been just her type ten years ago. She was curious to know his back story. He seemed to be a hard worker and had no problem taking orders from a woman...she had a good feeling about him.

She was going to have to rethink karaoke night. She didn't know if she could take it. She liked music way too much to tolerate the butchering of the classics. It was drawing a great crowd though. She might have to suck it up. It was close to closing time and a good thing because she was running low on energy and on bottled beer.

She shuddered to think what it would have been like tonight had Jesse and Ty not come through. She'd have been screwed. As it was, even with the three of them, they'd worked their butts off all night. Jesse hadn't even had time to sit down and have a beer with his friends. Things had finally slowed down enough to catch a breath.

"You missed it. Before you got here our 'friend' from the parking lot showed up. Sweet as pie and left a huge tip. I still have a funny feeling about him but I'm trying to give him the benefit of the doubt," Faye said.

"I guess we can all have a bad night."

"Jesse, go sit with your friends. Everyone's been served and things are slowing down."

"Only if you come over for one sec and let me formally introduce you to my crew."

She finished dunking the glass she was cleaning and put it on the drying rack, then wiped her hands on a towel. "Lead the way."

He took ahold of her hand and led her over to the group.

"Guys, this is Faye LeBlanc. My boss."

They all guffawed. The guy with a beard and salt and pepper hair spoke up and said, "Sure, that'll be the day."

"Faye the guy with the big mouth is Stan, my foreman, you met him before, and next to him is Jimmy, another guy on my crew. Last but not least," he cleared his throat, "you remember Joe."

Joe's dark eyes sparkled, and he grinned a bit sheepishly. And it seemed he couldn't resist ribbing Jesse, "Yeah, of course, who could forget that momentous occasion? I witnessed her put our boss in the doghouse. Quite the smack down. He didn't stand a chance."

They all raised their beers and nodded, "Cheers to that! Someone's got to put him in his place," Stan said.

Her cheeks turned slightly pink, "Just a misunderstanding. Don't want to disappoint y'all, but he didn't really deserve it. I jumped to some conclusions. But anyway, thanks for the support. Nice to officially meet you," Faye said.

Jimmy winked and said, "We'll accept any woman who puts a smile back on our Jess's face."

"You'll probably get sick of us. This is our new favorite spot to drink beer. And there's another half a dozen of us, but don't worry we won't bite," Stan said.

"Y'all are welcome anytime. The more the merrier. I'd better get behind the bar for last call. See you 'round."

*J*esse sat down and waited for the ball-busting he knew was coming, and they didn't disappoint.

"Damn Jess, she's even more beautiful close up and personal. You sure you're good enough?" Jimmy said.

"That's what I'm saying. I think I'm more her type," Joe chimed in.

"Maybe she likes an older man of distinction... like me," Stan said puffing out his chest.

The guys hooted with laughter. "You mean an older *married* man of distinction. What would Mimi have to say about that?"

"Oh, I forgot," he grinned, taking another big guzzle of beer.

Jesse looked around the table at his friends with true affection for his crew. He never had to doubt that they always had his back. Like now, they were all happy to help him out and pick up his slack, just so he could free up his time to help Faye. He'd never forget it. He knew he was lucky to have such a great group of friends and once the bar was done, he'd throw one hell of a party for them right here.

14

Faye's hands were slightly unsteady as she applied a shimmering pink lip gloss at the last minute. She had applied the barest of make-up, just a little mascara, and fragrant lotion to her body. Jesse would be there any minute to pick her up for their date. "Mads, why am I so nervous?"

"Um...because he's hot and you care?"

"It's not like I'm fifteen. I'm thirty-one. Hardly my first date."

"First one with Mr. Wonderful," Maddy said.

"What if it's awkward? What if we don't have anything in common when we're not at work...or anything to talk about? I hate those long stretches of silence when you go blank and want to squirm right out of your own skin."

"Quit worrying. I've seen you two in action; besides that, if it's not a good fit, better to know than not know," Maddy said.

Faye wrinkled her nose, "The problem is I want it to be...a good fit. I really like him."

"Just relax. You've practically been inseparable since he started working and you've been getting along just fine. Quit worrying...go and have a good time. He's totally smitten with you. He couldn't take his eyes off you. It was so hot, I thought *I'd* have to take a cold shower!"

Faye giggled, "I'll take your word for it." She heard Jess's motorcycle and her heart skipped a beat. "I hear the motorcycle now, see ya." She ran out the door to meet Jesse at the curb.

"Wow, you look amazing," he said.

He looked so good in his cargo shorts and faded black tee. The soft cotton fabric molded to his muscular frame, tempting her to run her hands across his chest. His strong tanned thighs straddled the bike. *Hmm.* She craved him and she missed seeing his eyes, which were hidden behind dark sunglasses. It made her feel more vulnerable, so she slipped on her own pair to hide behind before climbing on the bike. Handing her a helmet he said, "I have to make a quick stop by my folks' place before we head out. Okay with you?"

"Sure."

"Hang on beautiful."

She slipped her arms around his waist and couldn't resist hugging him tight for a moment. She breathed in his masculine scent. Today she detected a hint of soap, freshly laundered shirt and Old Spice.

"You can hold me like that forever," he said.

She rubbed her cheek against his back, the soft

material over the hard body wreaking havoc with her libido. What was it about this guy? She had never felt this turned on in her life. This was a new discovery for her and she kind of liked it. He waited for her to put on her helmet before starting up the bike.

"Ready?"

"Yes."

His large hand reached down and gripped her thigh giving it a squeeze. She responded by squeezing her legs tightly against him. She rubbed her hands softly up and down his stomach before coming to rest right below his navel.

It was a gorgeous spring day and there was no better place in the world to do spring than in the Carolinas. The air was aromatic with flowering trees and early perennials. The sky was bright blue with big white puffy clouds dotting the horizon. At Jesse's suggestion she had worn her swimsuit under the loose shirt and white linen slacks she had on. Despite her coaxing he wouldn't tell her what they were doing today, insisting that it be a surprise.

Faye felt exhilarated nestled so close behind this gorgeous guy, the wind in her face. By the time they pulled into the seaside cottage drive, her cheeks were flushed, and her eyes glittered with life. She playfully bit his shoulder before climbing off the bike.

"Ouch, you wench!"

"You deserve it. You practically laid the bike down going around a couple of those curves."

He grinned. "Did not, big scaredy cat!"

"I wasn't scared, it was invigorating. I'm just saying, I think you were testing me."

She loved the way his eyes crinkled when he full-on smiled, the way he was doing right now. "Ya think?" he said trying to look innocent.

She took off her helmet and shook out her hair, "I know."

He secured their helmets to the bike and grabbed her hand, interlacing their fingers.

"I'm a little nervous," Faye admitted.

"Don't be. My mom is the best and she's going to love you."

They walked up the weathered wooden stairs and entered through a screened in porch that wrapped around in an L shape. The back of the porch was ocean view with native sea grasses and dune swells leading to the white sandy shoreline. They had a large inground pool with inviting umbrellas and lounge chairs tempting one to pour a cocktail and chill.

"This is spectacular!" Faye enthused.

"Yeah it is. It's not where we grew up, that was inland, but I built this for mom and dad after I started making some serious cash."

She felt an ache in her chest and brought his hand to her lips and kissed the back of it. "Jesse, that is so sweet."

"It was nothing compared to what they did for us, raising four boys like they did *and* paying for and insisting that we all go to college."

"That is impressive. Where are you in the birth order?"

"Third in line. We didn't have much of a choice about college. Even if we didn't know what the hell we were going to do when we grew up, we were going to get an education. Pops was adamant. He worked construction his whole life and provided for his family just fine, but he wanted us to have options."

Faye squeezed his hand and said softly, "And you followed in his footsteps."

"Yep. He taught me everything he knew. I worked for him every summer through high school and college. I tried but I knew I wasn't cut out for an inside job sitting at a desk. I have to work with my hands. That's just who I am."

They walked inside with Jesse calling out, "Mom?"

"Coming!"

His mom came rushing out from the back of the house with a wide smile and a hug for her son. "Hi honey. I was doing laundry." She turned to Faye, eyes dancing. "And you must be Faye. We've heard so much about you. It's good to finally put a face to a name."

"It's so nice to meet you Mrs. Carlisle." Faye held out her hand, but his mom ignored it and gave her a hug instead.

"I'm a hugger. I hope you don't mind, and *please* call me Ruby. Mrs. Carlisle makes me feel old. Good lord and heaven forbid!" Her laughter was so free and infectious that Faye found herself laughing along, already half in love with Jesse's mom. She could see why he was so special. It made her think of her own mother, so self-centered and always poised and in control. More concerned with how she looked than how others felt in her presence, just the opposite of Ruby.

"I'd be honored," Faye said.

"How about a glass of sweet tea before you two go off on your date?"

"I'd love that," Faye said.

"Great, Jesse darling, take your beautiful date on out to the porch and I'll bring out the tea."

"Are you sure we can't help?" Faye asked.

Jesse snorted, "Don't even try Faye. My mom will cut off your hands and feed them to the alligators if you lift a finger. *That southern hospitality don't ya know*," he said, as he exaggerated his southern drawl for effect.

"Git you two!" Ruby swatted Jesse's butt as she shooed them out the screen door.

"I *love* her!" Faye said the minute they sat down.

"I told you."

"You're so lucky. She is like the quintessential perfect mom."

"I know, it doesn't suck."

Ruby joined them with a pitcher of iced tea and three glasses. "I'll be right back." She left then returned with a soft cooler which she placed by Jesse's feet.

He grabbed the pitcher and poured their tea, his eyes twinkling as they met Faye's. "Aren't you curious about the cooler?"

"Yes."

"That's our lunch. Nobody can beat Mom's cooking."

"Isn't that cheating?"

"Naw, I think it's good common sense. If I want to impress a girl, it's better to use every advantage I've got. And as you'll soon find out, my mom's picnic basket holds the key to your heart."

"I never did say my son lacked skill in the bragging department. I hope you're not disappointed in your lunch."

"I'm sure I won't be. Jesse does have a way with the words, Ruby. A real southern charmer."

"Wait til you meet his dad. Now he has the true gift."

"Where do y'all think I got it?" Jesse said downing the last of his tea. He stood up reaching for Faye's hand. "Let's go!"

"You two have a wonderful day and leave everything behind. Just enjoy each other and this beautiful weather."

Faye impulsively hugged Ruby, her throat tight. She couldn't imagine what it would have been like to grow up in such a normal household. "It was so great to meet you Ruby."

"Don't be a stranger. You're welcome anytime with or without my son. Ya hear?"

Faye's eyes glistened, and her chest felt tight as she held back her tears. She didn't know why she suddenly felt like crying. "Thank you, Ruby. That means a lot to me."

"Bye Mom. Thanks, love you." Jesse gave her a big bear hug and practically pulled Faye out the door.

She quickly slipped her sunglasses back on to hide her emotions. Before they got onto the bike Jesse wrapped both arms around her and held her against his chest. He kissed the top of her head and said, "My mom really liked you."

"I'm sure she likes everybody."

"No, not when it comes to her babies. She's a good judge of character, and she liked you."

Faye sniffled, "I liked her too."

"Are you crying?"

"No, I just got a little sentimental, that's all. She made me feel special. I can certainly see why you turned out the way that you did."

Jesse cupped his hand to his ear, "Tell me more about that, I'm all ears."

"Kind, strong, steady, honest."

She tilted her head to look up at him, then pushed his glasses to the top of his head to gaze into his eyes. "No matter what happens between us, I want you to know that I see you, Jesse Carlisle, and you are one of the most decent men I have ever met."

He dipped down and pressed his lips against hers. Lingering but not deepening the kiss, he seemed to be waiting for her. She parted her lips and he slid his tongue inside. She grasped her hands behind his head and met his tongue thrust for thrust. He broke away first, running his hands roughly through his hair, he took a deep breath and said, "Let's get out of here before I make a scene."

She dissolved into laughter, her heart full. "Yes, let's."

He used a bungie cord to secure their lunch to the back of the bike and they took off.

15

*A*n hour after they left Ruby, they were paddling their canoe down a lazy river. The current was slow which gave them plenty of opportunity to enjoy the protected wildlife refuge they were meandering through. The mammoth bald cypresses and rare white cedar trees provided some shade and the Spanish moss draping down made the rippling corridor seem mysterious... like the river held ancient secrets.

Jesse had taken his shirt off and was enjoying the warm sun on his back and the view in front of him, Faye in a bikini, her rounded bottom planted on the metal seat—didn't get much better than this. Her long legs reminded him of a young colt, and her slim back was sexy indeed, shoulder blades defined and delicate, long spine leading to the curve of her hips. Desire coursed through him.

"Faye," he said in a hushed tone. She turned, and Jesse held his fingers to his lips as he pointed up and to the left.

"Do you see that?"

"What?" She said as she scanned the treetops.

"That's a bald-assed eagle!"

She squealed, "I see it!"

"And look on that log over there, see those turtles sunning themselves?"

She nodded her head excitedly, "And there's a stork!"

He guffawed with laughter, "Honey girl, that's a heron."

"Quit laughing! It looks like a stork."

He shook his head, still chuckling. "Keep your eyes open, we could see anything. Since we seem to have the river to ourselves, we have a good chance of spotting lots of wildlife."

"Like what?"

"Snakes, beavers, deer, the occasional gator."

"As in alligator?"

"Yep. And we could even see black bear."

He dipped his paddle in leisurely pulling the oar back, the sound of the water splashing ripples onto the surface. The sun was warm, but the gentle breeze cooled at the same time. Time stood still...the sounds of nature, birds chattering, the trees rustling in the breeze, the warmth of the sun on their backs, only the two of them, everything serene and peaceful. He had stowed their clothes in a watertight satchel he'd brought along. After slathering sunscreen on each other, Jesse had stuck a Tilley hat on Faye's head for added protection. He was fantasizing about how her hands had felt on his back and let out a slight groan...

She glanced back eyebrows raised above her dark glasses. "Everything all right?"

He grinned a little sheepishly, "Couldn't *be* any better."

"Thanks for all of this," she said as she swept her arm wide.

"It's humbling."

"Yes, it is."

"Did I tell you that you're looking mighty hot in that bikini?"

"You don't say. Did I tell *you,* that your ripped bod is driving me crazy?" Faye said.

He waggled his eyebrows comically. "No, you *didn't* say. Are you hungry yet? I thought I'd look for a good spot to pull off and eat our lunch."

"Anytime."

"There." A few minutes later he pointed to a large fallen tree trunk with a bit of muddy beach front to dock their canoe. He began to paddle harder.

"Stay in. I'll jump out and pull the boat to shore."

"I hate to say this, but I've got to pee," Faye said.

"Tissues are in a plastic container and there's a baggie for the waste."

She smiled, "You've thought of everything. Be right back."

He liked that she wasn't fussy about peeing in nature. Some girls got all weird about not having a proper toilet. One more thing of many on his list of things that impressed him about her.

He pulled out the food from the cooler. Southern

fried chicken, Mom's famous potato salad and collard greens, his favorite. She'd also thrown in a couple of cookies for dessert. He was starving.

Faye returned and sat on the log, "Looks yummy."

"Wait until you sink your teeth into it."

"My mom doesn't cook," Faye said quietly.

"What?" he felt his eyes go wide with shock.

She shrugged, "No big deal. Sorry, I don't know where that came from, it just popped out."

He got real still as he watched a bunch of emotions flit across her face. It made him want to pull her into his arms and kiss away the pain he saw hiding just beneath the surface. She was a mystery, that was for sure. One that he intended to unveil. He wondered about the meaning behind her tattoos and what had made her fall. Was she flying yet?

Faye could have bit her tongue off after sharing that information about her mom. She didn't want to spoil the day with her pathetic, poor little rich girl upbringing. It was hard not to compare though. She'd grown up with the finest chefs catering to their family's every whim and yet she'd have traded it in a heartbeat for home cooked meals prepared with love.

Putting those thoughts aside, she took her first bite of chicken and almost had an orgasm. It was that good. "Oh my! You weren't kidding, were you? Would it be too soon for me to propose?"

Busy chewing a big mouthful himself, he swallowed before answering, "Nope."

"Nope what?" she asked already forgetting that seconds ago she had practically proposed.

"As long as you get down on one knee to do it. I'm kind of old fashioned that way."

"Oh you." Giggling, she reached out and pushed against his naked chest. Suddenly the air crackled between them. She unconsciously licked her lips and he groaned.

"Babe, you're killing me. You have no idea what you do to me," he said.

"Wanna bet?"

He caressed her cheek with his thumb then leaned in for a kiss. "Faye, you've got to promise to go easy on me. I'm in the palm of your hand."

She smiled against his lips, "Good. That's right where I want you."

"Let's finish lunch and head on in. Joe's picking us up at the Fox Run trestle. We're about a half hour out now. I'll give him a call. After we pick up the bike, I want to show you my place and maybe we can watch the sunset and take in a little Netflix action."

"Perfect." She fiddled with the strap on her hat. "Jesse?"

"Yes?"

"When I'm with you, I'm the happiest I've ever been. I feel like I'm exactly where I'm supposed to be. How do you do that? I'm not used to it. It kind of feels too good to be true."

His throat tightened, and he grabbed her, pulling her roughly against him. He wanted to give her everything she'd ever wanted. Burying his lips in her hair he whispered, "You deserve nothing less, if anyone ever told you *otherwise*, they were the fools. You make it so damn easy."

16

When they got back to Jesse's, he gave her the grand tour, then set out some towels and shampoo so she could take a quick shower. While she was in the guest bath, he disappeared into his own room to clean up. She hadn't brought any underwear and didn't want to put her damp swimsuit back on, so she went commando. Her slacks were a wrinkled mess, but they were clean and dry. She toweled off her hair and left it loose. How could it be that, already, she couldn't remember a time before Jesse was in her life?

She could hear Jesse singing and found him on the back deck waiting with a glass of wine poured for her. He was bare-chested, wearing only a pair of gray sweatpants that hung low on his hips. He took one look at her and his pupils dilated with heat... desire... and more... She knew it was about to get real and she wasn't sorry.

He had put on some music and Brett Eldredge crooned a romantic country tune, *Wanna Be That Song.* Grabbing her hand, Jesse pulled her tightly against his chest. His hands wandered up and down her spine, finally drifting to rest in the small of her back. Swaying with the music, he sang softly in her ear. "*I wanna be those words that fill you up... believe you're right where you belong...*"

Faye lost herself in a swirl of sensation so intense that she felt she might drown. Her body fit next to his like a missing puzzle piece. She wouldn't have been able to tell where she ended and he began, if not for his desire pressing against her belly. *How is it that she came to be in the arms of the sexiest guy she'd ever laid eyes on... and he was singing a song just for her...*

The song ended and he dipped his head down and gave her a soft kiss in the hollow of her throat, then led her over to a chaise lounge. He sat down, pulling her with him. Snuggled between his thighs, she relaxed her back against his chest. He grabbed her glass of wine from the side table and handed it to her. She took a sip as he nibbled on her ear.

"That tickles."

Jess whispered, "Faye, you take my breath away. I want to make love to you...but only if it's what you want. If you're not ready tell me now."

She stilled. Her mind said *too soon* but her body overrode her sensibilities. She tipped her head back and he buried his face in her neck. His bulge pressed against her bottom and she wiggled against him.

Groaning he said, "Either you're a sadist or that's a yes."

"Yes," she whispered.

*J*esse took her wine glass, then rolled them on their sides facing one another. He gripped her chin firmly, staring deeply into her eyes, as blue as any sapphires he'd ever seen. Her lips looked ripe for the pickin' and he covered them with his own. She moaned as he slowly seduced her with his tongue. He plunged in and out, each thrust deeper... their tongues in a sensual dance together. He traced her lips then thrust inside again, filling her.

He groaned as he pulled her shirt up exposing her lovely breasts, the nipples a soft petal pink and fully erect. He latched on and suckled greedily.

When he pulled away, she begged "No! Don't stop."

Smiling he said, "You've got too many clothes on," then pulled her top over her head tossing it aside, before skillfully returning to his ministrations. He squeezed and massaged one breast, which filled his cupped palm perfectly, while nursing the other. She cradled his head to her chest to hold him there. Still latched onto her nipple, he glanced up and was satisfied to see her eyes glazed with desire.

He lifted his head and began to remove her slacks. He tantalized her by licking and nibbling slowly as he stripped her. His cock felt like it was going to explode. When he discovered that she was naked underneath her pants, he came close to losing control. Trailing kisses down her thighs, he reached her feet, and the slacks joined her discarded shirt.

He licked her inner thighs as he worked his way

back up again, finally reaching her apex. She was wet and ready. He nuzzled her mound, his tongue flicking against her womanhood. He put his open mouth on the center of her heat, and she moaned and bucked, burying her fingers in his hair. He licked her, his tongue darting quickly, as she writhed beneath him. He pressed kisses until she cried out. As his mouth wandered up to her belly, he ran his tongue around her piercing before moving to the hollow of her throat.

Panting she said, "Jesse, please!"

"Tell me you want me," he said, his voice low and husky.

"Yes, I want you, only you. I want to feel you inside of me... Please."

He stood and pulled off his sweats, his cock springing out hard and ready. She stared hungrily then grasped him in her soft hand.

"Wait, I'll be right back," he said, breath ragged.

When he returned, he held a condom packet and passed it to her. She ripped it open with her teeth then pulled his hips toward her. He stood in front of her, his erection at her eye level. Before rolling the latex on she traced his length with her tongue; he jerked like he'd been shocked. She took him into her mouth and sucked. Her moist mouth tight around him felt incredible. "Babe, put the damn thing on before it's too late."

She rolled it over his hard shaft, then he pressed her onto her back. Crawling on top, he pushed her legs apart with his knees. He dipped his fingers into her moist center, testing to see if she was ready for him. Finding her wet he positioned himself over her. He pushed her legs up, then began to tease her mercilessly, pressing his tip against her then withdrawing. Each time he entered a little deeper until she was moaning with need.

"Open your eyes," he commanded.

She did as he asked; only then did he thrust inside of her. He rode her hard, plunging in and out, sweat beading his brow. Her breasts bounced, her soft pink buds inviting him to suckle. He dipped his head down while still riding her and licked her nipple. That was her undoing. He lifted his head to watch as her body convulsed with orgasm. Seeing her peak sent him over the edge, and he came inside of her as he felt her vagina pulsating against him.

They panted as they lay intertwined. He rolled off and lay beside her taking it all in...the smell of shampoo and soap mixed with sex, her soft skin, her beauty... he traced the tattoo under her collar bone with his fingertip.

"Who hurt you?" Then he kissed her there.

She wrapped her arms around him, resting her cheek on the top of his head. "The last relationship ended when I caught him in bed with one of his college students. I was devastated. I had trusted him without reservation."

"What a fool. But if he hadn't fucked up, I wouldn't be holding you in my arms. Fate may have had a hand. Faye, I've got it bad for you." He could feel her lips curve into a smile against his head.

"You do?" she asked quietly.

He kissed her throat then propped his head on his hand staring into her languid eyes. "I want everything with you." He skimmed his hand down the length of her...trailing slowly...down her neck... shoulder...arm... hip...thigh... then back up again. His voice was husky with longing, "You're so soft. So beautiful." He ran the pad of his thumb across her lips then kissed her, devouring, knowing he'd never get his fill.

His cock hardened again as she covered his chest with tiny kisses. She ran her fingertips over his nipples then stroked her palm down his toned hard belly, searing his skin. When she reached his erection, she gripped it and cupped his roundness in her other hand, gently rolling and squeezing with one hand while she slid her hand up and down his shaft with the other.

He reached between her legs and found her warm and wet. He inserted two fingers and plunged deeply, in and out while his thumb pressed against her sweet spot. She panted and rode his hand as he thrust against her grip. Their bodies reached a climax together, and he couldn't tell if the moan had come from her or from him.

"*J*ess?" she whispered.

Still breathing heavy he said, "Yes?"

"What you said earlier, about wanting everything?"

"Yeah?"

"Did you mean it?" Framing his face with her hands, she studied his smoldering eyes. His mouth curved into a smile.

"Yes. What do you want?"

"You. I think I was lost the first time I hopped on the back of your bike."

"I have you beat. You took my breath away the moment I laid eyes on you flitting around the bar and charming the pants off all of us."

Her nose crinkled, "Really? I'd have never known...I mean you were friendly and sweet, but I didn't have a clue that you were that interested."

"I didn't want you to think I was a jerk. I also had been keeping my eye on that dude at the bar. I had a bad feeling about him and so I waited around."

"You are my gallant fearless noble..."

Laughing he said, "Stop, it's going to my head. You ready for pizza? I thought I'd call in for a delivery."

"Have you ever known me to turn down food?"

"Come to think of it, no."

*J*esse had given Faye one of his old tee shirts to wear and she sat cross legged on the floor in front of the TV as she waited for him to settle up with the pizza delivery guy. She took another sip of wine, noticing that her body felt like a limp rag doll. She felt a little sore between her legs, a good sore, and her nipples still tingled from his hungry mouth.

If it weren't for that nagging voice in the back of her mind, her world would be almost perfect. She'd tell him...and soon...but not tonight. She wouldn't ruin this moment. She couldn't bear to see him angry right now. She wanted to hold on to this feeling for as long as she could.

He plopped down beside her with the pizza, paper plates and napkins and the bottle of wine. He refilled their glasses and raised his for a toast, "To the best date I've ever had with the most beautiful girl I've ever laid eyes on."

She suddenly felt shy and couldn't meet his gaze.

"Hey, is something wrong?" He asked, his brows drawn together.

"No! I just feel so tender that it hurts," she reached for his hand and placed his palm against her heart. "Right here."

His white teeth flashed with a wide grin. "You know how to get a guy don't you?" He nodded his head toward the pizza, "Dig in before it gets cold."

She grabbed a slice and took a big bite, the extra cheese dripping off the pie. "Jesse Carlisle, I am so stinking happy right now."

Winking he said, "That is my number one goal in life. To win over your cold, cold heart."

"Sweet talker."

"Gimme some sugar," he said leaning in for a kiss.

With her mouth full of pizza, she still managed to pucker up and kiss him.

"Tell me what your life was like before you bought the bar."

"Hmm, let's see...in college I majored in English, with a minor in fine art. Lasted until mid-junior year when I came down with a huge case of the travel bug. Dropped out and eventually, after several years of exploring the world, landed in New Zealand where I put the English to good use and started writing a travel blog. Landed a gig with a major travel magazine and did that until I moved back here."

"That's impressive."

"Funny that I ended up buying a bar...pretty much on a whim. I was rudderless when I first returned to the States. Healing from my breakup, grieving, then I ran into someone who told me the place was for sale, so I went for it." She bit her bottom lip. "Much to the dismay of my friends and family."

Jesse listened thoughtfully, then said, "I told you I went to college, but what I didn't tell you is that I quit my senior year." Faye caught a brief glimpse of sadness in his eyes before he continued. "Dad had a heart attack and I came home. When I dropped out Dad was so angry with me, he could've chewed up nails and spit out a barbed wire fence."

"It was important to him," Faye said, her eye's soft pools of warmth.

"Yeah, it became a battle of wills. He insisted I finish school and all I wanted was to take over the family construction business. Obviously, I won."

"How is your dad now?"

"I worry about him a lot. He likes his beer, he loves all the foods he shouldn't...bigger than life. My hero. But his heart attack was mild and after a double bypass they say he's as good as new."

"I'm glad. That must have been a huge shock for you and your family."

"Taught me to never take a day for granted. You never know if it's going to be the last time you do something. From the life altering to the mundane...last time you hug your mama, last time you wave goodbye, the last time you tie your shoes."

Faye tenderly brushed his hair back from his forehead. "I'm glad your dad is okay. I can't wait to meet him."

"He's going to love you." He reached for the TV remote and turned it on, channel surfing. "What do you want to watch? Your choice."

"Rom-Com for sure."

"I knew you were going to say that."

"I've been dying to see *Always Be My Maybe*. I heard it was really funny."

"Sounds good to me."

They both fell asleep halfway through the movie, wrapped in each other's arms. Sometime during the night, Jesse woke up and picked Faye up, carrying her to bed. She barely roused as he pulled back the duvet and tucked her in. He tenderly kissed her forehead and crawled in beside her, then promptly fell back to sleep with her spooned up against him.

17

*J*esse sat on the edge of the bed watching Faye's chest gently rise and fall in sleep. Her thick lashes rested against high cheekbones and her hair fanned out on his pillow just like he'd fantasized. He hated to wake her. All he wanted right now was to feel her smooth satiny skin writhing underneath him again.

Already showered and dressed, he had to leave to deal with some problems at the condo construction site. His vibrating cell phone had jarred him out of a deep sleep about an hour ago. He lightly caressed her cheek and her eyelids fluttered before opening sleepily.

"Hey you," Jesse said, softly.

She smiled shyly, "Hi." She stretched out sensuously, like a cat. "Did I oversleep?"

"No, I wanted to let you sleep in. I have to go to a job site; I've got some big problems. I didn't want to leave without saying goodbye. I won't be able to work at the bar today. I'm sorry."

"I understand. How did I get to bed last night? Did you carry me?"

"Yes." He leaned down and kissed her softly. "I'll call you later."

She pouted, "I don't want you to leave."

"You're killing me. Believe me baby, I don't want to go." His finger traced the outline of her lips. "Thank you for last night."

"It was everything," Faye said quietly.

After Jesse left, Faye stared at the ceiling, a roller coaster of emotions flooding her senses. The ache in her chest from watching him leave was running a close second to the feeling in her belly like she'd just bungee jumped off a sheer cliff. Her entire body felt like a live wire. She touched her lips still feeling the warmth of his kiss. Lord have mercy, it was going to be a long-ass day.

~

Faye had called Ty and asked if he could come work for a few hours. Currently she had him busy stocking the coolers and replacing the kegs while she caught up on bookkeeping.

Ty poked his head inside her office and said, "Faye where to you want me to put the empty cases?"

She leaned back in her chair studying him. "Stack them right next to the freezer in the kitchen. Thanks. Everything all right? You seem a little down today."

He mumbled and she had to strain to hear his reply. "Just life."

"Girl troubles?"

He shook his head. "Naw, my mom and I had an argument."

"Do you want to talk about it?"

"What good would that do?"

"Maybe my incredible wisdom will enlighten you." Smiling, Faye added, "Sometimes just talking about something helps."

Ty plopped down in the chair facing her desk. "I guess it can't hurt. Mom is mad that I took this job."

"Oh. Can I ask why?"

"A multitude of reasons...its complicated...but the one thing she made me promise is that I come clean with you about something. I hope you'll hear me out. I was in juvie some time back. I got myself in some trouble dealing a little pot. But I'm clean now, I promise. If you hadn't called me in on the fly, and we'd had that sit-down interview, I would've fessed up. The right time hasn't come up since...and I wasn't sorry about that."

"I see." Faye looked thoughtful as she tapped her pen against the desk. "I don't need any DEAs hounding my bar. Not good for business."

"That was a couple of years ago. I've kept my nose clean since. I don't ever want to be incarcerated again. Plus, now that I'm eighteen it would be much worse. Not to mention it broke my mama's heart. I'd never do that to her again."

"Look, I like you Ty. If I'm going to be one-hundred-percent honest, I'll admit that information might have influenced my decision before I had time to get to know you...but now that I have, I'm willing to give you the chance. I always trust my gut. You're a good kid. I'd bet the bar on it." Faye smiled.

"There's not a chance in hell I'd get into that world again."

"I believe you."

"Dope."

Faye cleared her throat, "Wrong choice of words."

He snorted with laughter, "Right. Sorry."

"It wouldn't be an easy topic to bring up. I would have struggled with it too. And you're only eighteen. Give yourself a break. And Ty? Now that tourist season is right around the corner, I could use more of your time, that is if you're available."

His eyes lit up. "Yes! I could use any extra hours you're willing to throw my way."

"Great. How are you with technology? I have a couple of big screen TVs that need to be installed. I can put them up, but can you program them?"

"Yeah, that's easy."

"Maybe we'll work on that tomorrow. I'd like to expand your hours."

"Sick!"

"And, since you're working out so well, I'll increase your pay to fifteen dollars an hour."

"Wow, thanks!" His whole face changed when he smiled. He was a real showstopper when that sullen look disappeared. Lordy help the poor girl who had to protect this guy from the girls who'd be throwing themselves at his feet. He had no idea how beautiful he was. And *that* was a good thing.

"Ty, one more thing...thank your mom for me."

He glanced down at the ground, "Yep."

"Ty you know you can come to me with anything?"

"It's all good."

Faye had a niggling feeling he wanted to say more but he stood up, his expression now poker faced, clearly done with their heart to heart.

"I'll be finished up with paperwork in a couple of minutes, then we can get started with organizing that storage room."

He slipped his hands in his front pockets and left. Faye shrugged. She'd probably only imagined the brief look of doubt that had darted across his face.

18

Faye's cell rang and she saw that it was her older brother Kyle. "Hey big brother. What's cooking?"

"I wanted to invite you out to dinner at the Yacht club tonight. I know it's last minute, but it's Ella's birthday and I thought I'd surprise her. Finn will be there, and Dad and Mom flew in unexpectedly this afternoon. Griffin's coming too."

"What time?"

"Around seven. You can meet us in the lounge."

"I'll have to close the bar, but I've been dead most Tuesdays anyway. I'm not too thrilled about the Mom and Dad part but maybe their attention will be on Finn, rather than on me and my bar endeavor."

"Don't count on it. Mom's been driving me crazy with questions in her own particularly smothering sort of way."

"Lovely."

"I'll try to run interference for you."

"While Griffin stirs the pot," she said, laughing.

"When do you expect to have your grand opening?"

"I'm looking at Saturday of Memorial Day weekend. I just hired a young guy named Ty to bus tables and do odd jobs around here. The construction company...well the owner himself, is moving right along on the outdoor seating area. I was actually slammed last Saturday night. Jesse stepped behind the bar and helped me serve customers. I advertised karaoke and had no idea of the crowd it would draw."

"Jesse huh? Griffin mentioned you had some hot construction dude working for you and you made him lie to him about his identity. What's that all about?"

"Long story and let's just say, I'm an idiot."

Kyle laughed, the warmth in his voice comforting and reassuring. He had always had her back while they were growing up, and with their crazy lifestyle, replete with boarding schools and nannies, she'd needed it. He'd run interference for her and Griffin more times than she could recall and had buffered them from the worst of their father and mother. Whereas her father had been cold and aloof with unrealistically high expectations, her mother, a famous French model prior to their marriage, had vacillated between her extreme preoccupation with self and smothering her children with a false sense of what mothering actually entailed.

"If it were anybody but you and Ella, I'd say no...but I'll come."

"Great, I miss you sis, it will be good to catch up. No gifts. We have everything we could possibly need...and then some."

Faye's lips twisted, "The downside of a billionaire lifestyle. I miss you too. See you at seven."

As she hung up the phone, Ty appeared at her door holding a gorgeous vase, filled with red roses and fern cuttings. Faye's cheeks flushed with pleasure at the surprise. *He must be missing me as much as I am him.* She tore open the card and inside it said *Forever yours, J.* And yes, she was living proof that hearts really *can* skip a beat... hers was racing while the butterflies in her stomach somersaulted.

Ty had a big grin on his face and said, "I'm taking notes."

She was still breathless but managed to croak out, "Did the florist just deliver these?"

"Yep. I'm taking off if there isn't anything else you need me to do."

"I'm right behind you." She rolled her eyes, "I'm meeting my dysfunctional family for dinner tonight. Fancy. I've got to figure out what I'm going to wear."

"Want me to wait for you?"

"No, go."

"Okay, see ya tomorrow." He stood shuffling from one foot to the other, hands stuffed in his pockets, obviously with something more to say.

Faye arched her eyebrows and waited.

"Um, Faye?"

"Yes?"

"I really appreciate you giving me a chance. Most people wouldn't have."

Faye beamed at him, "Anytime! Have a good night and see you tomorrow."

. . .

*A*s Faye was locking up, the creepy customer she'd had the run in with showed up. "Sorry I'm closing tonight for a birthday party."

"Damn, that's too bad. Guess I'll see you around another night. I was looking forward to that beer."

She shifted her heavy bag to the other shoulder. "Next time you're in, I'll give you a beer on the house."

A corner of his mouth lifted. "Got yourself a deal." He winked at Faye, "Nice flowers."

Faye felt a chill go down her spine. His smile never quite reached his eyes. After that initial altercation he couldn't be any more friendly. He'd come in with a bouquet of daisies the next day and a sheepish grin on his face. But still Faye wasn't convinced. He was pouring it on a little too thick.

"You know I never did catch your name," Faye said.

"Dave."

"Have a nice night, Dave."

He turned on his heels and left and she exhaled.

❧

*F*aye grumbled to Maddy as she slipped diamond earrings through her earlobes. "I don't miss this fancy smancy stuff one bit."

"Not even a little? I think it's fun to play dress up now and again."

"Maybe if it were for a hot date...but I'm already dreading the inquisition from my parents. I feel like a lamb going to slaughter."

"At least you're a beautiful lamb. That Christian

Dior dress is divine! The chiffon and that champagne color against your fair skin is *simply marvelous darling.*" Maddy said. The bodice was fitted with a short flirty skirt that gathered at the waist and swirled around her thighs with every movement.

"Good thing Romeo can't see you now. It might finish him off," Maddy said.

"What do you think of this ruby red lipstick on me?" Faye had decided to wear her hair pulled back tightly in a French chignon, which highlighted her fine bone structure and large eyes.

"Love it. You totally take after your mom. You could easily be a New York Fashion Week runway model. So jealous."

"Don't be. Look what that lifestyle did to my mom! Got her married to Dad," she laughed at her dark humor.

"They love each other."

Faye sighed. "Yeah I know. They just shouldn't have had kids. There wasn't room for children...so they paid others to raise us."

"So, you still haven't told me about your date yesterday. I know it went well since you didn't come home last night."

"It was truly perfect."

"And?"

Faye's shoulders slumped. "No, I didn't tell him if that's what you're asking, and I feel terrible about it. I've really dug myself a deep hole. I just don't know how to start that conversation. Then today he sent me a huge vase full of red roses...and the card read *forever yours.*"

"You have to tell him." Maddy said.

Faye held up her hand, "I know, I know, I'm waiting for the right time. I've tried. Something always seems to get in the way."

"He won't take too kindly to feeling like he's been played for a fool."

Faye covered her ears and said, "La la la la la."

"Okay, I get the message. Have fun tonight and tell everyone I said hi."

"I will. I'm going to tell him. I promise."

"I only nag you because I care. You two are perfect for each other. I wouldn't want some dumb mis-understanding to ruin it. He's one of the good ones."

Faye dabbed a bit of perfume behind her ears and grabbed her keys from the key holder. "I've got to run but it's at the top of my list. See ya later."

"Caio."

19

*F*aye hopped into her Fiat convertible, which literally hadn't been out of the garage for weeks. She was actually looking forward to her evening with the family. Despite their quirks she loved them, and they were hers. Nothing she could do about that. Can't choose your family.

She pulled up to the valet stand front of the Yacht Club. The young driver gawked and tripped over his tongue as he addressed her.

"I haven't seen you in a while Ms. Bennett."

"I know it's been a minute. Samuel, aren't you graduating this year?"

"Yes ma'am. Thank you for remembering."

"Congratulations. Will you be leaving us then?"

"No, I'm taking a year off before I go to college."

"Good for you. I lasted about three years then got bit by the wanderlust bug and skipped out."

He grinned, "I know all about your travel blog. You're kind of famous around here."

"Ha! I'll see you in a couple of hours. Do you know if my brothers are here yet?'

"Mr. Kyle Bennett is, he just arrived."

"Thanks again." She discreetly slipped him a fifty then headed inside.

Heads swiveled as she made her entrance, but Faye was so used to it that she hardly noticed. It had never boosted her self-esteem because it was so superficial. She had always longed to be loved for who she was beyond the flesh and blood.

For her mother, she'd been like a favorite doll that she'd liked to dress up and show off when it suited her. Her dad had ignored her unless she managed to do something to embarrass or displease him. For the most part, she'd managed to fly under her father's radar. She was sure being a girl hadn't hurt. Kyle, being the first-born, had received the brunt of their father's unreasonable expectations.

She spotted her parents before they saw her and as always was struck by what an imposing couple they made. They reeked of power and money. Kyle and Ella stood next to them and they were certainly a power-house couple in their own right. Kyle had his arm protectively around her waist as Ella laughed at something their mother was saying.

Ella and Kyle had met in the hospital after he'd been in a terrible car accident. She'd been his ICU nurse and they'd fallen in love. The transformation in her brother was astonishing. Kyle's seven-year-old son, Finn, was just as gaga over Ella as her brother was. Ella had not only helped him heal from the automobile accident, but also from the emotional trauma of his son's kidnapping.

As if that hadn't been devastating enough, his best friend and business partner, Peter, got caught embezzling money from their law firm. Kyle hadn't pressed charges, but instead had kept it private, with the condition that Peter turn in his law license and never practice again. Peter had also had to pay restitution to the firm for what he had 'borrowed' for his gambling debt. *Bad year... but he came out ahead with Ella by his side.*

Ella softened Kyle's edges and challenged his arrogance. He had definitely met his match. She was strong, intelligent and beautiful...not to mention fun. They were technically newlyweds since it had been less than three months since their quiet ceremony in a small local chapel. Faye sighed. What a magical wedding day that had been. She had been equal parts envious and delighted.

Would she ever get her happily ever after?

Her mom suddenly spotted her and rushed over enthusiastically, "*Cheri, mon bébé.*" She grabbed Faye's face between her hands and kissed both cheeks then stepped back looking her up and down... "*Tu es si mince.*"

Kyle came up to rescue her, "Now *maman',* don't start. She's no thinner than usual. She inherited your genes after all."

"Ah, but she is working too hard, *oui?*"

"Mom I'm right here," Faye said, already irritated.

"But you are still *belle ma chérie.*"

Her father stepped up and stiffly put his arm across

her shoulders and squeezed her briefly. The corners of his mouth turned down as he said, "How is the bar business going?"

"Just great!" Then she flushed because her answer had been a tad bit over enthusiastic and her dad never missed a beat.

Changing the subject as quickly as possible she said, "Where's Griffin?"

Her father gave a dismissive wave of his hand, "Late as usual."

Ella grabbed Faye and gave her a big hug as Finn wrapped his arms around her legs and held on.

"Aunt Faye where have you been? I've got to show you the tricks I taught my puppy."

"I'll stop by soon. I've been really busy. How are Miley and Cyrus?" She asked, referring to his goldfish.

"They're great. Ella bought me a huge and I mean *huge*," he held his arms wide to demonstrate, "fish tank. How big is it Ella?"

She smiled down at him, "Fifty gallons."

"Yeah, fifty gallons."

"Wow! I'll bet they're happy."

"Yeah, they really *really* like their new home."

"Ella, how are you feeling? Any morning sickness?"

"No thank God! I've been feeling great."

"I can't believe you're having twins! What do you think about that Finn?"

He scrunched his face up and bounced on the balls of his feet, "Can't wait!"

"You're going to be the best big brother. Just like your dad was to me. Ella you are glowing and so is my brother."

"We're over the moon."

"Do you miss going in to work?"

"Not one bit. I especially don't miss the head nurse. Good riddance," Ella said.

Griffin swept in and whispered in her ear, "How's the secret billionaire?"

She elbowed him *hard*. "Ouch!"

With gritted teeth she hissed, "I'm warning you."

"You're way too easy."

"And you're a jerk."

"Well looks like the gang's all here; should we be seated?" Kyle asked.

With a slight nod of his head, they were whisked to their favorite table outside, seated right next to the water. Much like her bar, a pier and marina abutted the restaurant, and many of the members docked their boats here.

To Faye's surprise, the evening was lovely, relaxed, and everyone seemed to be making honest attempts to avoid each other's soft spots. Ella was happily surprised when the birthday cake came out flaming and they sang to her. She teared up...making Faye tear up right along with her. She was truly sorry when they all said their goodbyes, with promises to get together very soon.

Driving home, her thoughts drifted back to Jesse, though they'd never strayed too far from him. She could hardly wait to see him tomorrow, assuming he had put all the fires out today. She commanded google to play the Brett Eldridge song they had danced to the night before and cranked it to full blast as she drove home.

Her heart hurt it was so full. The words stroked her

soul. He *was* that song for her. She had to tell him the truth. Until then, their relationship was built on sand. Sighing deeply, she pulled into the driveway parking under the car port and sat there until the last note was played.

As Faye was climbing into bed, she realized she had never turned her cell phone back on. There were three missed calls from Jesse but now it was too late to return them, so she sent him a text hoping the ping wouldn't wake him up.

Faye: Missed you so much. Can't wait to see you tomorrow.

Two seconds later her phone pinged.

Jesse: Not near as much as I missed you. I'll be there in the morning. Coffee's on me. I'm having withdrawal. For real!

20

Faye was disappointed when she saw that Jesse hadn't arrived yet but patted herself on the back that she had managed to beat him there for once. Parking her bike, she unlocked the bar and went in. She began opening things up and turning on lights. When she approached her office, the door was ajar. She mentally went over the night before, and distinctly remembered closing and locking the door. She knew she had. So why was it open?

With trepidation she looked for any other disturbances. As she entered the back room, she saw that the storage room door stood wide open. Her heart began to race, her hands clammy with sweat. Her body was shaking so hard she had trouble punching in the number for the police.

"Nine-one-one, what's your emergency?"

*J*esse frowned when he pulled in and saw the cop car in the parking lot. *What the hell?* He jumped off his bike and ran into the bar. Not seeing Faye in the main barroom, he panicked. He called out her name, "Faye?"

"Back here," she replied.

He took in a deep breath, not even realizing he'd been holding it. One look at her face drained of color and that momentary relief vanished.

"Babe, what's wrong?" He rushed to her side pulling her into his arms. His gut clenched when she wrapped her arms around him and began to cry.

"Shh, I'm here, whatever it is its going to be okay."

The police officer came out from the back room and nodded to Jesse. "What's going on?" he asked her.

She looked at Faye. "Can I speak freely?"

"Yes, he works here. I want him in on everything."

"A break in. Looks like they came in through the back. The door was kicked in and completely splintered. I'm afraid it will have to be replaced or boarded up. Broke the lock on the storage room, appears nothing was taken from there. Money from the cash register was taken, safe was untouched. Papers in the office were rifled through but other than that you're lucky. Could have been a lot worse."

"What comes next?" Jesse asked.

Her partner entered the room and they exchanged a glance. "We'll file a report but the chances of catching whoever did this are next to zero. I wish I had better news. My advice is to have security cameras installed and motion detector lights in the back."

With a tight-lipped smile, he said, "I'm on it."

The officer nodded toward Faye, "She's understandably upset. I wish there was more we could do, but we'll pick up patrol of this area, and be on the lookout for suspicious activity. Probably teenagers looking for cash money and found this to be an easy target. Get that security installed."

"*J*'m sorry I was late this morning, I should have been here first," Jesse said, kicking himself. "What if they'd still been in the building?"

"It's not your fault. You hear me? Don't you *dare* take this on! You have a life and other responsibilities besides this bar."

His lips curved, buried in her hair, "There's that spitfire I know and love."

His knuckles brushed across her cheek, then he tilted her head back. Seeing the lingering fear in her eyes filled him with a primal rage. He wanted to destroy something. His jaw clenched and he took a few deep calming breaths before he spoke.

"Faye, if I ever catch the bastards that did this, I will beat them within an inch of their life. I swear to you."

"Jesse kiss me."

He dipped his head and covered her mouth. His kiss was fueled by his anger and feelings of inadequacy. He hadn't been able to protect her, and he had never experienced this level of powerlessness before now. Breath ragged, he devoured her, tongue thrusting, holding her tightly against his body. She kissed him back, her fingers threaded through his hair.

Jesse pulled away and blew out his breath. "I hate that you were alone. It makes me feel crazy to think that someone could have been inside and hurt you." He sounded tormented.

"But they weren't and I'm okay. Just a little rattled is all."

"Faye I'm sorry I wasn't here first."

"Jess I'm a big girl. I was shook up, but I'm settling down and you're here now."

He framed her face with his hands, his eye's glittering with intensity, "If anything had happened to you...Faye... I'm not going to lie, you're it for me."

Faye chewed on her bottom lip. "Listen Jess, we have to talk."

"Not exactly what a guy wants to hear when he just tells a girl that he's falling for her."

"Don't take it that way. It's not what you think. I'm crazy about you."

A smile of relief lit up his face. "Then forget about the rest. That's all I needed to hear for right now. We can talk later. I have to get the door replaced and make some calls and get that security system installed. It can't wait. And no arguments, I'm paying. I know money is tight for you."

"Jesse..."

"I said, no arguments." He leaned in and softly kissed her.

"But..."

"Shh... I've got this babe."

She sighed heavily, "I guess we should get to work then. One step forward, two steps back it seems."

He planted a kiss on the tip of her nose. "You take my breath away," he murmured.

"Jess, I...um...I guess we'll talk later then."

She ran her fingers through his hair, then stroked it away from his brow, a frown on her face. What could she do? Timing was everything. She could no longer justify keeping it from Jess, they were in too deep.

"Will you promise we'll sit down and talk sometime today?" Faye asked.

"Yes. Now I'm going to go measure the door and see what others supplies I'm going to need."

21

"You want to go door shopping with me?' Jesse asked.

"Yes, I don't want to be alone here just yet and the break will do me some good. Let me grab my bag."

Jesse had already nailed up some plywood to cover the door. "You think we can be back by noon? Because Ty's coming in," Faye asked.

"Yep, for sure. I've got to trade in my bike for my truck on our way there, then it shouldn't take long to pick out the door and get back here."

She hopped on behind him and nuzzled his back before sliding her arms seductively around his waist. She tucked her hands up under his tee shirt so she could feel his bare skin. She loved the soft fur below his belly button and couldn't resist letting her fingertips follow the trail lower. He held his hand over hers briefly before starting up the bike.

After switching vehicles, it was a few short minutes to the home improvement store.

Jesse grinned, then said, "You know I feel like a kid in a candy store whenever I step in here."

Faye cracked up. "I get it. That's how I feel when I go to an art supply store."

Jesse reached for her hand and interlaced their fingers as they perused the aisles. When they arrived at the back of the store in the lumber section, Jesse glanced furtively around before reaching under her dress and running his hand up her inner thigh. "Hmm, your skin is so soft."

Giggling she hissed, "Jesse stop."

"I can't help it."

Faye squirmed and got away only to have him swoop her up from behind. Faye started giggling, unable to stop which only egged him on.

They both saw movement out of the corner of their eyes as someone joined them in the aisle. Faye dissolved into another fit of laughter.

"You are so bad," Faye said gasping for breath.

"Well if it isn't Jesse Carlisle as I live and breathe." A sultry southern drawl interrupted their intimacy.

Jesse stiffened. "Kelsey! What are you doing here?"

"Picking up some tools. Why haven't you been returning my calls? I've missed you and we need to talk."

She suddenly took a good long look at Faye and her eyes widened in recognition. Faye was shocked to see the bartender from The Yacht club, and even more surprised that she seemed to know Jesse and it appeared that she knew him quite well.

Kelsey's eyes narrowed as she looked Faye up and down. Before Jesse could make any introductions, Faye grabbed his hand and practically dragged him along behind her. "We have to hurry, remember, Ty's coming, and I don't want him to find everything locked up."

Kelsey put her hands on her curvy hips and opened her mouth to say something, but before she could get a word out, Faye interrupted her, and laying heavy on her own southern accent she said, "You have a real nice day. Come on Jess. Bye now."

Jesse gave a half shrug and apologized, as he was being hauled away. "Hey, we're kind of in a hurry. Sorry to run off like this."

When they got to the door section, Jesse cocked his head to the side and said, "What the hell was that all about?"

Faye's eyes went round, "What was what about."

"That little scene back there."

"Scene? What scene?"

"You know damn well what scene I'm talking about."

Relying on the old adage that the best defense is a good offense she went for it. "You two seem to know each other quite well. Why is she calling you and why haven't you returned her calls? Just who is she to you?"

It worked! As she watched him squirm, Faye felt just the tinsy-tiniest twinge of guilt right before it was swallowed up by relief.

He stuck his hands in his pockets and narrowed his eyes. "She happens to be my ex. Her names Kelsey. We split over a year ago. Nothing's going on between us. I'm not returning her calls because she's obsessed with getting back together with me and I'm not interested."

Faye's strategy backfired, the relief short-lived, as she grappled with this new threat. She crossed her arms over her chest as she was gripped by a different emotion...jealousy.

"Keeping secrets already?" she accused. *Girl you better quit while you're ahead. Isn't your own lying the whole reason you're even having this stupid discussion in the first place?*

"Faye are you *serious* right now? Having an ex-girl-friend is hardly keeping a secret."

"What about the phone calls?" Now that she was on a roll, she couldn't seem to stop herself. "She's beautiful. Quite the bombshell. I wonder how you can even look at me after being with someone like her. She looks like every man's fantasy."

He pinched the bridge of his nose, "I can't believe this."

"Believe it." She set her jaw stubbornly completely forgetting her own deception. She'd honestly never felt jealous over a man before. It was gut-wrenching. Her stomach cramped and she felt slightly nauseous.

"Let's pick the damn door and get out of here," she said.

"Fine by me," he said between gritted teeth.

The ride back to the bar was thick with tension. Faye sat turned away from Jesse her arms crossed, staring silently out the window.

"You know you're being unreasonable, right?" Jesse said.

Silence.

"Look, we broke up after I found out she had another guy on the side. Does that make you feel any better?"

He saw her shoulders soften out of the corner of his eye.

Progress.

"She might be every other guys' fantasy, but she's not mine. My dream girl is sitting right next to me acting as stubborn as a mule."

She finally turned and looked at him. He reached over and tweaked her nose. "I've had a dance or two with the green-eyed monster, and it's a dance with the devil."

"I'm *not* jealous."

"You sure about that?"

"Yes, I'm just surprised that's all."

"Well since you're *not* jealous I guess you don't need me to tell you how sexy and beautiful I find you. How I go to bed every night with you on my mind and wake up every morning rock hard thinking about you."

She tentatively reached for his hand and he took ahold of hers and brought it to his lips. "You don't ever have to worry about another woman. I'm a one-woman kind of guy. And you're it for me."

"Jess..."

"Here we are." They pulled into the parking lot and he jumped out and went around to open her door.

"I'm sorry, sorry for a lot of things," Faye said hugging him tightly around his hard body.

He kissed the top of her head. "Ain't no big thang. Let's get this door hung and leave that shit behind."

～

That evening as Faye lay in bed going over her list for the following day, she glanced over at the vase of roses and remembered that she'd never thanked Jesse. She'd have to do that first thing. She had changed her mind and decided to ask Ty to work evenings this week. She wasn't afraid to admit that she felt nervous to be there alone. His new shift would begin at five. He was young and didn't mind the later hours, so it worked for him.

Memorial Day Weekend would be here before she knew it. So much to do before the grand opening. The deck was almost ready. Jesse would start on the kitchen renovation right away. He was confident he'd be able to get the kitchen up and running before the big weekend. She almost couldn't believe it.

22

$\mathcal{I}$t was Saturday and Jesse had sent her out in his truck to get some supplies from the hardware store. The list would test the patience of a saint for sure. A half-dozen different sizes and shapes of screws. Who knew? She pulled one from the tiny plastic bag and held it up to the picture on the front of the bin full of screws. Nope, too long. She was going to have to find a clerk to help or she'd end up having a meltdown.

She finally tracked someone down and he was able to fill the order. Then on to the opposite side of the store to pick up some fittings for the kitchen sink. Glancing at her watch while waiting in line she sighed. *What a waste of time.* A whole hour had passed.

She got back to the bar and was getting out of the truck when Jesse ran out to greet her. He held up a scarf.

"Close your eyes. I'm going to blindfold you."

She put a hand on her hip, "What have you been up too? Did you just send me on a wild goose chase Jesse Carlisle?"

He grinned, "Who *moi?* Turn around." He slipped the scarf over her eyes and tied it behind her head. Taking her hand, he said, "Come with me."

She followed him until he stopped and said, "Keep your eyes closed til I say different." He removed the scarf and said, "Okay you can open your eyes now."

She gasped and covered her mouth with her hand. "Oh my Lord! I've pictured this a thousand times in my head, but it never looked this good!" Her eyes sparkled as tears threatened to spill out. She walked around the deck, touching every table and chair as if making sure they were real.

"I don't know what to say. It's everything I wanted. It's perfect!"

"You really like it?"

"I love it!" She threw her arms around his neck and planted a wet kiss on his lips.

"I still have a few finishing touches to do to the bar, but I'd say as soon as you've got the help you can open up out here."

"Can you help me bartend tonight? We can try it out. Ty will be here to help and to bus tables. And we do make a good team behind the bar."

"I'm in. It can be a test run."

"You've got to promise to show me some of your fancy bar moves."

Jesse grinned rakishly, "I'll show you, but full disclosure...it took many broken bottles to get to the master level I'm currently at." He glanced at his watch,

"Now I've got to go to a job site and meet with Stan. I'll catch up with you later."

"I'm in a daze over how beautiful it looks out here. Thank you, Jesse."

"You're my girl, right?"

Her throat tightened, moved by his goodness. "Yes."

He kissed the tip of her nose, "Be good. I'll see you this evening."

She twirled around in excitement then quickly punched in Maddy's number. "You've got to come over to the bar immediately."

"Why?"

"It's a surprise."

"On my way."

*M*addy shook her head in amazement. "You know this guy is head over heels in love with you right?"

Faye hugged herself. "I hope that's still true after he finds out who I really am."

"I can't believe you. You've had weeks to fess up."

"I swear every single time I've tried something derails me."

"No excuse."

"After we get off tonight, I'll tell him. He's helping me out behind the bar, so I'm sure I'll spend the night with him."

Maddy said, "Maybe you should soften him up first and wait til after the mind-blowing sex."

"Ha! You're coming tonight right? I'm having the DJ back again for another night of karaoke torture."

"I wouldn't miss it. With the two of you behind the bar they might decide to film you guys in a reality show. I can see the tag line now, 'If you like *Southern Charm* then you're gonna adore *Love Southern Style*."

Faye threw her head back and cackled, "That would be one boring show."

"Have you watched any reality TV lately? Girl, it would check all the boxes. I'm sure we'd have a hit on our hands."

"Get out of here, I have work to do. See you tonight."

~

*T*he inside of the bar was packed and overflowing to the outside deck. Faye had nabbed Maddy to wait tables and she and Jesse were cranking out drinks faster than a hot knife through butter. Ty was coming out of his shell and bantering with the customers as he mopped off tables and cleared the empty glasses and bottles.

Jesse's mom had sent a ton of Chex mix over with him and they couldn't fill the bowls fast enough. As quickly as the jerky and chips were going, she knew she'd do well once the kitchen was open. She was equal parts thrilled and terrified by the speed at which things were moving.

She glanced over at Jesse who was laughing with a customer as he showed off his juggling skills with three liquor bottles. His exhibition was drawing a crowd around that end of the bar and she stopped what she was doing to watch. He was so damn beautiful it took her breath away. She had earlier observed him handling the bottles with flair and showmanship, but this was another level. She clapped her hands along with the rest of the crowd when he finally finished with a flourish and took a bow.

He glanced over at her and winked, and her body pulse kicked up a notch. How had she gotten so lucky? She didn't deserve this man. He was everything that was good. She was falling hard, and she knew that if she hit the ground it was going to be a brutal landing.

She turned back to her customers and the hair on the back of her neck stood up. There sat Dave. His piercing dark eyes scanning the room with an intensity that implied he was looking for something or someone. Why the hell did he have to pick her bar to drink in? When he noticed her staring at him, he tipped his red ball cap and winked. Faye wiped her hands off on her apron and went to take his order.

"Hey Dave, the usual?"

"How about a *Coors* draft."

"Got it."

Jesse looked over and his jaw tightened. He strode purposefully over to the guy and said, "FYI, I've got my eye on you. If there's even a hint of trouble, I have no qualms about kicking your ass out. Got that?"

The guy held his palms up in mock surrender, "Hey, I thought there were no hard feelings, I did apologize."

"I'm just saying, check yourself."

Faye walked up and placed the frothy mug of beer in front of him, "It's okay, Jess."

He glared at the unwelcome guest and said, "It'd

better be." Jesse wasn't happy about it, but he backed off and went back to his end of the bar.

The crowd had thinned somewhat now that the DJ had quit. Everyone caught up with their tasks and took a much-appreciated breather. Ty came out from the back carrying a case of beer and set it down in front of the cooler.

"Thanks Ty." Faye said, then watched as Ty's eyes went wide and his face drained of color. "Ty? Is something wro..." She didn't even get the sentence out before he turned and rushed out from behind the bar into the back room.

"Jess, I'll be right back I'm going to go check on Ty."

Jesse, in the middle of serving a customer, nodded, acknowledging he had heard.

"Ty, are you okay?"

"I'm out of here. I've got to go," he hastily threw his backpack over his shoulder and ran out the back door. Faye followed him calling out, "Wait, Ty, talk to me."

"Later," he jumped onto his motorcycle and sped out of the parking lot like the devil was on his heels.

23

Faye sighed wearily as she locked the door behind their last customer. She sat on a bar stool and watched as Jesse lined up the last of the freshly washed mugs. "I don't know about you but I'm exhausted."

"Dog-tired. Show business is harder than it looks."

She had just taken a sip of beer and choked on it, her eyes dancing in merriment. She snorted with laughter. "You *are* quite the showman. I had no idea you were such a ham. I can hardly imagine what tales you have from your college bartending days. On second thought I'm sure I don't want to know."

"I never kiss and tell."

"Good to know."

"You're staying with me tonight right?" Jesse said.

"Yes, I was planning on it. Hey what do you think got into Ty tonight. He looked like he'd seen a ghost."

"Not sure, but I'm too tired to think about it. Let's get out of here."

~

The following morning Jesse woke up first and quietly slipped out of bed to make a donut run to the local bakery...hopefully before they sold out of their fresh baked pastries. He left a note for Faye in case she got up before he returned. He hopped onto his motorcycle and took off.

The parking lot was empty, and he whistled happily as he entered the shop, relieved to have beat the church crowd. He placed his order with the young girl behind the counter, who cheerfully filled the pastry box with a half dozen assorted delicacies. As he stepped outside, he slipped on his sunglasses. As he walked toward his bike, he heard a familiar and unwelcome drawl, his neck muscles immediately tightening.

"Jesse."

He turned. "Hey Kelsey."

"You're looking fine as all git-out. I miss you."

"Is that so. Odd, because you didn't seem to miss me much when you were fucking someone behind my back. I've got nothing to say to you."

"That's too bad. I suppose you think you're above me now."

"Why would I think that?"

"Oh, I don't know...maybe because you've moved up the social ladder."

His eyes narrowed, "What in God's name are you even talking about?"

"Just curious...how'd a construction worker like you hook the billionaire heiress? I mean you're gorgeous and all but..."

"I haven't a clue where you're going with this."

"Beautiful Faye? You know Faye Bennett? The one you're currently fucking?"

He tilted his head, eyes narrowed. "Faye LeBlanc?"

"Ha! Faye LeBlanc? Is that what she told you?" She studied his face, her eyes narrowing with sudden understanding. "You don't even know do you?"

"I guess not. What is it you're trying to tell me?"

"That girl you were fooling around with in the back aisles of *Lowe's*... I know her. She's a member of the Yacht Club. I wait on the Bennetts all the time. I'm her brother Griffin's favorite bartender."

His forehead creased. "Brother...Griffin?"

"Yes, you mean she hasn't brought you home to meet the family yet? Probably ashamed. Mr. Bennett would probably have a fit seeing his only daughter hooking up with a construction worker."

His face darkened, "Bennett as in Bennett developers?"

"Yes darlin, *that* Bennett. Old money and lots of it."

He turned away abruptly and tossed the box of pastries in the trash can. Hopping on his bike, his motor roared as he peeled out of the parking lot. His gut knotted and he felt like puking. What the fuck? Could it be true? Griffin...he remembered meeting him at the bar that day and her introducing him as her old friend. He recalled the jolt of jealousy he'd felt rip through him that day. *Fuck me. I've been duped. Why has she been hiding her identity from him?*

He screeched into his driveway and stomped up the stairs into his house. Faye was sitting at his kitchen island when he stormed in. Her eyes lit up... until she saw the dark scowl on his face.

"Who the fuck are you?"

Faye reeled back as if she'd been struck. Putting a hand to her throat her face went deathly pale. "Wait Jesse, I can explain."

"So, it's true? You're Faye Bennett... Jesus." He raked his hands through his hair. "You must think I'm the biggest schmuck on the planet."

Her hands were trembling as she reached for his arm, "Please listen to me..."

He jerked away as if he'd been burnt. His voice thick with emotion he said, "You've got no right to touch me anymore. Got that?"

Faye bowed her head and started crying. "My God Jesse, please don't do this. I can explain everything. I've tried telling you a thousand times. It took on a life of its own. The deeper we went the harder it was to tell you."

"Save it. I've been the biggest fuckin' fool."

"Don't you remember me saying I had something to talk about and you brushing me off? Don't you see? I was embarrassed to admit it to you. I wanted you to get to know *me*, not as a Bennett, but for me. Can you please try to understand? I never intended to hurt you."

"Well guess what? You did. And you sure as hell didn't try too hard to fill me in, now did you?" The disgust and anger made him sick to his stomach. The ache he felt in his heart was killing him.

He pointed to the door. "Get out."

Sobbing, Faye begged, "Please, don't do this. I'm falling in love with you."

"Falling in love? Tell me, which Faye is it that's falling in love? Faye LeBlanc or Faye Bennett? I don't even know who you are. It's all been a lie. You actually had the nerve to call *me* out because I owned a successful construction company? While the whole time you were lying to me about your entire life. The level of hypocrisy that took is beyond my comprehension. I'm only going to say it one more time, get out... now!"

Jesse couldn't even look at her and he definitely wouldn't watch her go. He stormed out the door, got on his bike and drove away.

24

Faye couldn't believe how quickly her world had turned inside out. Maddy hovered over her like a mother hen. She knew she looked like hell—she hardly recognized herself and worst of all it took nothing for her to burst into tears.

"Faye, just give it some time. I think he'll come around." Maddy said.

She lifted her thin shoulder in a half shrug, eyes bright with unshed tears. "I fucked it up. You were right all along. I should have come clean from the get-go."

"So what? You're not a criminal. It's not like you committed a mass murder or slept around on him."

"I lied. Pure and simple. If you don't have trust, you have nothing. I don't blame him."

"He'll cool off and realize what he's lost. Mark my words if he's even half the man I think he is, he'll come back."

"Mads it's over. It's been almost a week with no

word. I can't drive myself crazy hoping for the impossible. Not only that, maybe it's for the best. I need to focus on my business. Maybe I have some things to sort out within myself before I get into another relationship."

"You're right. You have to focus on yourself and your business... but that doesn't mean you have to do it alone! I'll do the hoping for the both of us. You'd better get it together enough to call in some people for interviews. You have to have more help."

"I know, I'll work on that today. I'll start scheduling interviews for next week."

"Good. If you need my help this weekend, I'm in."

"Yes, please."

"Okay. I've got to take off. Listen Faye, try to keep busy, take your mind off of things. Promise?"

"I'll try."

Maddy hugged her friend and left for work.

Faye dragged herself into the shower then threw on an old pair of cutoff jeans and a tank top. She stuck her hair up in a ponytail and rode her bike to the bar.

Stepping inside, it felt like the life had been sucked out of the place. More accurately it had been sucked out of her. She blew out a breath. You don't get sick days for a broken heart so get your ass moving. She raised her

chin and put one foot in front of the other. Mindless cleaning was just what the doctor ordered. It was as good as therapy. She filled a bucket with soap and water and got down onto her hands and knees and began scrubbing.

She was so focused she didn't hear Ty come in. Surprised to see him there she glanced at her watch.

"Noon already?"

"Yep. I see you're coming back to life."

She gave him a lopsided grin, "Don't be too sure about that."

"Faye, I've been meaning to talk to you about last Saturday night and why I ran off like I did."

"Yeah, I wanted to ask you about that."

"I told you a little about my past...you know the dealing..."

"Yes, I remember."

"Well I'd never want to set my bag of shit on your porch step..." he shifted uncomfortably.

Faye plopped her brush in the bucket and stood up. "Let's have a cool drink out on the deck. Sound good to you?" He didn't meet her eyes but mumbled in agreement. She grabbed a couple bottles of sweet tea from the cooler and met him out on the deck.

"Spill it."

"Well...when I came out from the back room, there was this guy from my past sitting at the bar. I don't know if you noticed him. Older dude, scruffy gray beard, shark eyes."

Faye felt a chill go down her spine, "Yeah, his name's Dave. Go on..."

Ty's eyes widened. "You know him?"

"He's been coming into the bar now and then. Not my favorite customer. How do you know him?"

Ty shuffled his feet. "Um...when I got busted, he was my supplier. I dealt for him. When I went to juvie, I owed him some money, and since I was locked up there was nothing I could do about it. They had confiscated my stuff."

"Wait, so you're telling me this guy is a drug dealer?"

"Yes, he's a bad dude. Bad mojo. When I saw him, I about shit myself. I'm not kidding he is evil. I don't know how he found me here."

"Ty, I don't think he was here because of you. I had a run in with him way before you started working for me."

He raised his thick brows. "Really?"

"Really. He's an asshole, but now that I know how he makes his living, I'm even more concerned about him hanging around my bar."

"Just be careful. He runs with some bad dudes."

"I'm worried about you." She ruffled his hair. "I'm glad you told me."

He lifted a corner of his mouth, "I hope I'm not stepping in shit but what's with you and Jesse?"

"There is no me and Jesse anymore."

He leaned back in his chair and sized her up. "Is it because he found out who you really are?" She froze and stared at him with wide eyes. He said, "Faye, I was born at night but not last night. This is a small town. Did you really think he wouldn't find out?"

She put a hand to her throat and whispered, "Was it you then?"

"Me what?"

"That told him."

"Hell no! I'd never do that to you."

"Thank God. I don't think I could have handled losing you too."

Ty tugged at his earring, looking thoughtful. "Do you mean what you just said?"

"What did I say?"

"About not wanting to lose me too."

"Yeah, I've grown quite fond of you, even if you're a bit on the cocky side. I know you're as soft as mush underneath all that." She gave him a playful shove.

He grinned, then looked down, "Faye, I'm guessing this secrecy thing must run in the family."

Her heart lurched. "Why's that?"

"Well, don't freak out on me...promise?"

"I promise, now spill it!"

"I don't know how else to say this...so I guess I'll just say it...okay...um...Marcus is my dad."

Her face was a total blank. "Marcus?"

"Marcus, your half-brother...you know...the one rotting in prison for blackmailing your family last year."

Her mouth dropped open, "Ty... I-I don't know what to say."

"Please hear me out. Don't judge me for the sins of my father. I didn't even know him growing up. They had me when they were teenagers and he split the scene shortly after I was born. Mom told me all about what happened. I guess dad never knew he was a Bennett until his mom died and told him on her death bed. Then my mom saw all that drama play out on TV and she told me."

"Why did you come looking for me?"

"I swear to you, I'm not after anything. I came to you because I was curious. It's just been me and Mom my whole life. We practically grew up together. She was only sixteen when she had me. I wanted to see who my family was. Remember when I told you about Mom and that fight? That was part of the reason we fought, and why she didn't want me to take the job. I didn't expect to like ya."

She burst out laughing. "Oh Ty, the tangled webs we weave. I'm glad you told me. And no, I don't hold it against you. Why would I? I was heartbroken when I found out I had a brother and lost him before we even met. In defense of my father, he didn't believe your dad was his until it was too late."

"Does that mean that I can keep my job?"

Faye slung her arm across his shoulder, "Yes. But don't think you get a free pass on work because you've got pull with me."

"Could we keep this between us for now?"

Faye narrowed her eyes, "I'm not sure... I guess for now, but I'd like you to get to know the rest of the family."

"They'll probably hate me."

"No, they won't. When the time comes, I'll be sure to break it to them gently. We'll ease into it. But not until you're ready. My father will be the last to know."

"Deal."

25

"You better clean that plate young man," Ruby said sternly, her tone belying the concern etched across her face. "Jesse, instead of moping around like a lonely bull moose, do something about it."

He pushed the plate aside, "I'm not hungry. Mom, best you leave sleeping dogs lie."

"You're my son and I love you dearly, but you have a stubborn streak a mile wide. That poor little thing deserves better than what you're giving her."

"Mom she lied. *And* it wasn't a little lie...it was about her entire identity. How would I ever be able to trust her again?"

"She lied because she didn't want you to judge her. I'm sorry but I've always thought being rich from the time you were born would be a curse not a blessin'."

"Mom, she's had weeks to tell me. I repeat, *weeks!* What does that say about her opinion of me if she didn't trust me or know me enough to come clean?" He folded his arms across his chest, jaw set.

"Jesse, darlin', can you imagine growing up not knowing whether someone liked you for who you were, or whether it was because of what you could do for them?"

His gaze was fixed and his expression mutinous. "I don't want to talk about it, okay? I know you mean well but I'm not going to go crawling back after being utterly humiliated. In front of my ex to boot. I've never felt so stupid in my entire life. And it was like pure crack for Kelsey. She practically rubbed her hands together in glee."

"Is that what this is about? Your pride? Oh Jesse, that is so disappointing. Didn't I raise you better than that?"

"No, it's not just my pride. It's her lack of faith in me. What did she think I was going to do just dump her because she's worth billions?"

"Believe it or not some guys couldn't handle that. They'd want to have all the power. Fortunately, I know I raised you four boys better than that. Am I right about that Jesse Carlisle?" When he didn't respond she put her hands on her hips and said, "Well, am I?"

"It's complicated. Kelsey's right about one thing. Faye's father would not take too kindly to his daughter being with some blue-collar guy."

"Do you hear yourself? You sound like a first-class snob."

"Mom you have to face facts. From her father's perspective, I'm just a working-class guy. He'd never accept me in a million years."

Ruby folded her arms across her ample bosom. "Why Jesse Carlisle, you've just gone and proved her point."

"Mom, we're talking billions, it's no small thing. There's a world of difference between us."

"You built our family business into one of the most sought after construction companies in this region. You have a stellar reputation; you make darn good money and you pay your workers well. A business to be envied if you were to ask me...which of course you haven't."

Jesse scrubbed his hands over his face. "I don't expect you to understand ma."

"Oh, I understand plenty. If you were still small, I'd march your butt right on over to her bar and make you stand there until you apologized."

He sputtered, "Apologize! Me? What the hell did I do?"

"It's what you're *not* doing that concerns me."

"I'm out of here. Thanks for supper. Love ya, Mom."

"I love you too, but I want you to think long and hard about what I just said. And I also want you to remember that she isn't Kelsey. I never did like that girl. I knew she wasn't the one for you the first time I met her. Now Faye, well, let's just say I've never seen you so happy and at ease as you are with her. And it goes both ways. You spark each other. That doesn't come along every day."

"Goodbye Ma." He couldn't get out of there fast enough. He loved his mom and normally found her counsel wise and comforting. Not today. He left feeling worse than he came. *Me apologize? That's just plain crazy!*

He decided to go for a long ride on his motorcycle.

Blow off some cobwebs. He couldn't think of anything but Faye. He saw her everywhere he went, she even followed him into his fucking dreams. He couldn't get away. Fortunately, his crew didn't pry or ask why he'd returned to the job site. But good thing they had a handle on everything because he was pretty much useless.

Against his better judgement he took the short cut which took him by the bar. And there she was. Standing in the parking lot with Tyler, pointing up at something on the roof. God, seeing her was like being punched in the gut. He twisted the throttle and blew past them. *Fuck me! How much more stupid can I get?*

⁓

"*W*hy that son of a bitch...I ought to..." Faye interrupted Ty by holding up her hand. "How would he know we'd be out in the parking lot? It's a small town. We won't be able to avoid each other forever."

"You're too kind. There's plenty of roads around this place."

"Ty just drop it. Besides I thought you and Jesse were cool. You don't have to choose sides you know."

"I'm just disappointed, I guess. I looked up to the dude. I didn't take him for a tool."

Faye sputtered with laughter. "He's not a tool. I hurt him. I did him wrong. That's on me Ty, not Jesse."

"Whatever. He should be finishing what he started at the very least. Leaving you hanging with the remodeling only half-done sucks."

"Look, before he came along, I wasn't planning on having the kitchen open before tourist season anyway. I thought it'd have to wait until winter when I could shut down for a few weeks. But jeez look what he's already done! Amazing work. He's a great carpenter and I was lucky to get what I did. Please be kind to him if you see him...for me, okay?"

"You're too good for him anyway. Any guy stupid enough to let you go is not worth your time. That's all I've gotta say about it."

Faye wrapped her arms around Ty in a big bear hug. "Ty, I feel like I've known you forever, but I sure am sorry that I missed out on the first eighteen years."

His eyes were a little brighter than usual, but he flashed his cocky grin and said, "Thanks *Aunt* Faye.

26

$\mathcal{S}$he had cancelled karaoke because she knew she wouldn't be able to handle it without another bartender. Saturdays had become busy enough without the added draw. The front door opened, and she looked up to see a girl standing there with another vase filled with roses. Faye's heart thudded in her chest.

"Hi, are you Faye Bennett?"

"Yes, that's me."

"Here ya go. Someone must really like you."

Faye took the vase out of her hands. "Thanks."

"You're welcome. You've done wonders with this place. Looks great."

"You'll have to stop in sometime when you're not working."

"I'll do that. Bye now."

"Bye." Faye's hands were shaking so hard she could barely open the card. *Yours forever J.* Just like before and she never had thanked him for them. She scrambled to find her cell phone then before her nerves could get the better of her, she punched in Jesse's number.

"Hello?"

"Jess it's me Faye."

"I know your number Faye."

She held her hand over her heart, almost overwhelmed from hearing his voice. "Um Jess, I'm just calling to thank you for the beautiful flowers and to say that I'm sorry I never got around to thanking you before."

"What flowers? I didn't send flowers."

She whispered, "You didn't?"

"Why would I send you flowers? It wasn't me."

"Oh God, I'm sorry to have bothered you, I've got to go." Faye hung up the phone, her heart racing. If it wasn't Jesse, then who? She got up and locked the door with trembling hands.

"Faye wait!" It was too late she'd already hung up the phone.

Jesse knew something wasn't right. He needed to check on Faye. He jumped on his bike and pulled out onto the road full throttle. When he got to the bar, he tried the door. It was locked.

Pounding he called out, "Faye, it's me Jesse. Can you let me in?" He heard the dead bolt sliding and then, there she was. His throat tightened when he saw the dark circles under her eyes. He could tell she'd been crying.

"Faye." Jesse cupped her shoulders in his hands. She wouldn't meet his eyes and that was like a kick in the gut. "Baby, what's happening? Talk to me."

Her voice was shaky but subdued. "The flowers were the last straw. I think I've been trying so hard not to overreact to things that I went too far in the other direction. I've been burying my head in the sand."

"What other things are you talking about?"

He could tell she was fighting back tears. "It's possible the flowers came from Julian... which could mean that he's behind the graffiti... which had a heart with J loves F right smack in the middle. I buried my concerns right under that paint roller. He could also have been the one to break in." She buried her face in her hands. "I don't know what to do...what to think."

"You don't have to carry this alone. We'll figure it out." A tear slipped down her cheek and it was all Jesse could do to keep himself from pulling her into his arms. He wasn't sure if she'd welcome it at this point.

"I'm going to call Maddy and get her to come over. Hand me your phone."

"Faye?" Maddy said.

"No, it's me Jesse."

"Oh, did you finally decide to man up?"

"We don't have time for that now, it's Faye, something's happened."

"What do you mean somethings happened? Is she okay?"

"Yes, I'll explain when you get here. We're at the bar."

"I'm on my way."

"Let's have a seat at a table. Can I get you a shot of whiskey or anything?" he asked.

Faye's lips turned up, "Actually that's not a bad idea."

The door opened and Ty stepped through. Seeing Faye's pale face and frightened expression he charged over, "What the fuck did you do to her?"

"Ty it's not the time. Settle your ass down," Jesse said, voice tight and clipped.

"Not until you tell me what the fuck is going on. Faye are you okay?"

"Ty, Jesse is here to help."

He glared at Jesse then squatted down beside her and grabbed Faye's hand, "I swear if he did anything more to hurt you, I'm going to kill him with my bare hands."

That brought a weak smile to her face. "No, it wasn't Jess. Please give me a minute and I'll tell you everything."

Jesse handed Faye a shot of bourbon and watched her throw it back in one gulp. He was pleased to see a little color return to her cheeks.

Ty stood up puffing out his chest like a rooster, still not convinced this wasn't Jesse's fault.

Maddy came running in and seeing Faye, swooped down to hug her. "Honey what happened?"

Jesse answered for her. "Some flowers were delivered, and she thought they were from me. The second time it's happened recently. They weren't from me. She suspects it was Julian."

"Oh no!"

"Is it that bad?" Jesse asked.

"Yes. After Faye kicked him out, he went off the deep end. Stalking her, sending cards and flowers, showing up everywhere uninvited. That's the main reason why she moved back to the States. He was obsessed with getting her back."

Ty paced the floor like a caged animal, "I'll fucking kill him."

Jesse tipped Faye's chin up and looked into her frightened eyes, "Can you think of anything else that's happened recently?" Jesse's eyes narrowed, then he remembered something. "That guy that came in looking for you...you said the description fit Julian."

Faye nodded her head slowly. "And that guy on the beach smoking, I went inside because it gave me the creeps. It seemed like he was staring right at me. But it was dark out and I convinced myself it was nothing."

"Was Julian violent, did he ever get physical with you?"

She shook her head no. "He just wouldn't let me go."

Jesse was all messed up. He felt powerless. Faye was at risk, and the danger swirling around her seemed like an elusive mist in the air that he couldn't grab ahold of.

Jesse kept his voice calm and measured, "We need to call the police and report this. Okay to do that now?"

She nodded yes.

"I'll call," Maddy said taking charge.

"I'm going to go outside and look around," Ty said.

"No! Wait until after the police get here. Please Ty." Faye begged, her voice sounding panicked.

"I'll wait," he said. "Don't worry."

"Promise me you won't do anything stupid."

His shoulders slumped and he stuck his hands in his front pockets. "I'll promise *for now.*"

"Thank you."

27

The police arrived and took her statement. "We'll file the complaint but understand, since we don't have an address and he's not a citizen, it will be difficult to monitor his movements or even find him. It's not against the law to send flowers and we have no proof he was behind the break in."

Faye nodded her head in understanding. She looked so fragile and alone, sitting at a table next to the burly police officer, her hands folded in her lap. It made Jesse want to howl at the top of his lungs. He felt the weight of his actions resting squarely on his shoulders. *I never should have bailed on her. I've was supposed to protect her.*

Ty hissed in his ear, "Can I have a word with you," he jerked his head toward the deck, "Outside?"

Jesse pinched the bridge of his nose but nodded his head and followed Ty out.

Ty was pacing back and forth then he stopped and

slammed his hand down on the table. "What the fuck man? Faye deserves better than what you did to her."

"Listen Ty, you're young, I don't expect you to understand, life's complicated."

"Fuck you. I may be young, but I've had my share of life's *complications* dude. That's bullshit and you know it. It was all about your ego."

Jesse clenched his fists. "I know you care, and I'm glad Faye has you in her corner. I like you Ty, I'm sorry I hurt Faye and its tearing me up that I wasn't here to protect her. But I'm here now."

"Too late dude, you blew it."

"That may be true, but I can still be there for her as a friend. If she'll have me."

"You know what bothers me the most? That you just cut out and didn't finish the job man, that's cold. This is her livelihood."

"I had full intentions of finishing the job! Did you see me taking my tools? No, because they're all still here. I just needed some time to get my head on straight."

Ty rubbed the back of his neck, "Well I'm relieved to hear that at least."

"I'm glad you're pissed at me. It shows that you're loyal and that you've got integrity."

"I don't need or want your approval anymore dude."

"Ouch! I guess I deserve that. But not for you to decide *dude*. Whether you want it or not, you've got it. I'm heading back inside to check on Faye. Good talk." He couldn't resist the dig. He respected Ty's gumption, but his words still stung.

. . .

The police had left and Maddy was hovering over Faye who still sat at the table. She had her hand protectively on Faye's shoulder as she turned toward them.

"They weren't much help. But the Bennett name did get their attention at least. You need to call your brother Kyle and get him to put the pressure on." Maddy said. "In the meantime, we've got to come up with our own plan to keep you safe. You should never be alone. Not until this guy is shipped back to New Zealand or sitting in jail."

"I agree," Jesse said.

Tyler puffed out his chest, "I can be her bodyguard." Faye's mouth curved into a smile.

"Everyone let's calm down and think this through. Obviously, he's been around for a while and hasn't done anything violent," Maddy said. "The biggest threat is when she's here alone and coming and going to work."

"Faye, you have to start driving your car or letting someone take you. Then either Ty or I will be here whenever you're here," Jesse said.

"I can't ask y'all to put your own lives on hold for me."

"You're not asking, we're telling you," Jesse said stubbornly. "Look I've been MIA for the past week, I know that, but I was always going to come back and finish the job. I gave you my word."

"Under the circumstances, I understand if you don't want to tackle the kitchen anymore," Faye said quietly.

"The circumstances are that I own a company and

you hired me to renovate your bar. Despite our personal problems, that's what we agreed to. This is my job and my reputation on the line. No arguments. That is...unless you're firing me?"

She bit her lip, eyes glistening with unshed tears. "No, I'm not firing you." Bowing her head, she said, "Thank you, Jesse. I don't deserve that after what I did to you."

Maddy and Ty snorted at the same time which made Faye giggle. "Okay you two pit bulls...stand down."

Maddy and Ty looked at each other, and seeing their defensive stances mirrored in one another, uncrossed their arms and relaxed their shoulders.

"So that solves the nine-to-five time slots; we'll have to do shifts for the rest of it."

"When I have customers, I'll be okay. He wouldn't try anything with people around," Faye said.

"When you open and close someone *must* be with you. Got that?" Jesse said.

"Yes."

Jesse rubbed his chin. "You know...I've got three brothers that have an overload of testosterone and would gladly step in to help."

"No. I couldn't ask them to do that."

"You aren't asking. I am. *If* we need them for back up. We don't know how long this is going to drag on."

"Good idea," Maddy said, a warmth creeping back into her voice, softening a bit toward Jesse.

"Well I'm here now, so I'm going to get back to work. I don't know about the rest of you."

"I need to head to my office. I'll be home tonight,

long before you are Faye. Call me when you're on your way," Maddy said.

"I will."

"We need to see a picture of this guy, so we'll know him if we see him, and then I can confirm if it's the same guy that stopped in to see you," Jesse said.

"Yeah," Ty said.

"I'll go home and see if I can dig one up. The police asked for one as well."

Ty jumped in, "I'll take you now. Then we can drop it off at the station."

Maddy chimed in, "Then head straight to Kyle's office. He may want to hire a private investigator to find Julian."

"Good plan," Jesse said.

Faye stood up rubbing her hands up and down her bare arms to warm them. "I don't think I can ever come up with the words...thank you all. I feel so taken care of."

"Good. We won't let anything happen to you," Maddy said.

Jesse was quiet, his expression pensive. "I never followed up on that security camera, I'll get on that today."

"I was supposed to do that. It hardly falls under your jurisdiction," Faye argued. "I'll do it when I get back."

"Better yet, get big brother on it," Maddy suggested.

"Yes, I could do that."

Ty tapped his foot impatiently and said, "Let's get this show on the road Faye."

"Can I have a moment before you go?" Jesse asked Faye quietly.

She nodded yes. He took her arm and led her outside. Facing her he put his hands on both her shoulders and stared into her blue depths. "Faye, I'm sorry. I don't expect you to understand or forgive me. I know it'll take some time to win your trust back, but I've got the time."

"Jesse, I understand more than you think I do. Everything moved way too fast for us and I should've known better than to mix business and pleasure. I don't blame you; I blame me. I'm glad to have you back in my life and I hope we can always remain friends. But for now, that's all it can be."

His chest felt like it was being squeezed. "I understand. I fucked everything up. I should have let you explain. You deserved better."

"Thank you for that but I take full responsibility for what happened. You have to quit beatin' yourself up, ya hear?"

His mouth twisted, "Yeah sure I will, just like that," he said, snapping his fingers. "Going to be pretty hard to do when I fucked up and lost the best thing God ever graced me with. I'm a damn fool. But I'll respect your wishes...like *you* said...for now. However, when you change your mind..."

"You'll be the second one to know."

Jesse's shoulders slumped. He would go along with it for now, but he didn't have to like it. He'd let the dust settle, give her some time, but he hadn't given up just yet.

28

$a$fter dropping off the photo of Julian at the police station, they headed over to Kyle's law firm. The secretary led them straight back to his office. When she and Tyler sat down, Kyle did a double take.

Faye made the introductions. Kyle's eyes narrowed and he asked, "How do you know my sister?"

"Kyle, he works for me."

Kyle stared at him for several long beats while Faye and Ty fidgeted in their chairs. She knew her brother was brilliant, and nothing ever seemed to escape him. Now that she was looking at him and Ty up close and personal, she saw a remarkable resemblance between them. Especially their eyes. That same cobalt blue. *Duh! How had that escaped her until now?*

After what felt like minutes, he turned back to Faye, "To what do I owe this pleasant surprise?"

"Kyle, Julian is here, in the States, he found me... found the bar."

"How do you know?"

Faye told him the entire story from beginning to end. He sat there tapping his fingers on the desk, his body tense. After she finished, he buzzed his secretary and told her to get Leroy Shay, the chief of police, on the line immediately. Faye and Ty exchanged a look.

As they were waiting, he looked Tyler up and down and said, "Are you from around here?"

Clearing his throat, he said, "Yes sir. Grew up inland...the neighboring town."

"Either of you two have something you want to tell me?"

Faye wrung her hands and looked helplessly at Ty and he shrugged.

"Kyle, we were waiting on the right time to tell y'all...I just found out myself. Tyler's our nephew... he's Marcus's son." At Kyles darkening expression, she rushed on.

"He came to me for a job. He never even knew his father. Marcus abandoned them when Ty was just a baby. He and his mama have been on their own his whole life. He only found out he had family after every-thing that went down last year. Since it was splashed all over the news, his mom put two and two together. He doesn't want anything...only to know his family."

Kyle's eyes narrowed as he stared at Ty. "What exactly do you want to know?"

"Kyle! I just told you, it's just been him and his mom; when he found out he had a family he wanted to meet us."

Kyle tapped his pen against the desk, as he contem-plated Faye's explanation.

"I don't need to tell you Faye that we can't be too careful. I know how trusting you can be and I'm sorry, but I can't indulge in the luxury of taking everything at face value. I don't need to remind you that my son was kidnapped, and my best friend and partner betrayed me. I'm sorry if I find Tyler's curiosity a little suspect."

Tyler jumped up and said, "Fuck you. Believe what you want. Faye I'll be outside waiting." And he stormed out of the office.

Faye's voice shook, "How dare you! You have no right. Tyler has been nothing but the sweetest most protective kid you ever want to meet."

"You expect me to automatically accept a complete stranger and take his word for it? Faye you can't be so trusting. When you're a Bennett, you can't afford to be."

"I had hoped you'd changed enough to give him a chance. You can't hold his father against him. He's a good kid."

"Hardly a kid. He seems pretty street smart to me."

"He gets his attitude honestly."

"Faye he's obviously a troubled kid. He conveniently finds out he's related to billionaires, looks them up because he feels all warm and fuzzy? You expect me to believe it's all on the up and up?"

"I'm with Ty, fuck you." Faye stood up and walked toward the door. "You know everything was handed to us. You can't help who you were born to. Try a little compassion for a change. It might be less painful than you think. I had hoped that Ella's influence would've opened your eyes to others' suffering. I guess it was too much to hope for."

"Faye," he called out to her, but she was already slamming the door behind her.

"Ty, I'm so sorry."

"It's not your fault. What a dick."

"He's really not, once you get to know him. He's just a shrewd businessman and as the oldest child, overbearing and protective at times. I love him with all my heart, but he can be pigheaded as all get out."

"I'll have to take your word for it, because I don't think he and I are going to be having any kumbayah moments any time soon."

"I feel terrible. He'll come around. I know my brother, and this won't sit well with him. He's going to feel guilty as hell and he'll be sniffing around before you know it."

Ty shrugged, then his shoulders slumped. "This is why I was hoping to keep it between us. You got to know me first, but he didn't have that opportunity. I don't really blame him for being suspicious."

She slung her arm across his shoulders as they headed toward his motorcycle. "At least you've got me."

He grinned and put his arm around her waist, "Yep, and that's even better than I could've hoped for."

29

"Faye can you hand me that wrench over there in my toolbox?" Jesse asked, as she passed by him on her way to her office.

"Sure." She squatted down next to Jesse, who was on his back working on the drain under the large utility sink. He was shirtless as usual, and his jean-clad legs were bent for leverage as he wrestled with the locknut. Faye had to catch her breath when his muscular abs flexed as he tried to loosen it.

She bit her lip, as her eyes wandered down from his navel, following the path of his soft hair until it disappeared into his pants. It was the temptation of Eve for sure, and she was ready to bite into that apple.

"Anything else?"

"Nope. Thanks."

"I'll be in my office, just holler if I can do anything."

His whiskey eyes looked penetratingly into hers... like he was reading her mind. Her cheeks grew warm and he grinned. Dang it! He *had* read her mind. He was like a drug. She jumped up and hurried away before she jumped on top of him and gave in to her desires.

So far, she'd managed to keep a tight rein on her feelings for Jesse. But it was getting harder every day. Kyle had hired a PI but the search for Julian had yet to turn up anything. Nothing else had happened. Julian appeared to have dropped from the face of the earth, but Faye wasn't entirely convinced. She had a hard time believing he would give up that easily.

Faye disappeared into her office and got busy working on her bookkeeping.

"Knock knock."

Faye glanced up to see Jesse at the door. "Hey, you never have to knock, come on in," she said softly.

He perched on the edge of her desk. "So how's it going for you?"

"How's what going?"

"Our arrangement."

She looked down, "Good, how about for you?"

"Terrible! I'm not going to lie, it's driving me crazy."

"Jess, I just can't go there right now."

"Are you sure about that, because I see the way you look at me...and it seems like you're as miserable as I am."

"That may be true, but it doesn't change the circumstances. I'm sorry."

"Well at least you're not denying it."

"No."

"Faye all I can think about is you...us. I miss you. I miss touching you, you touching me. I miss kissing you, smelling you, I miss listening to your stories."

"Don't you think I miss all that too? I do Jess. With all my heart, but I can't bear to go down that road with you again. Not now, I'm way too vulnerable. I can't make any promises right now."

"You know how good it is between us. No, it's more than good—it's phenomenal. We can't just let this slip away."

"It won't. If it's meant to be it will be. I truly believe that."

"How can I restore your faith in me?"

"Don't you see? It's my faith in myself that needs restored. Jess, you didn't do anything anyone else wouldn't have done. Your reaction was normal. I was a coward and I lied to the one I care the deepest about."

"If you cared that deeply, you'd put an end to this separation."

She wrapped her arms around herself. "Maybe, but I've got to clean up my past and stand on my own two feet before I can be ready to dive in with you. I didn't tell you who I was because I was ashamed. I was desperate to be loved for who I was."

"I get that now."

"The hypocrisy of wealth...well I had to run across to the other side of the planet to escape from my family name. Everyone saw me as this free-spirited girl, doing her thing, world traveler, writing my blog, doing my art, shacking up with my lover, throwing money around left and right. People hanging on to me because I had money and I liked to spend it. Money meant nothing to me...still doesn't. But it comes with a lot of baggage. It's empty. When I met your mom, I felt a pain so deep it almost took my breath away. She is everything I ever wanted when I was growing up. So grounded and strong and warm, good... just like you Jesse."

"Faye..."

She held up her hand, "Jess, the truth is I don't feel like I'm good enough for you. It was selfish of me to let you go on thinking I was some poor helpless victim when I could have just asked one of my billionaire brothers to flex their muscles and the work would have already been done by now."

"You wanted to make your own mark Faye. I totally get that. You weren't trying to hurt me."

"I'm so confused right now. I'm not even sure what I was doing. That's why it's best we just keep things the way they are right now. I've got no right to drag you through my emotional rollercoaster while I figure things out."

"Faye, that's what couples do. They walk through things together. Maybe you didn't see much modeling of that growing up, but I did. That's how it's done. If you wait until you have it all figured out, you'll be on your death bed, full of regrets."

A single tear escaped and trailed down her cheek before she wiped it away. "Jesse, I'm not closing any doors, I just need time."

He grabbed her wrist, exposing her tattoo before reading it out loud, "*Dream as if you'll live forever, live as if you'll die today.* Dammit Faye, do you think that's how you're really living right now?"

She remained quiet.

"I guess I have no choice but to do it your way."

"Don't be mad at me."

"I'm frustrated, not mad."

"I'm sorry Jess. And you know what else? Selfishly, I want you to wait for me," she whispered.

He blew out a deep breath. "What the hell else am I going to do?"

She grabbed his hand and kissed the back of it. He pulled her out of her chair and wrapped his arms around her hugging tight.

"Can I have one kiss?" he murmured.

She answered by tilting her head up. He placed his lips against hers and waited for her to respond. She parted her lips and he kissed her long and hard leaving her panting. When he lifted his head, her eyes were smoldering with passion. *He'd leave her right there, wanting for more. She may as well be as horny as he was.*

"I'm calling it quits for the day. Are you ready for me to walk you out?" he said.

Breathlessly she said, "Yes, let me put away a couple of files, then I'm good to go." Her hands were unsteady as she cleared her desk. He smiled in satisfaction, knowing she'd be missing his touch tonight, just as much as he was missing hers.

30

*J*esse was meeting a group of friends at his parents' for a pickup game of beach volleyball... followed by lots of beer and a seafood boil. His brothers and their families were coming, and Lord knew who else was going to show up. It was Sunday afternoon and Faye had decided that they should take a break, so he had a whole day to chill.

He had called Faye, but it'd gone straight to her voicemail. Instead of hanging up, he'd left a long rambling message inviting her and reassuring her not to feel pressured and why didn't she come for fun, they could keep it in the friend-zone and she didn't have to worry about him reading more into it...blah blah blah. The more he had said the stupider he'd sounded.

He raked his hands through his hair, blowing out a deep breath. The uncertainty was frustrating as hell. He wanted to shake her. Her excuses just seemed lame.

He could understand wanting to take things slow

and easy, he was all for that. He was just as invested in preserving his own heart as she was. But dammit, she wouldn't be the only one taking risks. Their feelings for each other had long passed the friend zone. Their chemistry was undeniable. He hoped that it was only a matter of time before they got back together anyway, so why wait?

He stomped up the stairs and let himself in. "Mom?"

Ruby came out from the back of the house, her usual cheerful countenance on display. "Hey sweetie. You're early. What time is the gang showing up?"

"It's loose. I told them any time after three."

"Good that gives us a little time to catch up."

"That's why I'm here."

"Let me pour us some tea and we can sit on the porch and talk."

He slung an arm across her shoulders and squeezed.

"Sounds good Mom. Where's Pops?"

"He'll be back. He's golfing with Bill."

"Extra ice please."

Hand on her hip, Ruby said, "Anything else prince Jess?"

He held his palms up as he backed away comically, "I'll just be heading on out then."

Reclining on the lounger he put his hands behind his head and watched the pelicans dive bomb straight down into the ocean, fishing for their next meal. It never got old. They were comical and he could almost hear a cartoon soundtrack in his head.

"Here ya go," Ruby said. "Is that darling Faye coming today?"

"Don't know. I left a message."

"Good. I hope she comes."

"Doubtful. Seems she has to keep me at arm's length... for my own protection no less."

"She'll come around."

"I hope so Ma. I'm starting to get frustrated. Why should it all be up to her? I'm the one that got lied to."

"That's oversimplifying it a bit, don't ya think? It's what's behind the deception that's the issue here."

"How are we ever going to find out if her billionaire status is a deal breaker if we don't try?"

"Give her time Jess. She's got all that other stuff you were telling me about as well. That's a lot to contend with. Which leads me to a point I want to make. If the ex is that obsessed with her, you can be sure he knows about you. I want you to be extremely careful. It's no longer just about Faye, but also about whoever gets in the way. I'll feel so much better when they find him."

"Me too and I'm aware of that fact."

"Just be extra alert."

"I am. You don't need to be worrying about me."

"That's a mother's number one duty," she said, laughing.

He rolled his eyes heavenward, "If you say so."

"What else is troubling you dear?"

"Besides the fact that my girl, who says she's no longer my girl, has an ex stalking her, and that even if we manage to climb those mountains and wind up at the top, what's waiting for me on the other side? Her father, who will have a hard time accepting a blue-collar suitor. I'll never be good enough."

"You don't know any such thing! And Jesse, everyone wants a family's blessing, but we don't always get it. If there is an issue at first, I think that given time, if he gets to know you, he will accept you. But you can't take on all of that. Remember what you have control over and what you don't. Then let what you can't change go."

"Uncle Jesse, Grandma!" Jesse's niece came flying onto the porch and threw herself at Jesse.

"Hey Matilda, how's my favorite niece?" Jesse said.

She rolled her eyes. "I'm your *only* niece."

"Oh, I forgot." He hugged her tight. "It's been a minute. How's school?"

"I'm ready for summer."

"Won't be long."

His oldest brother Dylan, along with his wife Jen, came up the stairs lugging a cooler. After depositing it in the kitchen they joined them on the deck.

"You ready to get your sorry butt kicked little brother?"

Jesse snorted, "Good luck with that old man. Remember what happened the last volleyball tournament? We took your team to the cleaners."

"I try not to live in the past. Today's a new day."

Jesse stood up. "Let's go set up the net."

Turning to Ruby, Jesse said, "Thanks for the talk Mom."

"You always were a mama's boy," Dylan said.

"Yeah? Look who's talking. You cried like a baby when you left for college."

Dylan grinned. "That's only because I was going to miss Mama's home cookin."

"Ha! If it makes you feel better."

"Get out of here you two!" Ruby said.

They set up the net, and more people started showing up.

Joe was the first to arrive, his sister tagging along. "Hey anything we can do to help?

"You can set up some chairs on the sideline," Jess said.

Jesse did a mental head count. Now that his other two brothers had showed up, there was at least enough for two teams and some bench warmers.

The Carlisle volleyball seafood boils were famous with their friends. It was always a great time. Fun and sun. Guys in their swim trunks, girls in their bikinis, some spiking and athletically diving to save the ball for their team, lots of laughter and teasing. Music, ocean breeze, salty air, gulls shrieking, it was a quintessential South Carolina beach party. Jesse's youngest brother Sam was in charge of the music and he had the speakers set up and the country tunes streaming. The drinks were already flowing.

Jesse and Dylan designated themselves as team captains on opposing teams. The competition had evolved over the years to become a legend of sorts. All in good fun, the Carlisle brothers took their bragging rights very seriously. Jesse and Sam always teamed up against Dylan and Connor, the two youngest verses the two oldest. Jesse was up first to serve the ball, and he easily muscled it over the net.

31

"Hello?" Faye called out, as she knocked on the screen door. She could hear the ruckus of laughter and music coming from the back of the house but felt shy about just barging in on the party. She had battled with herself about whether or not to even come, but in the end, it sounded like way too much fun to pass up. Jesse had told her tales about past tournaments and it had caused that familiar yearning for a normal upbringing.

"Faye! You made it." Ruby opened the screen and pulled her inside. She gave Faye a big hug and said, "Come on out here and have a drink with us before you jump into that wild group of savages. You can observe and see what you'll be getting yourself into."

Faye laughed. "Sounds good to me."

"Hank, this is Faye! Faye this is Jesse's dad, Big Hank."

Faye held out her hand and it was promptly swal-

lowed up in a hand as big as a dinner plate. A booming
voice with a major southern drawl said, "They told me
you were pretty, and they didn't exaggerate."

"Thank you, Mr. Carlisle."

He scowled, "There'll be none of that mister stuff in
my house. It's Hank."

"Hank it is."

"Have a seat, I'll go fetch you a drink. What'll it be?
We have beer, wine, wine coolers, vodka, tea, water, you
name it, we got it," Hank said.

"I'd love a beer. Thank you."

Patting the cushion next to her on the love seat,
Ruby said, "Sit right here beside me. You'll have an
excellent view of the game."

Faye's eyes zeroed in on Jesse immediately as he
leapt in the air, diving for the ball. He managed to
volley it before hitting the soft sand beneath him. A
voluptuous brunette laughingly held out her hand and
helped him up. After he stood, she brushed the sand off
his butt. Faye could see Jesse's dazzling white smile all
the way from where she was sitting. She gritted her
teeth. Maybe this hadn't been such a great idea after all.

Ruby drew Faye's attention away from the scene,
"So Faye, Jesse told me what happened; how are you
holding up? And it's fine if you don't want to talk
about it."

"I'm hanging in there. There isn't too much to tell.
My brother hired a private investigator, which I hope
uncovers something soon. I feel like my life isn't my
own anymore. Everything feels in limbo."

"I'm sure."

Like magnets her eyes strayed back to Jesse. She

couldn't help it. That same girl kept flirting with him, and she didn't seem to be able to keep her hands to herself. Faye realized that her fists were clenched and tried to relax. When she looked back at Ruby, she could see warmth and kindness in her eyes. She could also tell that Ruby had caught her staring at her son. Faye felt the familiar warmth creeping across her cheeks.

"She's just an old friend," Ruby said kindly. "Not that she wouldn't be interested if Jesse gave her the green light, but he's known her his whole life and doesn't see *her* in the same way." She patted Faye's hand.

"Um... I..."

"Honey you don't need to explain anything to me. I know I'm his mother, so I'm a bit partial, but all my boys are lookers. Fortunately, they all have a portion of humble pie in their characters. It hasn't gone to their heads...for the most part." She laughed.

Hank returned with a beer and bowl of Chex mix, setting both on the table.

"I'm going down to where the action is. Do you want to join me little lady?"

Faye looked at Ruby and she nodded her head, "Yes, go. We'll catch up later."

Faye stood and followed Hank downstairs and to the sidelines. A couple of middle school girls were sitting under the deck painting each other's nails.

"Grandpa, what do you think?" The girl with hair the same striking color as Jesse's, held up her hands to show Hank.

"Looks good kiddo. Faye this is my granddaughter

Matilda. My oldest son's daughter. He and her mom are in the game."

"Hi Matilda."

"Hi. Are you Jesse's girlfriend?"

Faye put her hand to her throat. "Um, we're friends, yes. He is helping me fix up my business property."

"Yeah I've heard all about it. Nice to meet you." She quickly turned her attention back to her friend.

Hank set up a lawn chair for Faye on the sidelines. "Do you play?" Hank asked her.

"Sort of. By the looks of things not nearly good enough for this crowd."

He guffawed. "Looks can be deceiving. Don't let 'em intimidate you. They're just a bunch of showoffs."

Faye laughed, already liking Big Hank as much as she did Ruby. Jesse was so lucky. He took that moment to look over and caught sight of Faye. He froze on the spot missing a ball coming right at him that landed on the ground at his feet. His teammates groaned, while the other team gave each other high fives. She felt a longing to touch him. His eyes blazed with hunger as they met hers. The ball was in play again, so Jesse turned his attention back to the game.

The brunette beauty was practically under his feet and Faye wanted to scream. Did she have to be so touchy feely? She was doing exactly what Faye wished *she* was doing right now. Putting her hands all over that hunk of perfection. Jesse called a time out and jogged over to where Faye was seated.

His eyes were golden amber flames and the natural highlights in his hair glinted like copper in the bright sunlight. Her heart raced as he approached.

Swallowing hard, she stood up when he reached her side.

"You made it." His voice was low and husky.

"Yes. Looks like I'm out of my league though."

He didn't miss her double entendre, glancing back over his shoulder at the girl. "Hardly. There's nobody in your league babe. Are you ready to jump in the game? I'm sure somebody's ready for a break."

"Sure. I'll give it a try."

He took her hand in his and led her over to the court. "Hey, everybody this is Faye. She's a Carlisle party virgin. Make her feel welcome! Who's ready for a break?"

His sister-in-law, from the opposing team, quickly volunteered and said, "Here please take my spot. Hi Faye, I'm Jen, with that guy in the flashy Hawaiian trunks." Jen nodded her head toward Dylan. "That's Connor in the back corner getting ready to serve."

Jesse said, "That means you'll be siding with my patronizing older brothers. But whatever. Dylan is your team captain."

Dylan winked at Faye. "We're going to kick some ass. Jump on in."

Faye smiled, taking over Jen's position in the sand. Connor served and the ball was in play. After several minutes Faye was warmed up and comfortable throwing herself into the game. Normally not competitive, the brothers had her fired up, and she found herself aggressively spiking the ball over the net whenever she had the opportunity.

. . .

*J*esse had lost his ability to concentrate on the game with Faye on the other side of the net distracting him. Those mile-long legs in cutoff jean shorts had his full attention. He'd already messed up some easy plays and his teammates were beginning to razz him.

"Dude, maybe you should take a time out. You're killing us!"

"Yeah we *were* ahead!"

Dylan was overjoyed with this turn of events. "Faye so glad you could join us!" He said grinning.

Faye was up to serve. She winked at her team captain and said, "Whatever it takes." Then easily lobbed the ball right to Jesse who *just* managed to pass it to a teammate.

At this point Jess couldn't wait for the game to be over so he could be close to Faye. When his team finally lost after giving up their huge lead, he couldn't have cared less. Everyone carried their hot and sweaty bodies to the huge in-ground pool and jumped in to cool off.

Jesse watched Faye dive underwater, looking like a sea nymph. She emerged next to him, water droplets trickling down her face and chest, tempting Jesse to lick them off. In the end, he couldn't keep his hands off her. He pulled her slick body against his and her eyes widened when she felt his erection press into her.

He blew out a breath, "Faye, what am I going to do about you?"

Her breath was quick and shallow, and her eyes were burning with want. His throat tightened. All the background noise and laughter disappeared, only the two of them existed. He dipped his head and pressed his lips softly against hers. She kissed him back then pushed playfully at his chest and ducked underwater to pull his legs out from under him.

He took in a big mouthful of water and came up sputtering. Her eyes were sparkling with laughter. "Remember you started it," Jesse said, before picking her up and tossing her high in the air as she shrieked. She made a big splash as she went under. When she didn't reappear, Jesse nervously looked under the water, and was caught off guard once again when she snuck up behind him and jumped on his back to pull him under. They wrestled under water for the upper hand, limbs entangled, the water heightening the sensations of her silky bare skin against his own.

He whispered in her ear, "You feel so good."

She dove back under and swam to the other end of the pool, before propping her elbows on the ledge, smiling teasingly from her safe perch. He raked his hands through his wet hair and sighed.

"Who is she?" A female voice whispered in his ear.

The brunette, Kelly, had snuck up behind him and jumped onto his back, wrapping her arms and legs around him, like she was riding piggyback.

"Technically she's a client. I'm renovating her bar, used to be Skully's."

"I saw it was open. The Pelican, right?"

"Yeah, that's the one."

"You two seem to have something more going on. Does this mean you're off the market again?"

He glanced over at Faye and caught her glaring

before she pulled herself out of the water and headed back toward the house.

"You could say that. Listen Kelly, I've got to go."

"My loss. Lucky girl. It's no secret that I've had a crush on you since I was ten. Let me know if you're ever up for more than a friendship."

"You know I care about you Kelly. You're one of my best friends and always will be, I hope anyway."

"No doubt. Go get her."

Jesse jumped out of the pool and went after Faye who had almost made it to her car.

"Nice car!" Jesse said when he caught up with her. *Silence.*

"Faye talk to me."

"Jesse, there's nothing to say. You don't owe me anything. I'm the one who said we could only be friends. You're a free agent."

"But that's just it. I'm not. You're the only one I want. Kelly is just an old friend."

"It sure looked like more than that from where I sat."

"Probably, but I'm telling you the truth."

"Does your *friend* Kelly know all this?"

"Yes, I just reminded her of it. She told me to 'go get her' as you were stomping away."

"I was *not* stomping, thank you very much!"

Jesses eyes twinkled, "Yeah, you seem to have some problems with ole greenie don't ya?"

Her eyes narrowed dangerously, "You seem to have a death wish."

He laughed out loud. Pulling her against his chest he said, "Listen, let's just see where this thing takes us.

We'll go real slow. I promise. Just don't close yourself off from me again. Please Faye."

She bit her lip, eyes bottomless pools of deep blue. "I guess we have no other choice, truth be told. I can't fight this anymore. It'd be like the ocean trying to fight the pull of the moon."

"Well said. Now about that kiss..." Jesse leaned down and covered her mouth with his. He plundered desperately, as she gripped his hair tightly in clenched fingers.

When he finally lifted his head, they were both breathing heavily. "I'd better get back to the party. Why don't you come back for some seafood boil?"

"I think I need to go home and rest up for tomorrow. I had a lovely time. Please tell your folks I said thank you."

"Okay. I'll see you tomorrow. And Faye?"

"Yes?"

"You know I'm crazy about you, don't you?"

"I'm kinda counting on that."

He ran his thumb across her bottom lip then opened her car door. When she looked up at him with that sultry look, he groaned. "Stop looking at me like that or all bets are off on taking it slow."

"Bye Jess. Be good."

32

Faye propped the front bar door open in preparation for the arrival of the newly painted statue. Jesse and Joe would be there any minute with the delivery. She had the perfect spot right next to the hostess stand at the front of the bar. It would sit nestled between the bench and the fountain. She couldn't wait to see what her friend had done with it.

The truck pulled in and she excitedly directed them to back the truck up to the front door. Both men hopped out and Jesse unlatched the back end of the pickup.

"Wow! It's amazing!" Faye said. It was ablaze with color. Just what she'd envisioned.

"And it hasn't lost any weight since we dropped it off," Joe said.

They huffed and puffed as they pulled it off the truck bed and muscled it through the door.

"Right here," Faye instructed.

Ty came out from the back and said, "That is cool as hell!"

"I know, right?" Faye smiled.

"This calls for a few selfies," Ty said.

"That's a great idea. We should send a photo to the newspaper. Good publicity," Jesse said.

"Joe will you do the honors?" Faye asked.

"Sure. You three gather round."

He snapped some shots with them getting increasingly goofy. He took a shot of Faye kissing the Mayan God on the cheek, one with Faye squatting in front and Jesse and Ty on either side with their arms around its neck. They ended up with some great shots which Joe forwarded to her email. She'd send them to the paper. Maybe they'd do a feature article about her bar. They were usually good about doing that for new businesses. The grand opening was only a couple weeks away.

"This is exactly what was missing. Must be fate!" Faye said.

"I have to admit, he's grown on me and the bright colors neutralize the creep factor," Joe said.

"He's adorable! He looks like a Mayan version of Buddha," Faye said.

"I wouldn't go that far. He looks too menacing to be Buddha, I'd say closer to Sasquatch."

"I think we just came up with his name," Faye said.

"I've got to get back to work on the kitchen. Thanks Joe. Tell the crew hi, and I'll check in tomorrow some time," Jesse said.

"Will do, see ya."

.   .   .

With the outdoor deck completed, Jesse had his sights set on having the kitchen finished by the grand opening. Ty was proving to be a real asset. He had a natural mechanical aptitude and enjoyed working with his hands. Reminded Jess of himself. He, Ty and Faye, The Three Musketeers. Ty had shared with Jess that he was related to Faye and that his father was in prison. That had taken a lot to admit, and it had sealed their friendship.

Jesse rubbed the tension in his neck. He had that weird sense that he was waiting for the other shoe to drop. Was Julian lurking around somewhere...just waiting for the perfect opportunity to show up? Faye had halfway convinced herself that he was gone. He hoped that was true.

He and Faye were back to their previous playful bantering. The lack of intimacy was starting to get to him though, and the sexual tension was building...she had to be just as frustrated as he was... There was some small consolation knowing that.

Faye had scheduled karaoke tonight and he was going to be bartending with her. He loved being behind the bar with her. This was the first night for the new waitress Faye had just hired, Addison. She was only twenty-one, but she'd already been a server at a couple of busy establishments and came highly recommended. Faye wasn't nervous about throwing her to the wolves on a Saturday night.

"Quit daydreaming and hand me that board," Jess said.

Ty distractedly handed the four by six to Jesse, and

said, "I've always liked older women."

"And who might you be referring to?"

"No one in particular."

"Yeah, I'm sure it couldn't be Addison you're talking about."

"She *is* hot. And we're only three years apart. Actually, I'll be nineteen in a couple of weeks."

"And you're *so* mature for your age, right?" Jesse said grinning.

"Yeah, how'd you know I was going to say that?"

"Just a hunch."

"I've always liked redheads."

"She's very cute, and seems like a nice person," Jesse agreed.

Tyler's eyes were glazed over, and Jesse saw the tell-tale signs of a full-blown crush blooming right before his eyes. "Let her get to know you, she'll be unable to resist your charms."

"You think so?"

"You've got a lot going for you. Let her see the real you. Don't try to act too cool, even though I know it comes naturally."

Ty extended his middle finger toward Jess, grinning.

"Girls like that shit though," Jesse said.

"Parents don't."

"You've got a point. Now hand me another board and get your head out of your ass."

"Sure chief."

They both turned in surprise when Faye entered the kitchen with Addison right behind her. Ty's jaw dropped, his eyes widening, before he schooled his features into a nonchalant expression.

"Ty, Jess, you both remember Addison?"

Ty looked down at the ground and mumbled, "Hello."

Addison's cheeks turned pink, "Hi Tyler, Jesse. Good to see you both again."

Faye looked back and forth between Ty and Addison then at Jesse and he winked. Faye arched a brow as her lips curved up.

"Tyler, maybe you could give Addison a tour? Show her the ropes, where things are. I've got to talk with Jess for a few minutes."

Ty cleared his throat, "Uh...yeah...sure. Follow me."

Addison grinned at Ty and followed him out.

"Well well, I never saw that coming," Faye said.

"That's because you're not a guy."

"I can totally see it now," Faye said.

"So can he," Jess shared.

"Aww, so now I'm in the matchmaking business. Who'd have ever guessed?"

Jesse pulled Faye into his arms, "Lets concentrate on our own relationship. When are you going to give in to me?"

"I'm definitely warming up to you."

"Is that so? Just now warming up huh?" He rubbed the bulge of his sex against her pubic bone, holding her tight against him.

He felt her breath quicken. Ducking his head down he traced the outline of her mouth with his tongue before settling on her lips. Her mouth parted and she hungrily latched onto his tongue. He jerked when she cupped his crotch and squeezed. The scent of shampoo and summer flowers were assailing his senses. Her soft skin as he slipped his hands down the waistband of her shorts made him crazy. He needed to feel her whole body naked next to his. He massaged her bottom as she pressed against him.

"Babe, I need you now," Jesse said.

She broke away panting, "Jess, Addison and Ty..."

"Send them away, on an errand or something."

"Okay."

Faye smoothed her hair and straighten her clothing then went to find them. Tyler was showing Addison where everything was stored behind the bar when Faye walked out.

"Hey Ty? Could you two go into town and grab a couple cases of mixers for me?"

"Sure. I have my bike though; can I use Jesse's truck?"

"Yeah, I'll go grab his keys."

She returned with the keys and a list, and they took off.

33

Faye entered the kitchen and said in her most sultry voice, "Urgent meeting in my office... *now*."

Her eyes blazed with desire and he picked her up and carried her into the office. Slamming the door shut with his foot, he locked it behind them. "Faye," he whispered hoarsely, setting her on the desk. He reached into his pocket to grab a condom out of his pocket before quickly unzipping his cargo shorts. His hard-on sprung out as she brushed her knuckles down the soft furry trail and pulled his shorts down over his hips.

"Well hello there," Faye said.

He hissed as she stroked him. He kissed her neck then behind her ear before planting tiny kisses all over her face. Her breath hitched as he reached under her shirt to tease her nipples, rolling his thumb over her nubs as she arched into his hand.

"Oh, baby you feel so damn good," Jesse murmured.

She put her arms around his neck and pulled him in for a long sensuous kiss. "Jess, I've missed you."

"I'm here now. You're going to have one heck of a time getting rid of me again." He lifted her shirt and pulled her bra aside, her breasts spilled out, nipples rosy and plump. He glanced up and found her looking at him eyes smoldering with desire. He dipped his head and latched onto her nub. She was achingly responsive to his lips and tongue suckling.

Faye gasped with pleasure as he sucked, each pull caused her vagina to throb. Gentle at first, when Faye cried out, "Yes, harder," he began tugging and pulling until she thought she'd lose her mind. He roughly pulled her shorts and underwear off, then got on his knees in front of her. Gripping her hips, he trailed tantalizing kisses up her inner thighs as she leaned back bracing her hands on the desk behind her. She watched him as he reached her center. He parted her labia with his fingers before inserting them into her vagina. She spread her legs wider as his tongue explored and his fingers moved in and out, going deeper with each thrust. He moved his lips to her belly then stood and positioned himself between her legs.

She watched him slip on a condom. He held his penis with one hand and parted her lips with his other. Faye pulled her knees to her chest and he plunged inside her hot juicy center. As he penetrated, she felt him fill her completely, his hardness pressing against her with every thrust.

He held her hips steady and plunged deeper and

faster inside her. She felt her vagina squeeze around him as he drove harder into her. He rode her like a wild stallion rutting, all the pent-up desire laid bare. She cried out as her orgasm pulled her under. Biting her bottom lip, her body shuddered in surrender.

Jesse suddenly stiffened as he exploded, moaning her name. Panting, he released her legs and leaned forward to bury his face into her neck while his body shuddered in climax. She licked him, tasting salt and smelling sex and spice. She tipped her head back and he rained kisses all over her face and neck.

"Jess," she said, breathlessly.

He moved to her lips and kissed her deeply, his tongue filling her mouth like his cock had filled her only moments before. She felt his tremors subside and his breath slowly return to normal.

"*That* was incredible," he said against her lips.

"Is this what they call make up sex?" Faye asked, her lips turning up.

He cradled her face between his hands, "Hey, from now on, can we please just skip over the fighting part and get straight to the make-up part."

"Yes."

"I'm crazy about you Faye. I will never get enough of you." He kissed her deeply.

She brushed her fingers lightly through his hair. Faye looked deeply into Jess's golden brown eyes, almost caramel today, and sighed. "Jess."

"Faye stay with me tonight. I need you in my bed. I need to see you right before I go to sleep and the first thing when I wake up in the morning."

Her mouth curved into a smile as she pulled his head toward hers, "I'd like that."

"Ty and Addison will be here any minute," Jesse said. After zipping up, he reached for her panties and slipped them over her ankles. The shorts followed, then she stood and held onto his shoulders while he dressed her the rest of the way. As he zipped up her shorts his knuckles brushed against her mound making her want to start all over again. She sunk her fingers into his flesh as his lips brushed her belly.

Jesse straightened and looked deeply into her eyes. He tucked her hair behind her ears then planted a kiss on the tip of her nose. She wrapped her arms around his waist and rested her cheek against his chest.

"I'm only slightly terrified right now," she admitted.

"How so?"

"I feel so vulnerable."

"We *are* vulnerable."

"Jesse, I feel like I'm diving off a sheer cliff. My belly's doing flip-flops and my heart is pounding."

"Just be here, with me now. You can't look ahead babe. All you need to know is what is happening right here, right now."

Faye's brows drew together. "I'm trying." She ran her fingers lightly across his chest. "You're so good Jess, so solid."

"We're good together."

"Faye? Jesse where are you guys?" Ty called loudly, right outside their door.

Faye dissolved into laughter at Jesse's guilty expression.

"Come here you," Faye said. She ran her fingers

through his hair trying unsuccessfully to tame his wild mop.

"One more kiss for the road," she whispered. He tenderly brushed his lips across hers before straightening and walking over to unlock the door.

34

Faye hung up the phone, her forehead creased with worry. Kyle had decided to throw a family get together and wanted her to bring Jesse and Ty along. Her stomach was tied up in knots. As she thought about their conversation, she knew she was being fickle.

On the one hand, she was getting what she'd hoped for...the family acknowledging Ty, and an opportunity to introduce Jesse. But now that she had to deal with the reality of Jesse and Ty meeting her family... She wanted to run as fast and far away from that scene as possible.

Despite Kyle's assurances that everyone was anxious to meet them both, when he'd told her that her parents were flying in on their private jet from Palm Springs, her nerves began to fray. As she'd suspected would happen, Kyle had had a change of heart and wanted to meet with Ty and have a do over. She was pretty sure Ella had nudged that along.

Her father though—*he* was in a league all his own. He was suspicious of everyone, domineering, controlling, overbearing, and had prevailed over the family for her entire life. He had been showing signs of mellowing, especially since the kidnapping last year. He'd made more attempts to be in their lives and in Finn's, but he was still a force to be reckoned with. She had thirty years of experience with her fucked up family and nothing was as it seemed with them.

She rubbed her temples, feeling a slight headache coming on. She was surprised at how protective she felt towards her two guys. They had become her go-to people and she felt like a mother tigress toward Ty. She wouldn't let anyone hurt him.

With Jess, she felt vulnerable. They were just getting back on track and their relationship was still new and fragile. She knew what her father was capable of. All she could do was prepare them both for the onslaught because she sure as hell couldn't control her family.

Maybe she was over analyzing, and everything would be easy. *Yeah sure and pigs could fly!* She stood up rubbing the back of her neck. She needed to move her body and do something mindless to distract herself. This usually resulted in a very clean bar.

She opened her office door and heard Jesse singing before she saw him. Her breath caught at the sight of him...*every time.* His eyes were sparkling as he belted out a Thomas Rhett tune, *The Day you Stop Lookin' Back.* He put his toolbox down and swept her up twirling her around. Faye giggled as he tickled her neck with his stubble. His scent was intoxicating.

"How's the most beautiful girl in the world?"

"Much better now."

"I missed you."

"Me too."

"Spend the night with me tonight?"

"Okay."

"Yee haw!" He swung her around one more time before placing her back on her feet. "Is Ty here yet?" Jesse asked.

"He was. He had to run an errand."

Faye stood on her tiptoes and put her arms around his neck, "I had a hard time falling asleep without your arms around me."

"Same. I was lonely as hell. Promise me some pillow talk tonight."

"I've never had *that* request from a guy before."

Jesse grinned, "I'm not just any guy, I'm one of those evolved kinds of guys. A developed feminine side, ya know what I'm talkin' about?"

She snorted with laughter, "You're a goof ball."

He feigned a hurt look, "What are you saying, I'm not a sensitive guy?"

Faye pulled his face down close to hers, "I never said that."

"My mama raised me right."

"Yes, she did. You'll get no arguments from me."

"Get a room," Ty said walking in with an armful of wood.

"Oh good, you remembered. Thanks for picking that up," Jesse said.

"Sure."

"Hey, I have to talk with you guys," Faye said.

"Let me put this in the kitchen, I'll be right back."

Ty returned and sat on a bar stool, hooking his feet around the chair legs.

"What's up?"

"A couple of things. I just got off the phone with my brother Kyle. The PI he hired thinks he might have a lead on Julian. He's getting close. That gives me some hope." She hesitated, "The other thing is that he and Ella are having a barbecue at his place on Sunday, and you're both invited. It's casual, poolside, a chance for you to meet the family."

Ty crossed his arms over his chest, "No thanks."

Jesse said, "If I have to go, you have to go, bro. I need the moral support."

"Nope. Find somebody else."

"But Ty, please, it's important to me," Faye said.

Ty lifted an eyebrow, "It must be for you to ask me, after the way your brother treated me last time. What's the big deal?"

"Kyle feels bad and wants to start fresh. I want you to be included...a part of the family because you *are* family."

"Faye, you may feel that way, but that doesn't mean everybody else is gonna accept me."

"If they get to know you, they'll love you, just the way that I do."

His eyes flickered for a moment before he looked down. "Faye, it sounds all well and good, but I come from the wrong side of the tracks. I'm from the streets.

I've got a record...I hardly fit in with the billionaire yacht club crowd."

"Ty, neither do I!" Faye said. "But they're my family. They're yours too, whether you like it or not. The good the bad and the ugly."

He scowled, "Faye, you're living in a fantasy world if you think they're gonna embrace a bastard nephew or grandson whose own father is rotting in prison."

Jesse held up his hands and said, "Okay you two, can I get a word in here?"

Ty scowled at him and Faye blew out her breath and said, "Go ahead."

Jesse rolled his eyes. "Gee thanks. Listen Ty, this is important to Faye. I'm not looking forward to being grilled either. I'm not exactly an aristocrat. But we may as well give it a try. At least you have blue blood running through your veins. The only blue I got is the blue-collar kind."

Ty's jaw remained clenched. "I'll think about it."

"Promise?' Faye asked.

"I said I would think about it." He got off the stool and marched out the front door.

"Nice talk," she yelled at his retreating back. "That went well."

"Look if I'm intimidated, imagine how he feels. I've got a few more miles on my tires and a solid upbringing. It must push every button he has." Jesse walked over and slung his arm across her shoulders. "Don't take it personal. I think he'll come around."

"Honestly, I'm just as nervous as he is but I want him to be part of the family. He deserves to be acknowledged and accepted."

"I know your intentions are good Faye, but you have to let go of the outcome. People are people. Everyone has baggage and not everyone plays well together in the sand box. Ty has a lot to overcome and he confided in me about his first meeting with your brother. That sure as hell didn't pave the way for a loving family reunion."

"I know, but I also know Kyle. He has a good heart underneath his heavy armor. He's always had my back and then some. He knows this is important to me and he always ends up doing the right thing. He feels bad about that first meeting. And as much as I hate to admit it, I understand why he reacted the way he did. It was kind of sprung on him."

"If you say so. So, tell me what I'm in for?"

Her lips twisted, "My parents will be there. I know my father's been asking about you. He is very protective of the family's reputation...much more than his actual family. What can I say? He's a control freak, but he's still my dad."

"I know that, and I want to meet him. I'm a big boy. You don't have to protect me Faye."

"He can be a bully."

Jesse's eyes crinkled, "I have two older brothers remember?"

"That's like comparing a couple of guppies to a barracuda."

He scratched his head, "I think you just insulted my brothers."

"No trust me. It's a compliment."

"I'm going to go find Ty and talk to him."

"Whatever he decides is okay with me. I can't really

know how he feels. As much as I may want it, and truth be told, I'm not so sure anymore, he has to want it too."

"He wants it...maybe too much."

Faye watched his retreating back and felt her eyes well up. What if she was making a mistake to introduce them to her family. Jesse might claim to be a big boy, but he also had feelings. Her dad was an expert at eviscerating any opponent who had ever gotten in his way. She just hoped her father saw what she saw and had good intentions. Faye sighed then put her hair up in a ponytail and started cleaning.

35

*J*esse dropped Faye off at the bar and left to meet with Stan to go over some problems at a job site they were on. Faye frowned; she knew Ty was there, but the door was locked. As Faye struggled with her keys to unlock, she whirled around when a male voice called out her name —a voice she knew far too well.

"Faye."

"Julian!"

"We have to talk."

"Leave now or I'll call the police."

"You look so frightened. Please, I'm not here to hurt you. I'm here to beg you for another chance."

"No. There is nothing you could say that would change the way I feel. The moment I saw you in bed with that student it was over. I don't love you anymore. The police are looking for you. You've vandalized my property, you've been stalking me, you have to leave right this minute!"

"Not until you hear me out. I've come all this way. Then after you've heard what I have to say I'll leave if you still want me too."

"No! We've already had this conversation... its over Julian."

His eyes were overly bright, and he looked strung out. Faye was struggling, way out of her depth here with how to play this. He didn't have any obvious weapons and he'd never tried to physically harm her in the past. What if she just heard him out? They had been lovers once and had been happy for several years before his betrayal.

She knew he could see her caving because his shoulders relaxed, and his lips tilted up in a slight smile. "Faye, I know you and I know how kind and caring you are. It's not like you to shut me out after all that we shared. I've missed you. My stupidity cost me everything. How could I have taken you for granted and lost the only person that has ever mattered to me?"

"Look, if I were the only thing that mattered, you wouldn't have been tempted by your nineteen-year-old art student."

"That was my dick, not my heart. That has always been yours."

"Regardless, even if that's true, I've changed, I can't go back. Julian I've moved on and you have to do the same."

Pacing now, he raked his fingers through his hair "I've tried. I can't. I'm no good without you."

Her mouth twisted, "Just go away. Leave me alone.

Go back to New Zealand. Please. I'm happy now. If you truly loved me, you'd let me go."

His fists clenched. "How can you even think like that? We're soul mates."

Faye blew out a breath, "Look we had our time together. It was fun while it lasted. You got to play the intellectual, I got to be your muse. Until I was replaced. It's done. Over."

"It's not like that! It never was. When did you get to be so cynical?"

"Um let's see...when my heart was shattered by finding the man I loved fucking another woman in *our* bed. That's when!"

His eyes darted around and something dark crossed over his face. She felt a chill go down her spine. Pointing to the street she said shakily, "Go, now, or I call the police, I really mean it!"

His face reddened. "Faye, you're making a huge mistake."

"You're the one making a mistake," a steely voice said, coming out from behind the building.

"Ty!"

He held his cell phone to his ear as he gave the dispatcher their address.

Julian glared at Ty. He glanced back at Faye and said, "I'll be back. Think about what we had. No one will ever love you like I do." He turned on his heels and jogged quickly away. By the time the police arrived he was long gone.

Faye gave the officers a rundown of what had transpired, and they left with a promise to patrol more frequently.

"A lot of good that's going to do," Ty grumbled.

"I'm glad you showed up." Faye's voice was trembling and her eye bright with unshed tears.

"I had just taken the trash out to the dumpster and heard voices. I locked the front door behind me after I got here. Sorry I probably shouldn't have."

"He came out of nowhere. Jess just dropped me off."

"Fucker. I'd like to kill the bastard."

"I'm okay. He didn't seem to want to hurt me. He wanted to talk."

His striking cobalt blue eyes, so much like her brothers, flashed in anger.

"No is no! If I see him again, I'll skip the phone call to the useless police and take things into my own hands."

"Ty you can't afford anything more on your record. It wouldn't be in the juvie system this time. A record is for keeps. Not worth it."

"*You* are worth it."

Faye put her hand to her heart, "Ty, I love you."

He shuffled his feet uncomfortably, then looked down mumbling something about getting back to work. Faye's heart squeezed in her chest. She slipped her arm through his and said, "Thanks Ty. You know how brave you are don't you? You didn't even hesitate. That took guts. Let's go inside."

As they walked arm in arm to the back door, Ty said, "Just wait till Jesse hears. He's going to lose his shit!"

"Maybe we should keep it between us and not worry him," Faye suggested.

"No fucking way. He needs to know."

"No, you're right. No more secrets."

He looked heavenward and put his palms together. "Thank you." His tone dripped with sarcasm. She shrugged and gave him a sheepish grin as they went inside.

36

Faye sat on her front porch stoop, unconsciously wringing her hands as she waited for Jesse and Ty to pick her up. She felt like a cat on a hot tin roof, half sick to her stomach with nerves. *What had she been thinking?* These men were two of the most important people in her life, and she was surely about to send them to slaughter.

She saw the truck round the corner and ran up to greet them. Her eyes widened when Ty jumped out to give her the front seat. He almost didn't look like her Ty. His jet black hair was slicked back with some kind of gel product and he had ironed his black tee shirt, tucked it into black jeans and even managed to put on a belt. Granted it was a biker style, black leather with silver studs, but still... He wore his signature wide-woven leather bracelet and the small silver hoop earring, but he almost looked conservative...at least by his usual standards.

"Wow Ty, you clean up nice!" Faye said.

He scowled. "I hope you're happy. I wouldn't do this for just anybody."

She impulsively gave him a big hug. "I know that, and I'm honored. Too bad Addison can't see you right now." That produced a slight curl of his lips.

Ty crawled into the back of the cab and Faye took the front seat next to Jesse. Her breath caught in her throat when she locked eyes with Jess. He hungrily took in every inch of her and her skin felt singed. He flashed a sexy crooked smile and her heart melted.

"You look amazing Faye."

His gaze heated her skin and she was glad she'd chosen this dress. It was short and flirty, and the strapless bodice left her shoulders bare. She had taken extra care with her hair and had added a bright red lipstick at the last minute.

He looked handsome and delicious, his muscles filling out the white polo shirt perfectly. His strong tanned forearms with the dusting of golden hair made her belly do flip-flops. She bit her lip as she stared at the outline of his muscular thighs, taunt against the gray linen fabric of his slacks.

Faye fanned herself and said, "My my, you sure know how to make a girl swoon Jesse Carlisle."

He reached for her hand and squeezed it. "Winning. That's what I'm talking about. Getting Faye Bennett to swoon is now my main objective in life."

"I just happen to be the lucky girl accompanied by the two most gorgeous men on the island," she replied.

"Don't think your flattery is going to get you out of this; paybacks are a bitch," Ty said.

"You'll be fine! I know I've been over this, but just don't let them get to you. I've warned you about my father, he'll try to intimidate you, just ignore him. Let it all roll off your back."

"Remind me again why I'm doing this?" Ty said.

"Because, you should know your own family and they should know you. It's a start."

Jesse pulled at his shirt collar uncomfortably. "I must admit, I'm looking forward to this about as much as a root canal."

"You got that right, bro," Ty said.

"You guys, it won't be that bad. Just try to relax and have a good time."

They pulled up to the drive and like magic the gates swung open. Jesse followed the winding cobbled path, pulling up the circular drive in front of what could only be described as a modern-day palace.

"Ho...ly...shit" Ty gulped. "I'll just be waiting in the car for y'all."

"If I have to do this so do you," Jesse said.

A young man dressed in a formal black and white uniform opened the truck door for Faye and she stepped out casually calling over her shoulder, "Jess, just leave your keys in the ignition, they'll park it for us."

Faye felt as if she was seeing everything for the first time...as if looking at the scene through the eyes of Jess and Ty. And her cheeks heated in embarrassment.

She sandwiched herself between the two and slipped her hands through their crooked elbows. Taking a deep calming breath, she said, "We've got this, guys." They entered the foyer and Richard, Kyle's house manager, was there to greet them.

His face lit up with a smile. "Faye, so glad to see you."

Faye gave Richard a hug then stepped back to introduce her dates.

"Richard Drake this is Tyler Anderson and Jesse Carlisle."

Richard bowed slightly, "Glad to make your acquaintance."

"Richard has been with our family forever! He *is* our family and we'd be lost without him," Faye said.

"Thank you for saying so," Richard said. "Follow me. The party is in full swing."

"Are we the last to get here?" Faye asked.

He raised is eyebrows and smiled, "Yes, that shouldn't come as any surprise."

"Hey not fair! I usually beat Griffin. He's always the last one to arrive," she said.

"Today he got a head start on you," Richard said, leading them to the festivities.

37

___

As they followed Richard through the grandiose home, Jesse glanced over at Ty. He felt a stab of pity for the kid. Seeing Faye's pinched expression and feeling her death grip on his arm made him question again just what they were in for. Jesse had built plenty of million-dollar houses, but this was on a whole other level.

When they finally made it outside, to the center of action, Jesse's eyes narrowed. Nothing could have prepared him for the scene before him. *Casual?* He had thought he'd landed it just right, but now he felt way under-dressed. The men all looked like they'd stepped out of a GQ magazine and the women...well let's just say he was a bit out of his comfort zone. He had his first unsettling moments of doubt creep in.

There was a jazz quartet playing poolside, waiters in black and white uniforms walking amongst the guests carrying trays of hors d'oeuvres and full glasses of champagne and wine. There were colorful bursts of flowers scattered everywhere, in large planters and in the surrounding flower beds. The Olympic-sized pool looked inviting as hell but currently had fake lily pads holding votive candles floating across the surface. A huge granite wall had water cascading down into a pool beneath, full of colorful koi fish swimming lazily as the sun reflected off the bubbling water.

Ty looked like a deer in the headlights as Faye's brother Griffin strode toward them. Jesse leaned in close and said, "Do you get the feeling we just walked onto a movie set?"

"Fuckin-a." Tyler agreed.

Griffin could only be described as stunningly hand-some. He had the self-possessed air of someone who'd never known hardship and had led a privileged life that most could only imagine. Arrogant or overly confident, maybe they were one in the same, but whatever you want to call it he had it in spades. He came off as a cocky playboy in Jesse's humble opinion. He knew it was going to take some work to keep an open mind.

Faye threw her arms around Griffin then kissed his cheek. "How's my baby brother?"

"Wishing I was on the golf course right about now."

"How is our father today?"

"Lukewarm, I'd say."

"I told you he's softening."

Turning toward her guests she said, "Griffin, remember Jesse?"

He bit back a laugh, "Yeah how could I forget. My friend Faye LeBlanc here. I tried to tell her you'd feel like a chump when you found out who she really was. But as usual she never listens to anyone."

Jesse worked at keeping his expression neutral even though he felt like sinking his fist into that perfect jawline.

Faye's eyes were overly bright as she pulled Ty forward into their circle. "This is Tyler Anderson our nephew."

"Hey Ty. The resemblance is uncanny," Griffin said casually. "Nice to finally meet you." He reached out his hand and gave Ty a warm handshake.

Jesse counted that as a point in Griffin's favor. If he'd been an ass to Ty, all bets would have been off. He took a long slow breath in and readjusted his attitude. He was doing this for Faye, so he'd better get a grip, or he'd blow it for sure. He didn't want to disappoint her.

Griffin turned toward Jesse. "Do you golf?"

"Some. I don't really have the time, but I get out on a course a couple times a year."

"How about you Ty?"

Ty's lips twisted, "Nope, never. That's a rich man's game."

"I'll take you out with me some time," Griffin said.

Ty crossed his arms and defiantly glared. "No thanks."

Just then Finn came running up and threw his arms around Faye. "Aunt Faye!"

"Hey Finn. I want you to meet a couple of incredibly special people. This is your cousin Tyler, and this is a very good friend of mine, Jesse."

Finn's eyes sparkled as he greeted the two men. "Hi, I'm seven."

Jesse squatted down to be eye level with Finn, "I've heard a lot about you Finn. Great to finally meet you."

"Are you Aunt Faye's boyfriend?"

Jesse's eyes crinkled as he smiled up at Faye, "I guess you could say that."

Finn studied Ty, his face open and friendly. "Wow! Tattoos. I'm going to get a tattoo when I get bigger. Did it hurt?"

Tyler turned his forearm to expose the inside and said, "This one hurt a bit. Nothing I couldn't stand though."

"It's a bird!"

"It's actually a Phoenix."

"What's a Phoenick?"

"It's like an eagle only mythical. I had it inked after I got out of juvie, it's a symbol of rebirth."

"What's juvie?"

"Prison for kids."

Finns eyes were huge saucers.

James Bennett, the patriarch, took that moment to appear. He had obviously overheard the tail end of the conversation and was decidedly unimpressed. "Do you really think that's appropriate conversation for a seven-year-old?"

"When I was seven, I was dumpster diving. So yeah, I think he can handle it," Ty said.

Jesse stifled a laugh and Faye over enthusiastically greeted her father. "Dad! You finally get to meet your grandson Ty!"

He stiffened then turned toward Ty. "I'm sure you'll understand that this all came as quite a shock to our family. Pardon me if I'm not prepared to accept everything at face value."

"Yeah we don't want to shock the old man, it's not as if he had any responsibility in any of this," Griffin said sarcastically. "I'm going to get a stiff drink. The bar with the real drinks is over there," he said pointing. "I'll catch up with you guys later."

James looked at Tyler's tattoos disapprovingly.

Jesse felt his jaw tighten and for the second time in less than fifteen minutes, felt his fists clench.

"I think they're really cool!" Finn said flashing his irresistible grin. He had no clue how relieved Faye was to have him there at that moment.

"And, *this* is Jesse," Faye said, slipping her arm around Jesse's waist.

James Bennett's piercing eye's sized Jesse up. "Hello. You're the contractor I presume?"

"More like my hero," Faye said correcting him. "If it weren't for Jesse and Ty, I'd have had to close before I even got to the grand opening."

"Now *that* would have been a blessing."

"*Ma fille chérie!*" Faye heard her mom Giselle's heavy French accent, as she came rushing over. Framing Faye's face with her palms she searched her eyes before planting a kiss on each cheek.

"Mom!" Faye hugged her mom before turning her around to face the others.

"Ah, you must be the builder. *Oh tu es si beau!*" She said approvingly, looking Jesse up and down.

"She said *oh you are so handsome,*" Faye translated.

Jesse grinned and held her hand, raising it to plant a kiss on the back of it.

"*Merci, Madame Bennett.* I see where Faye gets her beauty."

She laughed becomingly, "Ah but not only is he handsome but he is *charmant* as well."

"Mom, this is Tyler."

She greeted him as she had Faye, framing his face with her hands, studying him intently. "*Tu ressembles mon mari et mon fils.*"

"Giselle, speak in English," James interrupted.

Jesse pinched the bridge of his nose as he counted silently to ten. *What an ass.*

"Ty, she said you look like Dad and Kyle."

His cheeks reddened as he replied, "Dope, I think."

Giselle laughed and said, "*Oui!* It is a compliment. You are very handsome."

Giselle took ahold of Ty and Faye's hands and pulled them behind her saying "Come with me. I want you to meet Ella and Kyle told me to bring you to him the minute you arrived. Come along Finn."

Ty looked back at Jesse and shrugged as he allowed himself to be led away. Faye's forehead was creased with worry about leaving Jesse alone with her father. Jesse stayed silent, waiting for Mr. Bennett to speak first.

"You're working for my daughter?"

"Yes, we've been renovating the outside of her bar and now I'm working on the kitchen."

"Rumor has it that there is more to your relationship than contracted labor. Is that correct?"

"Yes sir. I care for your daughter."

James Bennett steepled his fingers staring thoughtfully at Jesse. "And can you...Care for my daughter?"

"What are you referring to sir?"

"I think you understand what I'm asking."

"You want to know if I can support her financially?"

"Yes, I hope you understand that I have to ask. A man in my position can never be too careful. I've learned that it's best not to beat around the bush. I saw the way Faye was looking at you. She's falling in love if she's not, in fact, already there."

"That would be an honor if it were true. Anyone would be lucky to have her attention, let alone her heart."

"Do you really think it can work for the two of you? You know she is an heiress to billions, don't you?"

"Unfortunately, I am aware of that fact."

"Can you handle that? It comes with its fair share of, shall we say, baggage."

"Honestly, it's not ideal."

"At the risk of sounding like an overprotective father, Faye has been taken advantage of by men before. She is way too trusting. I, on the other hand, am not."

"I can assure you sir, I couldn't care less about her money; in fact, for me it is an obstacle not an advantage."

James Bennett's lips twisted cynically, "I've been around the block a time or two, and excuse me if I seem a bit skeptical. I mean nothing personal; I only have my daughter's best interests at heart."

Jesse gritted his teeth, "I mean no disrespect *sir*, but it is personal. Your line of questioning is insulting, not only to me but to your daughter. I don't give a damn whether you believe me or not, but I'd think that you'd have a little more faith in Faye. And if you're implying that I have anything but Faye's best interests at heart, you're dead wrong."

"If it's true... that you have her best interests at heart, then maybe you should take a good hard look at the reality of your situation. That's all I'm suggesting. Will you be able to provide for her and keep her in the lifestyle she's accustomed to...or perhaps you're willing to let her carry the financial burden for the two of you."

"I think I've had enough of this conversation. Good talk Mr. Bennett." As he was turning James Bennett's parting shot stopped him in his tracks.

"And about this 'grandson' that suddenly appeared out of nowhere. His motives are highly suspect. I can only guess at how excited he must have been when he realized who his relatives were. I'm sure Faye has filled you in on the history there. His father is rotting in prison for kidnapping my grandson and blackmailing me."

"I feel sorry for you. Whether you like it or not, Tyler has Bennett blood running through his veins. I'm sure that galls you to no end. Your *grandson* was dealt a bad hand and had to overcome more obstacles than you could ever imagine. He's a great kid. Has a heart of gold and he'd do damn near anything to protect *your* daughter. He idolizes her. And you want to know something else? He didn't want to come today. He has no interest in anything other than connecting with family. He only reached out to Faye because his mom was all he had growing up. He mistakenly thought life might be a little less harsh and lonely with the love of family. Ha! He's better off without you anyway."

Jesse thought he caught a brief look of doubt cross over James Bennett's face before he turned and stormed back the way he had entered. He'd wait in the truck. If he stuck around any longer, he was afraid he'd do something he'd regret. Faye deserved better. But as furious as he felt, her father had just thrown gasoline on the kindling of doubt he'd had since he'd first found out who she really was. Mr. Bennett had managed to push almost every button Jesse had. Faye was a princess who'd grown up in a fairytale. *How the hell could he ever measure up to that?*

38

"Dad, where's Jesse?"

"He stormed out of here after our conversation."

Faye paled as she said through clenched teeth, "What did you say to him?"

"I was simply trying to have an honest conversation with him."

"I don't believe you. Jesse wouldn't be run off by an honest conversation unless you said something offensive."

"I'm your father. It is my job to protect you. I was trying to explain to him that it might prove difficult to accept your financial status and that he could end up feeling at a disadvantage at some point."

"How?"

"Faye there are certain realities that come with the kind of wealth you were born into. You've got to accept that you're different than most people."

"Different how? We're human beings not commodities. Jesse is the most decent person I've ever met. His family welcomed me like I was one of their own." Faye's eyes welled up with tears. "Couldn't you have done the same? If not for him then for me?"

"Faye be reasonable. Surely you can see my position?"

"No Dad, I can't. Don't you want me to be happy?"

"What kind of question is that. Of course, I want you to be happy."

Griffin walked up with his beautiful date clinging to his arm, "Everything all right here?"

Faye couldn't contain her vexation, "No it isn't. Our dear devoted father just ran off the best thing that's ever happened to me."

"Faye don't be over dramatic. I simply wanted him to be aware of what he was walking into. I meant no harm."

"He comes from a normal loving home, completely opposite of us. I can't even imagine what he must have thought. Why couldn't you have talked about golf or tried to get to know him?"

"You want to make me into the ogre, fine, but I've always tried to do what's best for the family. You have no clue how vulnerable your wealth makes you because we've sheltered you. Look at Finn, just last year, kidnapped! He could have been killed! His own trusted nanny set him up with Tyler's father—the one responsible! I'm his grandfather, how do you think I felt when I couldn't even protect my own?"

Ella approached the group her forehead furrowed with concern when she saw Faye's distress.

"I never should have left Jess alone with you!" Faye said to her father, her voice thick with emotion. "I'm so embarrassed right now."

Ella looked from Faye to her father-in-law and back again. James Bennett at least had the decency to look slightly sheepish when Ella sized him up. He had enormous respect for Ella and he suddenly lost his swagger.

"Dad?" Ella said, one eyebrow arched.

He cleared his throat, "Just a slight misunderstanding."

Griffin slung his arm across Faye's shoulder and glared at their father. "I hope you're right. I only caught the gist of the conversation, but in case you're wondering about Jesse's motives with regards to your daughter, I'll fill you in. Our dear Faye here was so embarrassed by her family fortune, that Jesse didn't even know she was a Bennett for the first six weeks they were together."

At his fathers shocked expression, he continued, "Yeah, that's right. Your daughter lied to him and gave him a fake name. She wanted to make it on her own. You know what else? He almost wouldn't take her back when he found out she *was* a Bennett. He didn't think he was good enough. You want to know what I think? We're the ones that aren't good enough!"

Tyler showed up with Finn following him like a puppy, his eyes dancing as he looked up at him with hero worship.

"Tyler said he'd take me for a ride on his motorcycle sometime and that he'd show me how to hunt crawfish!"

Ty, seeing Faye's distress, looked suspiciously at

James Bennett. Eyes narrowed, he said, "Where's Jess?" He scanned the crowded poolside and said, "Faye, where is he?"

He searched her face taking in her glassy eyes. "He left."

"He'd never leave us here. He's probably waiting in the truck. I'm going to go find him."

"I'm coming with you. Griffin, Ella, please give Kyle and Mom our best, and please offer our apologies for running off so quickly."

Finn's shoulders slumped in disappointment. "You're leaving? But you just got here."

Ty crouched down and put his hands on Finn's tiny shoulders. "Listen bro, I'll see you again. You've got to practice those tricks I showed you with your puppy then report back to Aunt Faye. She'll give me the low down. Maybe Faye can bring you around the bar to see me sometime soon."

Finn just nodded his head staring glumly at the ground.

"Hey, give me a fist," Ty said as he raised a clenched fist toward Finn. His irrepressible grin returned as he bumped his tiny fist against his newfound friend.

"See ya bro. Be good," Ty said.

"See ya bro. Bye Aunt Faye."

"Finny, I'll see you soon." Faye said.

"Okay. I'm sorry you're sad Aunt Faye. Tell Jesse goodbye for me."

Fighting back tears she said, "I will."

~

$\mathcal{T}$hey found Jesse waiting for them back in his truck, seat tipped back, music blaring, sunglasses concealing his eyes.

"Hey," Faye said quietly as she climbed in beside him.

"Back so soon?"

"Jess, I'm so sorry."

"Not your fault."

"But..."

"Drop it for now," he said, his voice tight and controlled.

"Jess...I..."

His jaw clenched, his words clipped and grim as he said,

"I...said...drop...it."

Tears shimmered in Faye's eyes, and she quickly swiped the back of her hand across them then turned to stare out her window.

Tyler stayed silent in the back seat, arms folded across his face, lips pressed tightly together.

The ride home was the longest fifteen minutes of Faye's life. Her heart literally ached. Before getting out of the truck she tried one last time to get through to Jesse, "Jess, I never should have agreed to the party. I know how cruel my father can be."

His face devoid of expression, Jesse waited for her to exit the vehicle.

She slipped out of the truck and ran inside. She stood in the foyer her back against the door. When she heard the truck peel out, she slid slowly down to the floor and buried her face in her hands, her body racked by sobs.

～

"*T*hat was salty bro," Ty said.

Jesse ground his jaw and stared mutinously ahead.

"Did you see how shook she was?"

"I think you heard me earlier, but just in case you missed it, shut the fuck up."

"Look you knew that party was going to be suspect, and her father's nothing but a tool, but Faye? Now, we both know Faye is a different story."

Jesse blew out a deep breath, "Look Ty, I need some time to think. Have you ever had someone emasculate you? Talk about 'shook'. Well, I'm shook."

"Hey man, you and Faye are tight, don't let him get to you."

"Her father didn't say anything that I haven't already wondered about myself. He just brought up my own doubts."

"Look, the dude is a noob. You heard him throw shade at me..."

Jesse snorted, "Yeah the 'dumpster dive' was epic."

Ty grinned, "I was kind of proud of that one myself."

"I just need a little time."

"Don't take too much time... man, her sad eyes, it slayed me."

Jesse pulled up to Ty's mobile home park entrance and sat looking straight ahead, "Listen, I know it might be a stretch for you to get where I'm coming from, but I don't want anything from Faye or her family. Call it pride, ego, whatever the fuck you want to call it, but that was the most insulting thing I've ever had to sit through. And it was Faye's dad. I don't want to come between her and her family. I'm not that guy."

"All I'm sayin' is Faye should have a say in this too. Later." Ty hopped out of the truck and disappeared through the row of trailers.

Jesse put it in gear and at the last minute headed for his parent's house. He needed the comfort of his family and a dose of reality. *I drew the winning number in the parental lottery.* He felt a pang of guilt remembering the look on Faye's face when she'd climbed into his truck.

He knew it wasn't her fault her father was an overprotective asshole; he'd make sure to let her know that. But family was such an important part of his life, he couldn't imagine moving forward in a relationship without her family's blessing. Her father would never approve of him. He'd never fit in with the billionaire lifestyle and truth be told, he was proud of it.

39

*J*esse walked into The Pelican the next day and found Faye in her office hunkered over some spread sheets. His eyes hungrily roamed over her and he hesitated before knocking. Taking in her pale face and dark circles beneath her eyes, his chest felt hollowed out. He tapped the door frame and she looked up startled.

She sucked in her breath, "Jesse!"

"Can I come in?"

"Yes, of course."

"Faye about yesterday... I'm sorry I wasn't able to talk to you. I just had to have some space."

She leaned back in her chair. "I know."

"I'm going to take a few days off from here, Stan needs me at the job site. The timing's good. I'll still be able to get the kitchen finished by the end of the week in time for the grand opening Saturday."

"Jess...I...please don't let my father ruin this for us. He's already taken so much, I couldn't bear to lose you because of him."

"Faye, its complicated. I'm not abandoning you here. I'll still bartend on Saturday; I'll finish the kitchen...we'll just have to give things some time."

"I understand," she said.

"I don't think you can, really. It's not your fault Faye. Maybe if I were a different person, less prideful, I'd see it differently. I'm working on it.

Plastering a fake smile on her lips she said, "Take whatever time you need. I don't blame you for running as fast as you can away from my family's baggage. You'd have to be a superhero to take it all on."

Jess bowed his head, "I'm not running Faye. But I'm no superhero, that's for sure. I wish I were a guy that takes everything in his stride, that lets stuff just slide off my back, but I'm not."

"I'm too much trouble...high maintenance, isn't that what you guys would say?"

"You're about the furthest from high maintenance of any girl I've ever known. Faye don't do this to yourself. You didn't do anything wrong!"

She turned her face away before saying quietly, "Then why does it feel like I'm the one being punished?"

Jesse squeezed his eyes shut. "Faye, all I'm asking for here is a little space to get my head on straight. As a guy, I'm conditioned to think of myself as the bread winner, the protector and provider. I know that makes me sound like some Neanderthal, believe me, I'm disappointed as hell in myself. I thought I was coming to terms with the juxtaposition of our situation, until I realized I'd just buried it...never really dealt with it at all."

"I'd walk away from it all...to be with you...money, wealth...it all means nothing to me."

"I believe that, I know that about you. I'm the one with the problem and I'm sorting it out. Give me time, that's all I'm asking for right now."

She lifted her shoulder in a half shrug, "I don't have much of a choice."

"I'll be back tomorrow, Wednesday at the latest."

She raised her chin, then said, "I hope you find that clarity you're looking for. It takes courage for a man to walk beside his woman instead of always leading the way."

Jesse winced. "I guess I deserve that. Faye, when you put it that way, it makes me sound like the most pathetic bastard on the face of the earth. I want you to understand, my family is everything to me. I don't want to be the one that comes between you and yours."

She gave a mirthless laugh, "I'm afraid that there isn't much to come between with me and my father. I'm sorry Jess, I know that wasn't fair to imply you lack courage. Go, do your thing. Get your answers. I won't try to stop you."

Jesse turned and quietly left the room. Seeing her blue eyes filled with pain would haunt him. He had done that to her. *Damn. Why did love have to be so complicated?*

∽

"*H*ey Faye, I just passed Jesse. Is he coming back?" Ty asked.

"In a couple of days. He's got to catch up on some things at his own business for a change."

"He loves you. You know that don't you?"

Faye smiled sadly, "I'm not so sure about that. More importantly, what they don't tell you in the romance novels is that sometimes love isn't enough."

"It's enough. It takes courage is all."

"Ty, how did you get to be so old?"

He looked away, then back at her, "Faye, don't give up on Jess. He's one of the good ones. He'll get it."

She sighed, "I hope you're right."

"Should I start filling the coolers?"

"Yes, then if you'd go pick up some extra ice at the beverage dock to tide us over until Friday's delivery, that'd be great."

"Done."

"And Ty?"

He turned and raised an eyebrow. "*You* are one of the good ones!"

He grinned, "Faye, you're so extra." Then he left her sitting there trying to figure out exactly what he'd meant by that. She'd have to download a slang app onto her phone to keep up.

❧

*J*esse and Stan leaned over the drafting table, studying a blueprint. Jesse scratched his head then said, "I triple checked this floorplan, there has to be a mistake, the electrical layout included all the extras for a theater room."

Stans brow furrowed as he ran his finger across the sheet, "Yep, there it is," Stan said pointing to those details. "We fucked up on our end. Sorry Jess. That'll cost us two extra days of work, but at least we caught it before the customers did."

"Yeah, no biggie. Otherwise, everything else seems to be humming along."

"I miss our bromance is all," Stan said grinning.

"You're coming to the grand opening on Saturday, right?"

"Yep, we all are. Wouldn't miss it."

"Great...or as Ty would say, dope."

"Ty working out then?"

"Real well. He may be joining our crew when all is said and done. He's a natural. He's been helping me out. Saved me from pulling the crew away from you."

"On the job training from the best. We can use him, that's for sure."

"Let's head over to the site and tell the guys the bad news about the do-over."

"Sounds good. I'd like you to look over the model home; it's about ready to display."

Jesse rolled up the blueprint and wrapped a rubber band around it before stuffing it back into his backpack. "I'll follow you on the bike."

"Okay see you there."

Jesse was satisfied with the way the projects were moving along. There was always some glitch. This electrical snafu was minor in the scheme of things. He didn't know how he'd manage without Stan.

40

Tyler came in with an armful of local tourist guide periodicals and excitedly thrust one at Faye.

"Look who made the front page!"

Faye squealed when she saw the photograph of the three of them perched around the statue. She tried to push aside the ache in her chest remembering that day, when things were still good between her and Jess.

"Let's put some of these on the table right next to Sasquatch," Faye said.

"Wait till Jesse see's this. Speaking of...is he coming in today?"

"As far as I know. That's what he said the other day."

"So the schmuck hasn't called you?"

"Nope. I wasn't expecting him to."

The door opened at that exact moment and Jesse stepped through. A wave of longing hit Faye. Jesse's eyes blazed with raw hunger and he only had eyes for Faye.

"Look what the cat dragged in," Ty said dryly.

Jesse nodded at Ty then walked toward them. "Faye." His eyes searched hers intently.

"Hey Jess."

"I'm back."

"I see that."

Clearing his throat, Tyler said, "Maybe I'll go take the trash out."

Jesse reached for her hand and turned her palm up before planting a soft kiss in the center. "Forgive me Faye."

Her palm tingled where his lips had just been. "I do, but damn you, nothing has changed."

"I just needed to process the whole thing."

"Feels different when it's on the other foot doesn't it Jess? We could have worked through it together."

His voice was tight with pent up emotion. "I know, I realize that now. But that's what I'm trying to do now. Faye, I don't want to lose you, ever. I don't give a fuck if your father approves or not."

"You hurt me Jess."

"I know I did. I'm sorry."

"I'm embarrassed at the way my father handled himself."

"I didn't handle it so great myself. I let him get to me. Maybe you'll never be able to understand...I'm not sure I completely understand myself, but he managed to find my weakest spot and attack me there. It was sudden and unexpected. I was trying to wrap my head around the posh surroundings...felt completely out of

my depth, then he went all in. Hit me right in my gut."
He gave her a lopsided grin, "At least Ty was spared,
that's some consolation."

"He would have probably been next, if we hadn't
left. I hate the way you just disappeared on me, but I
shouldn't have left your side."

Jesse pulled Faye into his arms and buried his nose
in her fragrant hair. "You're right. I need you right by
my side," Jesse kissed her softly.

Faye melted into his body, parting her lips. She
brushed her fingers across the smooth skin of his neck
then ran them through his hair. She closed her eyes as
he planted tiny kisses all over her face.

"Mm you smell so good." His tongue licked her
bottom lip before sucking it gently into his mouth. Her
pulse fluttered as his tongue flicked against her lips.

Faye took his hand and led him back to her office.
She closed the door and locked it then turned to stand
on her tiptoes, kissing him softly on the lips. His eyes
were warm pools of honey as he slipped his hands
under her shirt. Faye opened her mouth inviting him to
deepen the kiss. Her knuckles grazed his toned belly as
she snuck her hand down the waistband of his jeans,
smiling when she found him fully erect.

She walked him backwards until his knees were up
against the club chair and with a tiny push he plopped
down. She straddled his lap and smoothed her palms
up his chest. She could feel his hardness between her
legs and rubbed against him. She tore her mouth away
to quickly drag his shirt over his head. She licked his
bare skin, her fingertips rubbing his nipples until he
groaned.

His eyes were heavy lidded with desire as he watched her remove first her top then her bra. His pupils dilated seeing her naked breasts. He reached for them gently massaging and kneading, driving Faye crazy with want. He pulled on her nipples and she bit down hard on her lip to keep from crying out. Leaning forward he put his open mouth between her breasts, he licked and kissed his way to her nipple, then latched on and pulled and sucked until she was squirming in abandon.

"Stand up," he said.

She stood in front of him while he pulled her pants down, kissing her soft mound through the silk panties before tugging them the rest of the way. He held her hips steady while he nuzzled her center and dipped his tongue into her sweet spot. Her hands gripped his broad shoulders as she through her head back, biting her bottom lip in fiery passion. He inserted two fingers inside while his tongue continued its onslaught. She was on the brink of surrender when he pulled away. She cried out, "Don't stop!"

He kissed her belly then stood up to remove his pants. "I want to come inside of you, I want to feel your orgasm...your tightness throbbing against me."

He slid on a condom then sat back down pulling her with him. She rubbed her hot wet core against his large erection until, voice hoarse with passion he said, "Faye now!"

She slowly took him inside her and rode him. He filled her completely, snug around his hardness, she gripped him with her taut thighs as she lifted her pelvis up and down. He felt so good inside of her. He pressed his thumb against her clit with one hand while teasing her nipple with the other. She could feel his shaft penetrate deeper with every thrust.

She watched his beautiful face as his body suddenly shuddered in climax. His jaw tightened, his gaze never leaving her face, his eyes liquid amber and hot with desire. She sat down fully onto his shaft and wiggled her pelvis against him until she was overcome with her own powerful rush of sensation. Wave after wave tore through her as she collapsed against his chest panting.

She felt his lips in her hair as he tenderly brushed it back from her face. He cupped her bottom with his other hand. She could feel him throbbing inside of her and the smell of sex heavy in the air. It was sensual and erotic, and she never wanted to move. They lay motionless, spent, except for the rapid rise and fall of their chests which slowly returned to normal.

*J*esse felt a possessiveness he'd never experienced before. Fiercely protective... and the only way he could describe it was primitive. Mine! With her long sensuous body melting into his, he didn't want this moment to end. He could feel her breasts pressed against his chest and her breath against his skin. He never wanted to let her go. He put his knuckles under her chin and tipped her head back gazing at her kiss swollen lips. So sexy.

Her eyes were deep pools of blue, almost navy, her lids lowered alluringly.

"I need you Faye. These last two days have been hell."

Her voice still smokey from sex she said, "I need you too."

Nibbling her neck, he said, "Now that we have that settled."

She rubbed her cheek against him. "Jess?"

"Hm?"

"Don't ever leave me like that again. I don't care if you can't talk about things right away but don't leave. It's too much for me."

"I won't."

"Promise?" Her voice sounded small and vulnerable.

"Yes." He put his open mouth over hers and they shared a torrid kiss, one that held all of the pent up emotions from the last two days. She pushed against his chest and gracefully uncurled from his lap to stand. His eyes burned a path from her face all the way down her delicious body.

Jesse's voice was husky, "You take my breath away."

She reached for his hands and pulled him up from the chair. "Let's finish this conversation tonight, at your place."

"That's the best idea I've heard all week."

They reluctantly dressed each other then forced themselves to focus on the long list of things they had to get done by Saturday.

41

"Well I think we've got everything checked off the list. Ty said he'd help Maddy out in the kitchen with the pizza orders in between busing tables. Maddy said she could help wait tables too, we can put her wherever we need her." The kitchen was functional, but Faye was only going to serve frozen pizzas and nachos until she could hire a cook.

"You and me behind the bar, Ty bussing and helping Mads, Addison waiting tables, we should be able to handle it. Thank God your seating capacity is only sixty, plus the twelve at the bar," Jesse said.

Faye looked around at all they'd accomplished. The deck was stunning. It had thousands of twinkle lights strung across the overhang, gigantic urns with colorful annuals and vines trailing down, and hurricane lanterns on each table. He'd built the outside bar counter under the arbor, which had potted Morning

Glories full of blooms trailing up and providing splashes of color. The deck bar would only be used for catered private parties for now. And of course, there was the view—waterfront, right on the marina.

"You are so beautiful," Jesse said, his eyes roaming over her in her long navy tube skirt and fitted white crop top. Her arms were bare, and she'd left her hair down to fall thick and wavy around her shoulders. She had silver bangles around her wrist and a delicate chain around her exposed waist that was sexy as hell. Her ankle bracelet jingled with every step she took. He wanted to trail kisses from her belly down the curve of her hips to her rounded ass before carrying her off to his cave.

She tucked a strand of hair behind her ear and said, "Quit looking at me like that or I'll have to change my underwear."

"Damn, you wore underwear?"

She dimpled as her lips curved up.

"Hey y'all we're here," Tyler called out, holding hands with Addison as they came through from the back room.

Jess and Faye exchanged an amused glance. "Hey you two. I'm just getting ready to open. Ty you want to put the open sign out for me?"

"Sure." He tugged on Addison's hand, pulling her along behind him.

Jesse said, "That was quick."

"They're young. They look cute together."

"They look like they can't keep their hands off each other."

Faye arched a brow, "Remind you of anyone?"

He gave her his big sexy smile and winked as Ty and Addy returned ready for their instructions.

"Mike Taylor is going to start setting up at six and play from eight to midnight," Faye said.

Addison said, "He played at the last place I worked. He's really good."

"I heard him play at the Yacht Club a few times, that's how I knew about him," Faye said.

Ty and Jess gave each other a look, Ty added an eyeroll for posterity.

"I saw that," Faye said.

Ty's eyes widened in mock innocence, "What I'd do?"

She glared at him and playfully punched his arm. The door opened and their first customers arrived, a group of six who opted to sit at the bar. Jess stepped behind the bar and began serving.

Faye watched him with hungry eyes. She'd never grow tired of seeing him charm the pants off everyone he encountered. His wide toothy grin, his warm eyes, his playfulness and sense of fun, and for now anyway, he was hers. She was in love. *Love!* It hit her like a ton of bricks. This was no crush...no affair... this was the forever, fairytale kind of love. The one she hadn't thought really existed six months ago. She was in danger of losing herself completely to this man. Who was she kidding? Losing? She was already lost.

Her hands shook slightly with this sudden realization. Taking a couple deep slow breaths to calm her nerves, she plastered a welcoming smile on her face then went to greet the new arrivals. The guests were now lined up waiting to be seated, and she decided to help Addison with the tables until she was needed behind the bar. Jesse had everything under control.

As she was returning from seating customers outside, her eyes widened when she saw Kyle, Ella and Griffin along with Griffin's latest arm candy walking in. Her eyes strayed immediately to Jesse. *Too soon.* They'd barely got through the most recent family drama and here they were. Oh well... there was nothing she could do but suck it up and hope for the best.

"Hey! You made it," Faye said.

"Hey sis, the place looks great," Kyle said approvingly.

"Thanks to Jesse. Please make sure you're extra nice; we've barely recovered from Dad's attack last week."

Kyle grimaced, "That's one of the reasons we're here. To celebrate with you of course, but also to offer an olive branch to both him and Ty. We're only going to have a pre-dinner cocktail. We've got dinner reservations at the club."

Ella stepped forward and hugged Faye. "I'm so sorry. If I'd have known what my father-in-law was up to, I'd have interceded."

"You had fifty people to contend with, how could you have known? It's not your fault," Faye said.

"There's four bar stools left with our names on them," Griffin said. "Let's take them."

Faye caught Jess's eye as she followed them to the bar. Her stomach was in knots until she saw that Jesse was relaxed and friendly when he greeted them. He took their orders and even teased Griffin's date about her choice of drink, a Kamikaze, sharing a bartender war story about the possible repercussions of one too many.

With her family tucked safely away she went to find Ty, leaving them in Jesse's capable hands. "Ty, FYI the Bennett family is in the house."

"Shit and here I was enjoying myself."

"You still can."

"Doubtful."

"Why don't you give it a try. They're here to show their support. You know you're stuck with me...which means you're kind of stuck with them too."

His intense blue eyes sparkled today. "I'll go make nice. I'm in a good mood."

"And I think I know who to thank for that."

He flashed his devilish grin as his eyes searched the bar until they lighted onto Addison. When he found her, his whole face softened. "She's so beautiful," he said.

"She is." Faye had to bite back the words *'be careful'* because they'd serve exactly no one.

She watched like a proud mama bear as Tyler approached the bar and shook hands with Kyle then Griffin. Ella pulled him in for an affectionate hug and Griffin's date batted her lashes at him. He *was* a gorgeous young man and Griffin's date was probably not much older than Ty was. After reassuring herself that things weren't going to explode, she jumped back into service.

42

Ty was excitedly telling Faye about his earlier conversation with Kyle, "He even promised that I could take his boat out after he's taught me how to sail!"

"That's great Ty." The musician was playing his last set and the bar was down to about half full. Her family was long gone, and this was the first chance they'd had to catch up since they'd opened.

"And Griffin is going to teach me how to golf."

Faye bit back a grin and it was hard not to tease him about his previous scorn for golfing. It put a smile in her heart.

"Jesse was invited too. Right Jess?"

"Yep."

"He said he'd take him up on it. At the Yacht Club's golf course."

"Will wonders never cease," Faye said, raising her eyebrows.

Addison passed by on her way to the back room and Ty hurried after her. Faye turned as the front door opened and pressed a hand to her throat. Dang it! Just when she thought the evening was just short of perfection, Dave waltzed in like he owned the place. What an awful man, and now that she knew what he did for a living she was even more uncomfortable serving him. He checked out their new mascot, sasquatch, then sidled up to the bar.

Faye casually walked over to Jess and said, "Don't look now but Dave, our favorite customer just came in."

Jesse's brows drew together. "Do you want me to kick him out?"

"No, but will you serve him?"

"Yeah. Are you sure you want to do that?"

"Yes. I don't want to cause a scene. And he did apologize. My biggest concern is his history with Ty and the company I'm sure he keeps."

"Yeah that's why I think he should go somewhere else to drink." Throwing his bar towel across his shoulder he went to take the man's order.

Jesse poured from the tap into a frosty mug and glared as he slid it across the bar.

"Keep the change."

Without a word Jess stuck the change into the tip jar and turned his back on the unwelcome patron. Jesse went to the back kitchen to ask Faye something as Tyler came out lugging a couple cases of beer. He set them in front of the coolers to refill. He grabbed a tub intending to clear some tables, but as he was walking toward the deck, a loud gravelly voice said, "Well, well, if it isn't the mule, Tyler."

Tyler whirled around and his eyes flashed with rage when he saw the old man sitting at the end of the bar. He slammed the tub down on the first table he passed and stomped over to him. "What the fuck are you doing here?"

"Just a paying customer. I caught the photograph of your smiling mug in the tourist rag, thought I'd come see for myself."

"Get out."

"Oh so now you're the boss? I thought that pretty little blonde was the owner."

"Don't even talk about her! Get the fuck out now!"

"You've got balls, I'll give ya that. But aren't ya forgettin something? Like about five grand, as I recall."

"Your reward is that I didn't rat you out...should have though."

The man chuckled mirthlessly, "Regrets already and so young. Tsk tsk."

Addison took that moment to approach Ty, she touched his arm about to ask a question, he shook her hand off and snapped, "Go, get out of here."

Her eyes widened with hurt, but she pivoted and walked away.

"She's a real beauty."

That was the fuse that lit the fire, Ty exploded. He tackled the man off his bar stool then jumped on top of him. He pounded his face with both fists as the guy fought back. They rolled around on the floor each trying to gain the upper hand, but the old man was no match for Tyler. Jesse and Faye hearing the commotion and shrieks from customers came running out from the back.

"Tyler!" Faye squealed. "Get off him!"

Jesse tried pulling Ty off but with adrenalin on Ty's side, it was a struggle. He was finally able to grip him around his waist and lift him off. Faye was visibly shaking as she knelt beside the bleeding man trying to help him up off the floor.

His lip was cut and bleeding and his nose looked like it could be broken. He swiped the blood off on his arm and Faye yelled for Addison to get some towels and ice.

Jesse had hauled Tyler to the back and was making sure he stayed put.

"I'm going to sue you and this bar for everything ya got, ya hear me?' he screamed, his face red with anger.

Faye winced, "I'm so sorry this happened. But why did you come back anyway? We never should have let you through that front door. You're nothing but trouble. Sue if you like but I'm sure you'd rather avoid the attention."

"What I'd like is the money that two-bit dealer owes me."

"Get out or I'll call the police. If you need medical care, I'll call the squad and you can wait outside for it."

Jesse came out from the back with a subdued but angry Ty following. "You heard her, get the hell out unless you want me to call the police."

Ty stood behind Jesse with his arms folded across his chest and wearing an expression of utter contempt.

"You disgust me...you're a vile excuse for a human," Ty said.

"Ty...enough," Faye said firmly.

"I'm leaving but you haven't seen the last of me." He held the ice pack wrapped in the bloodied white towel to his face as he shuffled out the door.

43

"Ty! What the hell were you thinking?" Jesse said.

"I wasn't thinking! I don't need a drug dealing pimp leering at Faye or my girl. He was up to no good."

"That doesn't give you the right to attack somebody completely unprovoked."

"I was provoked," Tyler stared rebelliously at the ground, his jaw set like granite.

"What's your idea of being provoked? Did he throw the first punch?"

"No, I did."

"What did he say that was so threatening that you had to get physical?"

"He made a couple of suggestive comments about Faye and Addison that I took offense to. That was enough."

Jesse blew out his breath, his anger deflated. "I

agree he is a douche and if I'd heard him say anything about those two, I might have done the same."

"Thanks for that," Ty mumbled.

"You're going to have to watch your back and be extra careful. He's not the forgiving kind."

"If I see him again, I won't go so easy on him," Ty said.

"Listen tough guy, after hearing about your history with him, I wouldn't be so cocky. I'm sure he's got some pretty bad players on his team."

"I'm not scared. Fuck him."

"That's adrenalin talking. Just watch your back is all I'm saying."

Faye came over, her forehead creased with worry. "The customers seem to be taking the bar brawl in their stride. Nobody left anyway."

"I'm sorry for that Faye but I'm not sorry I hit him."

"But you do realize that now I'm going to have to worry about you? He is going to want a payback."

"Let him. He's old and out of shape."

"That's fine in theory, but your youth and muscles won't have much impact against a gun. Don't be careless. Are you hurt?" she asked.

"Naw, he got in a couple of kicks and scratches but no biggie."

"I'm going to pay him what you owe. If you feel you need to, you can work it off a little at a time."

"Forget it. He owes me for not ratting him out."

"I want you safe. I don't care about the money."

Jesse nodded his head. "I agree. Best to put the past where it belongs and get a fresh start."

"Please, Ty let me do this."

Faye's eyes were his undoing, he couldn't stand seeing her stressed out. "Okay. I'll find him and make sure he gets his money."

"Thank you!" Faye gave him a big squeeze.

"Can you cover for Addison for a few? I have some splainin' to do."

"Sure."

*T*yler grabbed Addison's hand and dragged her outside behind the bar. She stood with her arms folded glaring.

"Listen Adds, I'm real sorry for speaking to you like I did. I wanted you as far away from that tool as I could get ya."

"A simple 'not now' would have sufficed."

"One hundred, but my head wasn't on straight. When he made a suggestive comment about you, I lost it." Tyler leaned his forehead against hers and pulled her snug against his hips. "Forgive me?"

She sighed, "Yes, I can't stay mad at you."

Ty tipped her chin back and softly kissed her.

"Your lips are so sweet," he said. He cupped her cheek. "Addison, besides Faye, you're the best thing that's ever happened to me." He tried pushing away the niggling voice of self-doubt. Ty wasn't sure he deserved the good things that were coming his way. Ever since Faye had come into his life it felt like his luck had turned. *I might not deserve it but I sure as hell will take it.* That settled, he got out of his own way and deepened the kiss.

~

"*I* don't know about you guys but I'm exhausted. I say let's leave the cleanup for me to tackle tomorrow."

"I can come in," Ty offered.

"I'm in," Jesse said. "We can come in after a leisurely breakfast. I'm hoping to sleep in...with you tucked up against me."

"Let's say noon then. Does that work for everybody?"

"I'd like to help. You don't have to pay me. I may be a little late because I'll be coming from church," Addison offered.

"I'll pick you up," Ty said.

"We need all the help we can get, and of course I'll pay you," Faye said.

Faye suppressed a smile as she saw Tyler's eyes practically smoldering as he and Addison looked at each other.

"I'll take you home now. I know you have to get up early," Ty said to her.

"Thanks, let me grab my purse." She came back out moments later and they left hand in hand.

Jesse pulled Faye into his arms. "Finally! I thought we'd never be alone."

"Let's get out of here. I'm not lifting another finger."

"Good idea. Save your energy for more important things." He wiggled his eyebrows playfully.

Faye set the security alarm then locked the door behind them. "Somehow I don't think that's going to be an issue."

"Let's get the hell out of here. I want to kiss every inch of you."

He let her settle in behind him before he kick-started the bike. She held him tight, craving the feel of his warm body close to hers. Suddenly she wasn't the least bit tired anymore.

44

*J*esse and Faye pulled into the bar parking lot about a quarter till noon.

When they stepped into the bar, the previous night's chaos still awaited them.

"Apparently the cleaning fairies had better things to do while we were sleeping. I was hoping for a miracle but it's just as bad as I remembered," Faye said.

"We'll have it done in no time."

"I'll start by cleaning the tables and then I'll do the dishes before I tackle scrubbing the floors."

"Where do you want me?" Jesse said.

"Let's keep our minds out of the bedroom," she teased, eyes twinkling.

"Just the way I like my women...insatiable." Grinning he playfully pulled her against him and kissed her.

She kissed him back then stilled. "I swear I never knew it could be like this. I've never considered myself to be overly sexual, not that I didn't like sex, but I've never fantasized continuously about someone like I do with you."

"I feel like a horny teenager...it doesn't suck," Jesse said.

She giggled, then pulled away to begin the dreaded cleanup.

"I'll round up the trash and take it out to the dumpster. Then I'm going to sacrifice myself for love and clean the bathrooms."

"No way!"

"Yes, I'll do it... for you."

"How about you do the guys' bathroom, since we know how careless y'all can be with your aim."

"Hey, don't lump us all together. I told you my mama raised me right."

"I'm sure that's true and all, but I'd rather clean ten women's restrooms than just one of the mens'."

"You know when you look at me with those big baby blues, I'd say yes to about anything."

Faye watched him disappear out the back door lugging the recyclables first. She grabbed a rolling cart and plastic tub from the storage room and began loading it with the empty bottles and glasses from the barroom, wiping the tables off as she cleared them.

Jesse suddenly reappeared, his face drained of color.

"Jesse! What's wrong?"

"Faye, I need for you to sit down. We have a situation."

Her face blanched, "Is it Ty? What? Tell me!"

"Faye, when I went out back to take the trash out... I

don't know how to say this...there is a dead body floating right off the dock."

Faye's hand flew to cover her mouth. "Oh my God, who? Is it anyone we know?"

His voice grim he said, "It's not good. It's the guy from last night. Dave, the one Ty had the altercation with. I'm going to call the police now."

"Wait! Are you sure its him? How do you know?" Faye was babbling and she knew it but couldn't seem to stop herself. "Why here? How did he die? I'm going out to look."

"No!" Jesse shouted, grabbing her arm as she started for the door. "Faye, just no. Trust me, you don't need to see it. I'm going to be having nightmares for the next ten years—why would you want to subject yourself to that?"

"I need to get ahold of Ty before he gets here. I don't want him walking into a scene without a warning," Faye said, pulling out her cell.

Holding the phone to her ear with a trembling hand, she looked at Jesse. "It went straight to voice mail. I'll try a text."

"He's probably picking Addison up right about now. They might already be on their way. Text him then try calling him back and leave a message. I'm going to call the police."

Jesse went to the back room to place the call leaving Faye alone to call Ty.

"Tyler, this is Faye. We have an issue at the bar. The police are on their way. I just didn't want you to be blindsided when you got here. Call me. It's important!"

She felt compelled to go look at the crime scene for

herself. Just a quick glimpse. She wasn't sure if she'd believe it without seeing it with her own two eyes. As she headed for the back door Jesse blocked her, grabbing ahold of her shoulders he gripped them tight.

"Faye listen to me. You-do-not-want-to-go-out-there! It's not like a TV show. It's gruesomely real. You'll regret it for the rest of your life. I won't let you do it. You have to take my word on this. Plus, it *is* a crime scene. You don't want to disturb anything."

Her eyes flooded with tears. "I can't believe this is happening. Why here? Maybe he came back to make trouble and fell and hit his head."

Jesse pulled her into his arms. He tenderly brushed her hair back from her brow. "Shh, Faye, it's not for us to figure out." He kissed the top of her head. "We'll let the cops solve it," he said, his voice calm and steady. Faye's entire body trembled in his arms.

"The police are going to want to question all of us. What am I supposed to say when they ask me if I knew the guy?"

"The truth. We had a full bar witness the altercation he and Ty had. If you lie, it's only going to make things look worse for him."

"But Ty will think I'm throwing him under the bus," she said, as Jesse brushed away her tears with his thumb.

"We know Ty and we know he's innocent. He didn't do this, and they'll know it too. It was just a coincidence. Just stick with the truth. It's always the best idea."

Ty ran in with Addison trailing behind just as they heard sirens approaching.

45

"What happened?" Ty said, eyes narrowed with concern.

Jesse looked at Faye and she nodded. "Ty, listen, when we got here, I took out the trash...and...there was a body," Jesse said.

"What? Dude what do you mean a 'body'?"

"I'm sorry—as in I found someone dead floating in the water right off the dock."

"H...ol...y...shit! Faye are you all right?"

She nodded, "I didn't see it. Jess stopped me from looking. It's shocking enough in my imagination, I'm glad I wasn't the one to find him."

"The thing is Ty, I hate to tell you this, but it's the guy you punched out last night. Your old supplier."

Ty's body coiled like a panther ready to leap, "Dave? I've got to get out of here man. Why didn't you tell me that on the phone? Fuck! They'll think it was me!" He turned to leave, and Jess grabbed his arm.

"Don't do it man. You can't run. You'll look guilty as hell."

His eyes were wide with panic, "Dude let me go! You know they're going to pin it on me. I'll hide out until they find who the real killers are. I can't be locked up again...I just can't!"

"You've got to calm down and think rationally. Yes, they're going to have questions for you. But you didn't do it. If you run or lie...well, they'll only have one person in their crosshairs and that my friend, will be you. If you cooperate, they'll be more likely to keep an open mind and do a full investigation."

Tyler sat down heavily onto a chair and buried his face in his hands. His shoulder shook as he began to sob.

Faye's heart broke into a million pieces. "Ty I will do everything in my power to make sure this isn't pinned on you." She leaned down and held him tightly to her. "You hear me? I'm going to call Kyle right now. He is the very best and he will help you."

His voice muffled he said, "Why would he? Your whole family thinks I'm nothing but a trailer park lowlife."

"No Ty, he doesn't think that. He will do it."

Addison who had stood silently taking it all in said, "Ty, if you can't do it for yourself, do it for me. Listen to what they're telling you. It's the truth."

They all looked at the door with dread when the police charged in. Jesse and Faye went to meet them at the entrance. Jess gave a brief summary of events then led them to the crime scene.

The minute they disappeared Faye dialed her

brothers' number. "Kyle, I need you to come down to the bar right away!"

"Sorry I can't. We're entertaining some friends and I'm in the middle of barbecuing chops. Can't this wait until tomorrow?"

"No! It's urgent."

"What's so urgent that it can't wait?"

"A dead body, police and Ty could wind up as their main suspect."

"I'm on my way."

"Thank you. Be safe."

He disconnected without saying goodbye and Faye felt like a thousand pounds had been lifted from her shoulders. Her big brother had always had her back and he'd have Ty's back now. He was the best attorney around and he'd know the best way to handle things.

"Ty, Kyle is on his way. Don't answer any questions until he gets here."

The female officer came back inside and approached them. "Mr. Carlisle tells me the victim was a customer of yours?" she said, directing the question at Faye.

"Not a regular, but he'd been in here a couple of times since I've opened."

"Did you know him outside of the bar?"

"No, just from serving him here."

"What can you tell me about last night?"

Tyler sat with his arms crossed tightly over his chest, His eyes downcast and his jaw set. Addison's hand rested on Ty's thigh. Her eyes were glassy with unshed tears. Faye glanced at him before continuing.

"The first time I served him I practically had to kick

him out. When I closed up and left for the night, he was waiting outside the bar, acting threateningly. Fortunately, Mr. Carlisle was there to intercede so nothing more happened. He was here a couple other times before last night."

"Tell me everything you remember pertaining to last evening."

"Well, he hadn't been in the bar long," she glanced at Ty and hesitated before continuing.

"Go on," the officer encouraged.

"He'd just ordered his first beer when Ty, who works for me" she nodded her head at him, "came from the back with cases of beer to refill the cooler."

"They exchanged words, he provoked Ty, making insinuating remarks about myself and Addison, who is a waitress here. Ty is very protective of us and unfortunately, he let the guy bait him. A tussle ensued and some blows were exchanged. Jess broke up the fight and he left on his own accord, with an ice pack and a bloody nose. That was the last time we saw him," a sob caught in her throat, "Until Jess found him this morning."

She had been jotting down notes then she turned to Tyler. "Can you tell me your version? Why did he pick you to spar with? I want an account of the full verbal exchange between the two of you."

Faye jumped in, "My brother is an attorney, Kyle Bennett, and he's on his way. I think its best that he be present when you question Ty."

"So you're not going to talk without a lawyer? Got something to hide? We just need to ask a few routine questions. From all of you."

"Look, Ty had a fight with the guy, and he winds up dead. It doesn't take a rocket scientist to know he'll be a suspect," Faye said. "That doesn't mean he's guilty, it means we've watched enough cop shows to see where this is going."

"Have it your way," she said. "I'll get the waitresses' statement then Mr. Carlisle's and hopefully the attorney shows up by then."

Ty who had remained quiet throughout the exchange said, "I can answer your questions. I've got nothing to hide. I won't say anything different either way."

The cop forced a smile, "That's a wise decision. If you haven't done anything wrong, no need to complicate things."

"Ty, I said no!" Faye said, her voice steely.

"Faye, I know what I'm doing. I'm not playing their game."

Kyle stepped through the door coming in from the back entrance. Faye got up and practically flew into his arms. "Thank God!"

Kyle, seeing his sister's stricken face, hugged her protectively, before slinging his arm across her shoulder and walking with her toward the small group.

"I ventured out to the crime scene before I came in, and I see you have the scene taped off. The coroner arrived as I was pulling in."

The officer nodded hello. "Good to know. I'm officer Randall. I've already got the owner's statement and was getting ready to question the employees."

"I guess I'm here just in time then."

Kyle carried himself with a self-assurance that brooked no argument. "Shall we proceed?"

Faye felt such relief at having her brother take over, that it felt like all the air had been sucked out of her. He must have jumped immediately in his car because he was dressed casually in faded jeans and a black tee shirt...with only flip flops on his feet. She was also aware that the police officer seemed slightly shell shocked; her brother just happened to be drop dead gorgeous and built like a Greek god. That had to give them a slight tactical advantage...at least it couldn't hurt. His cobalt blue eyes were piercing in their intensity. Right now, he had them trained on Ty.

46

Ty visibly stiffened as Kyle studied him. "On second thought, I'd like a word alone with my client before you proceed, would you excuse us please?"

"Have at it," Officer Randall said, waving her arm wide.

"Come on, son, let's go outside where we can have some privacy."

Ty got up, hands in his pockets, and followed Kyle outside.

"I'm royally screwed dude."

"Talk to me Ty. Who was this guy to you?"

"From my past. I wound up in juvie for dealing. He supplied the dope. When I got busted, I owed him money. Couldn't pay it back. First time I saw him in the bar I thought he was there to find me, turns out he'd been there before I started working for Faye. He came in last night, rubbed me the wrong way, I lit into him. The rest is history."

"Unfortunately, it's not history. They'll be gunning for you. The faster they can wrap it up into a neat bow the better for them. You've got to help us point them in a different direction. Who supplied to him, who he hung out with, anything you can remember."

"He said he'd seen the photograph of Faye, Jesse and me posing with that statue. It's in those tourist rags all over town. He said he wanted to come in and see for himself if it was really me."

"You were his mule but who was he working for. He had to be low on the food chain. Who'd want him dead and why?"

"How would I fucking know?"

"Let's get something straight right now. I'm here to help you. I'm on your side. Got that?"

"Why would you believe me anyway?"

"Two reasons, one, I trust my sister and two, I trust my own instincts. You might have a chip on your shoulder, but you're not a murderer. I'd bet my law degree on that."

Ty didn't know how to respond. He pinched the bridge of his nose as he tried to drum up the past. "Listen, I was only fifteen, it was pot for Chrissakes, I didn't hang out with the slimeball. I remember him mentioning that if I was interested in expanding my brand, he could supply me with just about anything I wanted to deal. He mentioned that there was good money in meth. I told him no way. Pot was it for me."

"Was he always alone?"

Ty closed his eyes in concentration, "One time there

was someone waiting in the car. Gnarly, covered in tats, older than dirt."

"Could you pick him out of a lineup if it came down to that?"

"Don't know man. It was so long ago."

"Okay, we're going back in there. Be honest but don't elaborate on anything. Make it short and sweet. No feelings, opinions, just the facts. Think you can handle that?" Kyle asked, kindly.

"Yeah."

Kyle clapped Ty on the back and said, "Let's get this initial interview over with. I can't make any promises about how they'll proceed but if they do take you into custody, don't freak out. I've got your back and I'll make your bail."

Tears glistened in Ty's frightened eyes, reminding Kyle that underneath his defensive bravado was a terrified eighteen-year-old kid.

"Ready?"

Ty nodded and followed Kyle back into the bar.

They were greeted by three more officers who been added to the mix. Officer Randall had acquiesced her role as interrogator and an older officer with a shaved head and serious scowl was now asking the questions.

Kyle whispered to Ty, "Easy now."

Ty looked up at him with a glimmer of trust in eyes that were mirror images of his own. Something twisted in Kyle's gut. He would do everything in his power to keep this kid safe. He smiled reassuringly then said, "It's show time."

47

Faye rocked in Jesse's arms, inconsolable. After only thirty minutes of questioning, the officer in charge had read Ty his rights, cuffed him and taken him into custody. Despite Kyle's reassurances that he'd be released on bail, it had shattered her to see him being hauled away. All she could see was his stricken face, utterly defeated. When she'd asked him about notifying his mom, he'd lost it. His strangled *'no, please Faye,'* had been tormented.

He was in Kyle's hands now and she had to let go. There was nothing to do. Since the Pelican was now a crime scene, she couldn't re-open until forensics had done their thing.

They'd taken the video from the security cameras and Faye prayed they'd find evidence to vindicate Ty. Poor Addison had been beside herself and her best friend had come to pick her up. She'd promised to keep in touch. Now the hard part...waiting.

Faye's cell phone rang and seeing it was her sister-in-law Ella, she picked up.

"Hey," Faye said.

"How are you holding up?"

"Not so good. It's just so unfair."

"I know but Kyle is the best and he'll get him out."

"I hope you're right."

"Faye, why don't you and Jesse come over and wait with Finn and me? We can hang out by the pool and be miserable together. And our company left so we have tons of food I don't want to go to waste."

"I don't know...I just don't feel like doing anything right now."

"I know, but it will be good for all of us. Finn would love to see you and Jess and so would I. We haven't had any time together since you bought the bar...please?"

Sniffling, Faye said, "I suppose... let me check with Jess."

"Yes, to whatever it is," he said.

"I guess it's a go."

"Bring your swimsuits."

"Okay. We'll see you soon."

The ride over, sitting tucked behind her man with the wind in her face, had helped clear her head. Ty was innocent, she knew that, and she also knew her big brother was fierce in battle. He was in good hands. That's what she intended to cling to.

"*A*unt Faye, Jesse! Come play with me!" Finn yelled, as he held onto his noodle, splashing water with each kick.

Faye smiled affectionately at her nephew. He was so dang adorable, who could resist. "We'll be right there."

Now that Ella didn't have on clothing to disguise her baby bump, it was obvious she was pregnant. She still rocked her bikini but there was a decided swell to her belly above her bikini bottom. It was so beautiful to see. She wondered if she'd ever be lucky enough to have what Ella and Kyle had. They were so happy together and such a tight family unit. She hoped so.

"I'm going to grill some burgers and brats when we're ready to eat. I have potato salad made up, chips, and a homemade key lime pie. Can I get either of you anything now?"

"No rush but I'll have a bottle of water when you get a chance," Faye said.

"Me too," Jess said.

"Two waters coming up. Finny, do you need anything?"

"Nope, just somebody to play with," he said.

"We're coming already," Faye grumbled, her lips curving up in a smile.

Faye watched as Jess peeled off his white tee-shirt, her gaze drifted over his body resting on his strong thighs...remembering their lovemaking the night before.

He caught her staring and his eyes smoldered and heated her skin as he returned the favor and watched her strip down to her bikini. He reached for her hand and they walked to the pool's edge. Faye dipped her toes in, testing the temperature of the water.

"Dad always says make it quick, just jump," Finn said.

Jesse jumped into the air and tucked his body into a cannonball and yelled "Yee haw!" as he plunged, spraying Faye from head to toe. She shrieked as the cold water splashed her.

"You're toast now!" Faye said, before diving in.

Finn cheered Faye on as she chased Jesse, finally catching up and jumping on his back to pull him under. They wrestled, their water slicked skin making them both even hotter. Faye's knee accidently brushed against his hardness and she let out a little gasp, "Oh!"

"I would like to kiss every inch of you right now," he whispered.

She bit her lip then dove under again and swam over to Finn.

"Aunt Faye, can you pretend to be my horse?"

"Sure, hop on."

Jess floated over and said, "But Finn, wouldn't you rather ride a wild stallion?"

Faye sputtered with laughter and Finn said, "Yes."

"You little traitor. See if I ever let you saddle me up again."

Finn giggled and wrapped his scrawny arms around Jesse's neck, holding on tight while Jess called, "Hold your breath I'm going under."

With a powerful kick he dove under and as graceful as a dolphin swam to the other end with Finn laughing in delight when they resurfaced.

"That was dope!" Finn said.

"Um where have I heard that before?" Jess said, as it reminded him of why they were there in the first place. *Ty.*

"Ella says that Dad is going to bring Ty home."

"Yes, I have no doubt."

"Maybe he'll be here in time to eat with us."

"That would be pretty great Finn." Jess said, "Hold your nose."

Finn's eyes got wide and he grinned from ear to ear. Jesse picked Finn up over his head and threw him high into the air.

He made a big splash then came up sputtering, "Do that again!"

Jesse tossed him a few more times until he realized Finn would never grow tired of this game. "Buddy my arms are getting tired. I'm going to have to take a break."

"Aunt F-a-y-e...your turn."

"I think Jesse should throw you a few more times. I'm enjoying the view."

He winked at her, "One more time just for your Aunt Faye."

Finn surfaced sputtering, shaking his hair like a dog after a bath. He rubbed the water out of his eyes with his fists, then his eyes lit up.

"Ty!"

48

Faye's eyes widened in shock when she saw Kyle and Tyler standing under the arbor.

"Ty!" she shouted as she scrambled out of the pool. She ran over to Tyler and hugged him with her dripping wet body, laughing and crying at the same time. "You're here."

"Thanks to Kyle. He's a badass!"

"I told you."

Jesse walked over wrapping his beach towel around his waist. "Dude."

"Dude," Tyler said, grinning.

Jess's voice was thick with emotion as he said, "Man is it ever good to see you."

Ty shrugged and looked down, "The security tape cleared me."

Faye gasped, "It did?"

"Yep, showed the whole thing. It also showed your

ex snooping around in the middle of the night, but not last night."

"Julian?"

"Yep."

Faye arched her brows as she looked at her brother. "So, Ty is completely in the clear?"

"Yes. The video shows the whole thing. There was some kind of scuffle, the victim fell and hit his head on a metal cleat. The murder probably wasn't intentional. Shows the other guy throwing him off the dock and hightailing it out of there. Problem for him came because the victims clothing got snagged so he didn't float out to sea. We still don't know why they were there in the first place."

"Ty recognized the other guy from the good old days. Saw him with the vic once; he was waiting in the car when they were making an exchange."

"I brought a still shot for you to look at...see if you recognize him," Kyle said as he pulled out the photo.

Faye gasped and held a hand to her throat, "Jess, it's the guy from the boat, the one who insisted on using my dock and entrance."

Jesse looked down and said, "I'll be damned. That's him all right."

"Unfortunately, we don't know who he is, or where he came from, but he claimed he'd been using my dock for convenience and was mad that I'd bought the place and ruined his perfect setup," Faye said. Faye's eyes narrowed deep in thought. "Now that we know those two were connected and both seemed to be lurking around my bar, the next question is why? They showed up way before Ty did, so that connection has to be a coincidence."

Kyle smiled at Ella and pulled her against his side before saying, "It's possible they were using your place for their drug operation and that would surely have pissed them off when you blew it by buying the place."

"That's the most obvious reason. But why keep showing up when their setup was blown?" Ty said. He looked past them, and a dazzling smile lit up his face.

"Addison!"

She rushed over, "Faye called and invited me. I hope that's okay?"

"Are you kidding me?" He grabbed her up in a bear hug and lifted her off her feet.

He leaned down and planted a kiss on her surprised open lips. He kept his arm slung across her shoulders as they discussed different scenarios.

"Bottom line, we won't know until the guy is caught. He's probably long gone by now," Jess predicted.

"Ella can you go grab some swim trunks for Ty? The rest of you can take a dip while I start the grill." Kyle said.

Faye's eyes sparkled as she teased, "I'd never thought I'd see the day my big brother would be so domesticated. I love it."

"I won't argue with you. I'm smart enough to know that I'm the luckiest guy on the planet. Ella is the best thing that ever happened to me. I'm going to spend the rest of my life proving to her that she picked the right guy. It took a lot of convincing to get her to give me a chance." He squeezed her before she left to grab the swimsuit. Kyle watched her, his eyes warm pools of love.

Faye sighed. "You two are wonderful together. You're the happiest I've ever seen you. You used to be so restless, now... you're totally content."

Ella returned a few minutes later and threw a pair of trunks at Ty. He went into the pool house to change. Addison took off her clothes and when Ty returned his eyes practically bulged out of his head.

"Wow! You look amazing!" he said.

Addison smiled shyly, "You're not so hard to look at yourself."

He grabbed her hand and they held hands as they jumped in the pool together.

"Ah, to be eighteen again," Faye said.

Jesse looked at her, his face serious, "I wouldn't go back, the best day of my life was the day I walked into The Pelican and saw the girl of my dreams."

Faye's cheeks grew warm, "You sweet talker."

Finn had wrangled Ty into taking over where Jesse had left off, tossing him into the air, his shrieks and laughter lifting everyone's spirits. Faye looked around and felt her heart ache in her chest. She was so happy. These were her people. She looked at Jess, in deep conversation with Kyle and knew he was her mate. Tonight...he'll be all mine ...and she intended to take full advantage of that.

∾

*H*ours later as they lay in bed together, both of them languid from the wine, water and sun, Jesse felt his cock respond to her naked breasts flattened against his chest. He held her tight against him and breathed in her sweet scent. Nuzzling her hair, his hands caressed her back, stroking up and down. He moved his hips slowly and slid his erection between her thighs rubbing up against her sweet spot.

Faye took in a sharp breath, then sighed his name, "Jess."

"Faye," he responded his voice low and seductive. "I need you."

She bit her bottom lip then said, "I'm yours."

"Mine," he said, and covered her mouth with his.

Faye's breath quickened as he began thrusting slowly between her legs. After sliding on a condom, he rolled her onto her back, parting her thighs with his knees. He slid into her, voice gruff and said, "Tell me again."

"I'm yours Jesse. All yours."

He pushed hard into her and stilled until she began writhing beneath him begging, "Jess, please!"

"Please what?" Then he plunged in and stilled again, waiting.

"Please, take me," she pleaded. He smiled against her lips and thrust again.

She raked her nails down his back. "Jess," she was panting lifting her pelvis her legs wrapped tightly around him squeezing.

"Look at me," he commanded.

When she looked up at him her eyes glazed and

heavy lidded with desire, he couldn't hold back any longer, he began to ride her hard and fast. When he felt her climax pulsating against his shaft, he exploded with his own orgasm. His body shuddered until he collapsed on top of her burying his face in her hair.

He kissed her all over her neck and shoulders, which was torture to her over sensitive skin, still tingling from her climax. A long while later as she was just about to doze off, Jesse whispered in her ear, "I love you Faye Bennett."

49

Faye grabbed at the envelope taped to her door before it blew away. She unlocked and went inside taking off her drenched clothing in the foyer. The letter had stayed dry under the cover of the storm door, but by the time she got inside it was soggy and her written name smeared almost beyond recognition. The whole condo rattled as the wind howled outside. The forecasters had predicted it would only reach a level two by the time it made land. They didn't call for an evacuation, since the storm was losing steam rather than gaining in intensity. Still, one hundred-mile-per-hour winds were nothing to scoff at, but they didn't feel it was necessary to evacuate and move inland.

The hurricane was expected to hit land sometime late evening but even now the rain was torrential, coming down so heavy you couldn't see your own hand in front of your face. It was eerie. Jesse was taking last minute precautions to batten down Ruby and Hank's house. Maddy was on her way home and due any minute. She hated being alone in this storm. She headed to the bathroom to towel dry her hair then changed into some dry clothes.

After putting the tea kettle on the stove, she picked up the letter, her chest heavy with dread. Her hands shook slightly as she opened the card. 'My Dearest Faye. I had to make contact with you, to say goodbye. I thought by moving here temporarily I could convince you of how much I love you and what lengths I'm willing to go to win you back. But I can see that you are happy and in love. I've finally accepted it, and I want that for you. I'm sorry...for everything. I lost the only thing that ever mattered to me. It was never about the money. It was always you and I'm sorry I ever gave you a reason to doubt that. You will always be my biggest regret. I'd like to see you one last time before I leave. Please. For old time's sake. Forever yours, J.'

The kettle whistled, and she poured the boiling water over her herbal tea bag. She added honey and waited for it to steep. She didn't know what to think of the note. There was no way in hell she was going to meet with him, but could it actually be true? Was he leaving? She hadn't realized how much anxiety she'd been burying until she felt the relief sweep through her body. Suddenly the door opened and Maddy entered drenched to the bone and looking like a drowned rat.

"Oh my God! It is wicked out there. You can't see an inch in front of your face."

"I know I just got home myself. Let me go get you a couple of towels."

She reached for the towels and suddenly remembered that she hadn't boarded up the large window in the back of the bar. Dammit! It would only take about fifteen minutes tops.

"Maddy I forgot to board up the large back window. Will you go over there with me?"

"Are you nuts? I'd just leave it."

"If we go now, we'll beat the worst of the squall and we can get back before Jesse gets here. I've got everything ready for our hurricane lock down party, alcohol, flashlights, candles, snacks, cards and games...all ready and waiting."

"I still don't think it's a smart idea."

"I can't just leave it! We've put so much work into the place, I'd feel sick if it got destroyed over my stupid mistake."

"Fine, I'll go. I'm not letting you go alone. Let's get this over with."

"Let me leave a note for Jess, then I'm ready."

She scrawled a quick message for Jesse, and they ran outside. The front door was suddenly ripped out of Faye's hands and slammed back violently against the wall. The street was deserted, not a car or person in sight. Her hair whipped painfully against her face and she was drenched to the bone within seconds. She and Maddy held hands as they made a run for it. The rain stung as it pelted her skin and the wind pushed them back. Faye felt like she was trying to go up on a downward moving escalator. She imagined that a gale might pick them both up bodily and blow them out to sea. Maybe this wasn't such a smart idea.

Trash blew around and the trees were bent so far

over that it was a miracle they didn't break or completely uproot. And this was a level two. She'd witnessed the aftermath of a level three and it had been devastating to their community. They finally made it to her vehicle. She gripped the steering wheel tightly, her shoulders knotted with tension as she drove the three blocks to her bar. The car was being blown about and she prayed it would get them there safely.

She pulled right up to the entrance and hunkering down, they raced to get inside as quickly as possible. The whole building creaked and shook, and she could hear banging from something that had blown loose outside.

She flipped the light switch, and nothing happened. "Damn Mads the electricity is out. Hold on I have a mag light behind the bar." She felt her way along until she found the flashlight.

"Let there be light. Thank God!" Maddy said.

"Follow me," Faye led the way to the storage room to grab the plywood and cordless drill. It was right where she'd left it. Now that she was here though, she wondered if she and Maddy could even do the job by themselves. With the wind they probably wouldn't be strong enough to secure the board and drill at the same time. It would be hard enough under good weather conditions. Nope, this was an exercise in futility. Change of plans. We're going home!

"Mads not my brightest move. I think this is a hopeless cause. I'm sorry."

"I agree. Let's get home. Dry clothes, a bourbon and coke, a few games sound like heaven."

As they walked out of the back storage room, the

front door banged open. Thinking it was from the wind, they both screamed when a figure came toward them in the dim light. The man came towards Faye and raised his arm overhead, then her world went dark.

"Should we lock them up in the storage room?"

"Naw, we don't have time for that. Let's grab the statue and get the hell out of here."

"You're the boss."

The two men huffed, panting as they pushed and dragged the heavy 'Sasquatch' out the front door. The wind practically ripped the door from its hinges. They had to scream to be heard over the roar of the mighty ocean and storm. They had backed up right behind her small sports car, so they didn't have far to go.

The grizzled leader yelled, "On a count a three... one...two...three..." they managed to lift it onto the truck bed and claw their way against the wind, to get into the vehicle. They raced out of the parking lot despite limited visibility.

Julian hung back weighing his options. When fifteen minutes had passed with no sign of Faye or her friend reappearing, he began to wonder. Pulling his hoodie tight around his head he jumped out of the rental car and hunched down low against the wind he ran inside.

He shined his phone's flashlight around the room. He found Faye lying motionless on the floor, a pool of blood around her head. He panicked. He didn't know what to do. Should he move her? He couldn't leave her here to die. He felt for a pulse and was relieved to find it strong and steady. But he also knew they might not believe that he wasn't responsible for harming her.

The other woman was sitting up and appeared groggy but awake. He made a split-second decision and then tenderly slipped one arm under her knees and the other supporting her neck and lifted Faye into his arms. He brushed his lips softly against hers, squeezing his eyes tightly shut against the wave of longing he felt. She smelled like flowers. He'd always loved the way she smelled.

Brushing her hair back from her forehead, she moaned. "Shh, you're safe. I'm here my beautiful Faye. I'll take care of you." She was so pale, all of the color drained from her face. He wanted to cradle her against his chest and never let her go. He stepped out into the storm.

50

_J_esse arrived at Faye's place and was surprised that her car wasn't there. He mentally braced himself for the onslaught of driving wind and rain as he pushed open the truck door. He ran in slow motion as the wind pressed him back and the relentless rain pounded. Where the hell is she? And Maddy. He spied a note on the kitchen counter and the letter from Julian sitting right next to it. His blood turned to ice when he read Julian's note. Had she gone out to meet him? No way. She would never do something that risky. Then he picked up her note to him and was flooded with relief. She was with Maddy. They were at the bar. He raced back out into the storm and headed to The Pelican.

· · ·

*J*ulian opened the car door and tenderly slid Faye onto the passenger side seat. As he was buckling her in, he was grabbed from behind and picked up with so much strength, that at first, he thought the hurricane had done it. As he was thrown to the ground he looked up and saw the outline of a man standing over him. The rain made visibility next to zero, and he feared the men had come back to finish Faye off.

"Leave her please. Don't hurt her."

"You crazy fucker. What did you do to her?" the male voice yelled, just barely heard above the screaming winds.

"Nothing! It wasn't me! I saw two men follow her in, they came out with a statue, she didn't come out, so I went in and found her lying in a pool of blood."

The wind kept blowing the man back even as he held onto the car door to anchor himself.

"I memorized the license plate number. I swear, I'd never hurt Faye."

*J*esse forced himself to keep from jumping on top of Julian and beating him within an inch of his life...but for some strange reason he believed him. "Where's Maddy?"

"Inside, she was just coming to."

"I'm going to go in and get her. If you leave with Faye, I'll hunt you down, I swear!" he yelled.

Maddy appeared at the door just as Jesse got there.

He shouted, "Maddy, come on. Faye's hurt, she's unconscious, we've got to get her to the hospital."

Maddy held onto Jesse as they fought their way back to the car. Her eyes went wide with shock when she saw Julian in the driver's seat. "You!" Maddy hissed, "What the hell is he doing here?"

"Just get in Maddy. We've got to get help. You need to be checked out as well."

"I'm fine."

"No arguments."

They climbed into the back seat and Julian sped away. Jesse called out directions and when they arrived, he had Julian drive straight up to the emergency room entrance. Jess jumped out and ripped open the passenger door, then gently pulled Faye from the car and raced inside. Julian parked then he and Maddy followed him.

They took her back immediately for testing. Over Maddy's protests, she was getting checked out as well. Jesse felt like puking. She had appeared lifeless, her delicate face as pale as a ghost. Her lips colorless. Her hair was matted with blood. *Fuck fuck fuck!* What had she been thinking? *Why the hell would she ever think that was a good idea?*

Jesse paced the floor. He'd just hung up from talking to Kyle and he was going to notify the police, then head over to the hospital. The storm complicated everything. Julian sat huddled in the corner, off by himself.

∽

*A*n hour after Kyle arrived a nurse came to get them. "Follow me. She's been moved to her room. Dr. Thompson is the doctor on call. He'll come in to speak with you soon."

Relief flooded Kyle. Dr. Thompson had been his doc after the car accident that had almost killed him. The same accident that brought Ella into his life. Ella and Andy Thompson were former colleagues and good friends.

Julian looked uncertain about what to do, but Jesse gestured with his thumb for him to follow, so he did. Getting off the elevator, they passed a waiting room and Julian said, "I'll wait here. I don't want to cause any trouble."

"We'll let you know once we talk to the doctor," Jesse said.

Jesse stepped into Faye's room and saw that she was awake. In that exact instant he realized how tightly he'd been wound. He was finally able to take a deep breath. His eyes were glassy as he approached her bedside.

She was still pale as hell, but she was smiling at him and he knew she was going to be okay. Jess leaned down and softly kissed her, then rubbed his thumb across her cheek. The doctor entered the room, his expression relaxed, exuding confidence as he filled them in on Fays condition.

"She's going to be fine. As I told her, she's suffered a mild concussion, we'll keep her in overnight as a precaution. She'll have to take it easy for a few weeks, but the CT scan was negative for swelling or bleeding.

The blood you saw was from a superficial cut from the blow."

"Thank God!" Kyle said, scrubbing his hands across his face.

Dr. Thompson smiled, "Always a good night when I can give loved ones good news. How's Ella? Tell her to stop in and visit the old gang. We miss her."

"I'll tell her."

"How about her friend?" Jesse asked.

"She's fine. Not even a concussion. She says she never completely lost consciousness, just got her 'bell rung' quote unquote." He smiled. "I'll be here for another couple of hours, but the nurses know I'm available by phone if I'm needed. By the way. I just heard that the storm has changed its course and is heading back out to sea."

"Great news! And Doc, thanks."

"You're welcome. Don't forget to tell Ella what I said."

"I won't. Did you know we're pregnant with twins?" Kyle said.

Andy Thompson's eyes widened in surprise then a smile spread across his face, "Congratulations. I don't think I need to tell you, you're one lucky man. Ella is something special."

Kyle nodded his head, "Yes, I don't know what I did to deserve her but I'm not questioning it."

He gave Faye an encouraging smile, "You might have a headache for a few days. I recommend over-the-counter acetaminophen, but your concussion is a very mild one. Take it easy, listen to your body, and you'll be as good as new in no time." He pivoted on his heels and briskly left the room with the nurse following him out.

Faye smiled weakly at Jesse and Kyle. "I'm sorry to put you guys through this. What happened?"

"What do you remember?" Jesse asked.

Faye's brows drew together, "I remember realizing I hadn't boarded up the back window, so when Maddy got home we went over to do that. We went inside and that's the last I can recall. Who found me? What happened?"

"Some men followed you in, apparently hit you over the head, and made off with the statue."

"Sasquatch? Why would they want to take him?"

"Good question," Kyle said. "We have no idea. Here's the part that gets even more bizarre. Julian was there and saw you go in, followed by the men, when they came out and you guys didn't, he went inside and found you lying unconscious. He said Maddy was already awake, so he wasn't worried about her. He claims he was taking you to the ER when Jesse showed up and they brought you here."

Faye's eyes were huge in her pale face. She looked at Jesse, "Is this true?"

"Yep, but I'm not entirely convinced he would have brought you here if I hadn't shown up. I guess we'll never know."

"Where's Julian now?"

"In the waiting room. He managed to get the license plate of the men that did this to you. The police issued an APB. The storm isn't helping any, but at least we have something to go on."

Jesse held onto her hand stroking it with his fingers.

Faye brought his hand to her lips. "I'm going to be fine, but *you* look like you just buried your favorite puppy."

The corner of his mouth turned up. "I think this shaved about ten years off my life."

"God, I hope not!" she said, laughing. She grimaced and put a hand to her head, causing Jesse to jump up from his seat.

"Are you okay? Should I call the nurse?"

Faye held up her hand, "No I'm fine. My brain's just rattled."

Kyle said, "You should get some rest. I'm heading out. I love you sis," he said as he leaned down to kiss her forehead. "I'll let Julian know how you're doing on my way out."

Tears shimmered in Faye's eyes. "Okay. Tell him I got his note and that I understand and tell him I said goodbye."

"I'll tell him. I'll also tell him as grateful as we are, I'll be escorting him to the airport myself on the next flight out of here."

Faye smiled, "That will be so sweet!" Then she closed her eyes.

"I'll be here until she gets released. I'll update you if anything changes," Jess said.

Kyle gave him a quick hug. "Thanks. I'm glad Faye has you."

"Likewise."

51

It had been a week since Faye had been released from the hospital. Jesse had insisted on bringing Faye home to his house. He was so solicitous that Faye had to fight to even pour her own cup of coffee.

"You're spoiling me, you know that?"

"Your point?"

"I'm fine. It's been a week already!"

"I like taking care of you."

Faye hesitated, then said, "And I *love* having you take care of me, but I'm not going to break. We haven't made love since the accident."

"I'm afraid I'll hurt you."

She smiled tenderly at him, "Come here, you big lug."

He sat down on the edge of the chaise lounge and took the hand she held out to him. He raised it to his lips and kissed her soft palm. "Faye, I don't know how to describe what it was like to see you unconscious and bleeding." His voice cracked, "I thought I was going to lose you."

She tugged and pulled him down on top of her. "Kiss me."

He tentatively brushed his lips across hers. Faye put her hands behind his head, her voice low and sexy, she said, "You're going to have to do better than that." Her tongue darted out and licked his bottom lip. He groaned.

"Are you sure?" he asked.

"If you don't make love to me now, I'm going to lose my mind."

He stood and leaned down to scoop her up into his arms. He carried her to his bed and laid her on top of the covers. As he straddled her, he slowly began to remove her clothes. She held up her arms as he pulled her shirt over her head. His whiskey eyes that she got lost in every time, smoldered with desire *for her*. He kissed and licked seductively as her skin was laid bare.

"Faye," he whispered. She felt his erection throb against her as he covered her body with his own. He trailed open mouthed kisses...her neck, her breasts, her belly, until he reached her sweet moist center. Parting her thighs with his forearms he licked her until she was delirious with need.

Her fingers gripped his hair, holding him as she moaned. "Jess...Jess..."

Kissing his way back up he found her lush swollen nipple and put his mouth over her and suckled until she cried out, "I need to feel you inside of me!"

Jesse rolled on a condom then kneeled between her thighs. His knees spread her legs wider as he guided his shaft to her wet entry. He pushed inside, her snug vagina enveloping his hardness. He moved his hips gently at first, but as she bucked beneath him, he thrust faster... almost desperately, until he exploded inside of her, his whole body shuddering with the intensity of his orgasm.

Faye peaked seconds later. "Oh, God, Jess..." panting, her body continued to tremble as wave after wave of sensation had its way with her.

As their breathing slowly returned to normal, Faye said, "Now that's what I'm talking about."

Jess smiled, "Why didn't you just say so."

She began tickling him as he tried to escape her fingers. He rolled onto his back pulling her on top of him. Faye looked down at her man. He was golden and beautiful. His eyes often sparkling like he was in on some great joke. Joyful, kind, sexy as hell...and *she* was the lucky girl that got to wake up in his arms.

~

*J*ess hung up the phone. "That was Mom. She wants to have another seafood boil and invite your family. She thinks it's time everyone meets."

Faye grinned, "This must be getting serious."

He shrugged, "Oh I don't know..."

Faye punched his arm, "You don't huh?"

"Can you round everybody up for this Sunday?"

Her mouth curved into a smile. "I'll try."

"Good. I'll let Ty know to bring Addison. You'll let Maddy know too?"

"Yes. Sounds like fun. Good timing since the bar reopens next week. It'll be a celebration."

Jesse's eyes twinkled. "Yes, I think that's what Mom has in mind."

"I'll make some calls now, while you cook for me."

"You weren't kidding about getting spoiled. I think I've created a monster."

Faye pouted, "I thought you liked it."

He dazzled her with his smile, "I wouldn't have it any other way."

Faye stretched her arms lazily overhead, then crooked her finger at him. "Come over here."

He leaned in for a kiss. "What can I make for you your highness?"

"A cheese omelet with a side of bacon please."

"I draw the line at delivery."

"Spoilsport."

52

*L*ike last time, Faye had to admit, the Carlisle clan sure knew how to throw a party. Her whole family had made it. That is, everyone but her parents, whom she'd left off the invitation list. There was plenty of time to introduce them later.

She was still taking it easy, so she and Ruby cheered for the volleyball teams from the sidelines. Finn and Jess's niece Matilda were playing in the pool with Big Hank, while the rest of the group fought for the bragging rights of the volleyball championship.

Her heart felt achy but full in her chest as she watched the people she loved most in the world gathered in the same place at the same time. As before, the Carlisle lines were drawn, Dylan and Connor teamed against Jesse and Sam. Kyle, Ella, Ty and Addison teamed up with Jess, while Griffin, Dylan's wife Jen, and Maddy joined team Dylan.

Ruby patted Faye's arm. "Your brothers are certainly

handsome devils. That Griffin, he could be a movie star. Makes even a granny like me swoon. Why if I were forty years younger, Hank would have to worry," she cackled.

"Please don't let Griffin hear you say that. His head is already big enough."

"He seems like a charming young man."

"Three words...baby, billionaire, playboy. That's all I'm saying. Don't get me wrong, I love him to death, but he's just a tad bit spoiled. I may have contributed to that."

Ruby laughed, "I'll keep it to myself." She looked at Faye out of the corner of her eye.

"You know Jesse really cares for you. I've never seen him like this."

Faye smiled, "I care for him too, Ruby. If you're asking me what my intentions are with your son, I'm in it for keeps. I'm in love with him."

"Have you told *him* that," she asked kindly.

"Not in those words, but I think he knows."

"People need to hear it. My son, well... he comes off as confident, he's as good looking as all get out, girls were always crazy about him, but... he's my sensitive one. He was always rescuing baby birds, bringing strays home, he's got the kindest heart...just like my Hank."

Faye reached for Ruby's hand and squeezed it. "That's why I love him. You did a great job of raising strong sensitive men that respect women. Thank you Ruby. I take it we have your blessing?"

"We love you Faye. I knew the first time I met you that you were perfect for my Jesse. He's head over heels in love with you."

Faye's eyes shimmered with tears. "Ruby, you know

the first time I met you, when I left here, I almost bawled my eyes out. You were all I'd ever dreamed about as a little girl. *You* were the mama I'd wished I'd been born to. I'm not trying to put my own mama down. She did the best she could. Motherhood just didn't come natural to her...not in her DNA. I'm not sure I deserve Jess, or you and Hank, I'm working on that. Thank you for accepting me." Ruby looked at her with such maternal warmth that Faye's tears spilled over.

"Darling Faye, you deserve everything good that comes your way. I'm an excellent judge of character, and so is my son. If I'd have handpicked his mate, it would have been you. Hank feels the same. I *never* want to hear another word about deservin' from you again. Ya hear me?" Faye wiped her tears and smiled shyly.

"I hear."

"Jesse tells me they caught those guys that clunked you over the head."

"Yes, and it was all over drugs. Turns out that our statue was stuffed with about fifty pounds of meth... street value over half a million dollars. They'd been smuggling drugs and using my bar as a place to store them until they could be distributed. Me buying that building really messed it up for them. They hadn't been able to get their hands on Sasquatch before I had him shipped off to be painted. Imagine their panic when they couldn't find him during the break in."

"Jesse said that photograph of you three tipped them off."

"Yes. The night that guy was killed at my bar, he said he'd come back to check out Ty, but we're pretty sure it was really about the statue. What Ty owed was small potatoes compared to all that meth they'd misplaced. I'm sure their hide was on the line."

"Oh my! You're lucky you weren't killed over it."

"Someone up above is looking out for me," Faye agreed.

~

*M*uch later, they all sprawled around the campfire, bellies full, but not so full that there wasn't room for smores. By this time Matilda was acting like a bossy big sister to Finn, who was eating it up. They were in charge of roasting the marshmallows and Matilda ran a tight ship.

Griffin and Maddy had left earlier, Maddy had to work the next day and Griffin supposedly had a hot date waiting. The couples were now paired up, much teasing and laughter being shared. It was a hot summer night and the sky was star-filled, the ocean breeze and sound of the surf a perfect backdrop to a perfect gathering. The kids had excitedly called out when they saw a shooting star and made a big deal out of making a wish, just as Faye had done as a child...and still did.

"Did you see the falling star?" she asked, looking up at Jesse through her lashes.

"Yeah."

"What was your wish?"

"Not telling."

"You're allowed to tell. That's only a superstition that it will jinx the wish."

Jesse laughed, "And the wish itself isn't superstitious at all, right?"

She smiled, "Course not. Have you lost your magic Jesse Carlisle?"

"At one time I had, but then I ran into a sexy secret billionaire and the magic returned. Which is why, I'm not telling you my wish. Our family believes it goes against the spell to tell anyone your wish." Jesse squinted. "What about you? Did you make a wish?"

Her dimples appeared as she flashed a wide smile. "Not telling. Just in case."

"Maddening," he said, kissing the top of her head.

She was sandwiched between his legs, leaning against his chest and his arms were wrapped around her. She became lost in thought, thinking about a conversation she'd had earlier when Kyle had pulled her aside. It was some pretty big news and it still had her reeling.

With a little arm-twisting from Kyle, their father had agreed to put a ten-million-dollar trust fund, originally intended for Marcus, in Tyler's name, to be transferred to him on his twenty-first birthday. Since Kyle was the family attorney, he'd been the one to draw up the documents. Her father had also offered up an apology of sorts by inviting her and Jesse to come visit them in Palm Springs after tourist season died down.

She was beyond gob smacked. Just thinking about it brought tears to her eyes. Everything seemed to make her teary these days. Kyle had also convinced him to pay for Tyler to go to college if he was interested. Faye was going to make sure that he was.

"Everything all right?" Jesse whispered in her ear.

It amazed her... how he got her. He always knew. "Yeah, why?"

"You got so quiet."

"Just taking it all in. I've got some big news I'll share later. Has to be kept on the downlow. For now."

"Good or bad?" He nuzzled her neck.

"Real good."

"That's all I need to know."

Tyler got up pulling Addison with him, then he brushed the sand from her back side, and she returned the favor. "We've got to go."

"Thanks for everything. This was the best party I've ever been too!" Addison said.

"Yeah, what she said," Ty agreed.

"I'll see you guys Tuesday when we re-open," Faye said.

"Yep, back to the grind."

"Be prepared, we'll probably have loads of extra business, the looky-loos wanting to visit the scene of the crime. Just like a *Dateline* episode." Faye said.

"Sick." Ty grumbled.

"We may as well get something good out of it," Jesse said.

"Tyler, tell your mom we're sorry she couldn't make it. One of these days we're going to convince her to join us." Faye said.

"I'll tell her you said that."

After they left, everyone else began making moves to go. Jesse and Faye were the last to leave, staying behind to help with the cleanup.

Faye hugged Ruby extra tight as she said goodbye. "Bye Ruby, Hank, you guys are the very best!"

Ruby whispered in her ear, "You remember what I said."

"Cross my heart," Faye replied.

Jesse picked his mom up in a big bear hug while she giggled and demanded he put her down. Hank smiled, wearing his big heart on his sleeve, as he stared adoringly at his wife of forty years.

As they pulled away on Jesse's motorcycle, his parents stood in the driveway waving them off.

53

They had made passionate love almost the minute they got inside the door. Later as they lay snuggled together in bed, Faye said, "This is one of my favorite parts."

"What's that?"

"Pillow talk."

"Mine too."

"You'll never guess what my father did."

"Probably not," Jesse agreed.

"He had started to set up a trust for Ty's dad when all hell broke loose last year. He made the decision to set it up for Ty...when he turns twenty-one, he'll receive the trust. Isn't that amazing?" Faye's eyes sparkled with joy.

"Yeah, that's really something. Redemption for real."

"My brother Kyle strong armed him but I still have to give him credit for doing it. I've been assigned the task of telling Ty. I'm just not sure when or how. Should I wait? Do I tell him now? What's best for him? If I wait, it gives him a little more time to mature. If I tell him now, he gets time to get used to the idea of becoming a millionaire. Father is also paying for his college, if we can convince him to go."

"My advice...let the dust settle. You'll know when the time is right."

"Kyle kept his promise and literally paid for the ticket and escorted Julian to the airport. He didn't leave until the plane took off. He said Julian was ready to go. It's just so sad," Faye said.

"After all is said and done, he did the right thing. That's a better note to end things on."

Jesse laid back against the pillows and Faye climbed on top of him. She propped her arms on either side of his head, her hands cradling his face, her face only inches from his. She stared into his warm pools of amber and felt like she was in a freefall. She kissed the tip of his nose, then his eyelids, then his soft lips.

"Jess...I..."

His eyebrows rose, "Yes?"

Suddenly overwhelmed she hesitated, then said, "Are you hungry?"

He bit back a laugh, "Really? Is that all you have to say?"

She kissed him again and started to roll off. He held her tight, stopping her.

"I love you," Jesse said.

Her body stilled. "What?"

"I love you Faye Bennett. I belong to you. I'm all yours...that is...if you want me."

She began to plant tiny kisses all over his face. "Yes, yes, I want you. Every sexy inch of you."

"Move in with me...for good. Marry me. Let's have a half dozen little munchkins together."

Faye raised an eyebrow, "Only six?"

"Give or take."

"Jesse Carlisle, I want it all with you. I love you, with all my heart." His earnest expression and twinkling eyes tugged at her heart. "Thank you."

"For what?" Jess asked, tucking a strand of hair behind her ear.

"For seeing me, really seeing me..." She softly kissed his lips. "For showing me what love really looks like..." She licked his neck. "For knowing just how to touch me..." She moved lower to his chest, her tongue flicking his nipple. "for being decent..." Lower still she tongued his navel. "And for being kind and brave." She followed the triangle of hair, then took him into her mouth. He groaned.

The End for Now....

Thanks for reading Secret Billionaire, Book Two of The Carolina Series. I so loved these characters and hope you did too! Faye and Jesse were a perfect match. I hope you enjoy the rest of the series and will then take a deep, satisfying dive into love, life and family with my Triple C Ranch Series! Look for me on Facebook under Author Jill Downey! **And *please* consider leaving a rating and/or review! It really means a lot!**

Here's the universal links to the Carolina Series and
The Triple C Ranch Series.

https://mybook.to/SeducedbyaBillionaire
https://mybook.to/SecretBillionaire
https://mybook.to/Playboybillionaire
https://mybook.to/billinairexmas

The Triple C Ranch

https://mybook.to/cowboymagic
https://mybook.to/Cowboysurprise
mybook.to/cowboyheatTripleC

Please join my Facebook readers group, where I have
giveaways, teasers and pre-release excerpts:
https://www.facebook.com/groups/179183050062278/

BOOKS BY JILL DOWNEY

Books by Jill Downey

The Heartland Series:

More Than A Boss

More Than A Memory

More Than A Fling

The Carolina Series:

Seduced by a Billionaire

Secret Billionaire

Playboy Billionaire

A Billionaire's Christmas

The Triple C Series:

Cowboy Magic

Cowboy Surprise

Cowboy Heat

Cowboy Confidential

Made in the USA
Middletown, DE
18 January 2023

22381751R00210